THE
BIG HYPE

AVERY CORMAN

SIMON & SCHUSTER

NEW YORK · LONDON · TORONTO · SYDNEY · TOKYO · SINGAPORE

SIMON & SCHUSTER
Simon & Schuster Building
Rockefeller Center
1230 Avenue of the Americas
New York, New York 10020

Designed by Laurie Jewell
Manufactured in the United States of America

1   3   5   7   9   10   8   6   4   2

Library of Congress Cataloging in Publication Data
Corman, Avery.
The big hype / by Avery Corman.
p.   cm.
I. Title.
PS3553.0649B5   1992
813'.54—dc20   92-6684
CIP
ISBN: 0-671-69297-6

FOR ED KLEBAN

1.

AT TIMES I FELT LIKE the bear in the penny arcade game who scurried back and forth and spun around when you hit the target. I was a semibicoastal bear going back and forth between the Polo Lounge in Beverly Hills and the Russian Tea Room in New York.

I worked as a television scriptwriter and had written about forty scripts for television dramas. It was an unending struggle to find interesting projects to work on, so I was constantly in meetings with people, pitching ideas I wanted to write, listening to their proposals. I had won four Emmys and each of those movies for television went on to another life in videocassettes. Several producers referred to me as their "quality guy" and without embarrassment actually used that expression in conversation. I was "doing well" in my work, but like many scriptwriters, I was writing The Novel on the side. I also had written some short stories that were published. A two-month period when I was able to concentrate on the book was coming to an end; I needed a television assignment for money again, so it was time to put on my bear outfit and scuttle for work.

My immediate hope was Tod Martin, a producer in from the West Coast. These California producers were so tan and healthy-looking that as a New Yorker sitting opposite them, I thought I looked like a character in a black and white movie who had been colorized imperfectly and turned out faintly green.

I had worked with Tod Martin before on a worthwhile project about the Wright Brothers. He had called, eager to offer me an assignment so important, he said, that he had to present it to me face to face. We met for lunch in the Russian Tea Room, the tanned one and the green one. Martin was a rangy man in his late thirties, six feet two, in a pink cashmere sweater and white slacks, shirt open at the neck.

"Paul, I'm offering you my best," he said. "A movie-of-the week. I have a go from ABC."

"Good, Tod."

"It's scary, but quality. You ready for this? *Lyme disease!*"

He leaned back, self-satisfied, allowing me to savor the beauty of his suggestion.

"Tod, I appreciate the thought, but I don't do diseases-of-the-week."

"We're going first class on this one. That's why I called my quality guy. We do it as a medical mystery. You know, like it's transmitted to somebody from the family dog and somebody's sick but they don't know how or why."

"Lyme disease. You're making me itch."

"*That's* what we're looking for, that kind of audience involvement. People sitting in front of their sets, scratching, looking at their dogs funny."

"Let me rise to the occasion. The closing shot is like that last image from *Viva Zapata* where the white horse lives on in the hills. The last thing you see is the family dog, a cocker spaniel, roaming the grounds of a house rendered vacant by the disease."

"That's goddamn poetic."

"No, I didn't mean it. It's a lousy illness to get and I don't want to do this kind of work."

"You pass?"

"I pass. The hives that await me if I did it—the dermatologist's bills alone wouldn't make it worth my while."

. . .

I made several counterproposals to him. Tod Martin declined, having been in a one-project, one-disease frame of mind. Over the next couple of days I made several calls to producers and couldn't extract a commitment over the phone from anyone. I was going to have to pitch my ideas in person and make another trip to the West

Coast. In the meantime, in the remaining hours I had available for it, I worked on the novel. I was unsure about a chapter I was writing and took a lunch break. I made a sandwich at home and walked over to Central Park, where I sat on a bench.

. . .

As I was sitting there, Mario Puzo and Robert Ludlum came walking along.

"Hey, fellas, how are you?" I said to them.

They nodded coolly.

"I'm a writer, too. Ever get stuck where you have to just walk around the block, take a break?"

"I take breaks," Robert Ludlum said. "But I never get stuck."

"What kind of writer are you?" Mario Puzo said.

"TV mainly, but I've had three short stories published in *Esquire* and now I'm trying to break out and write a novel."

"What kind of novel?" Robert Ludlum asked.

"About the way we live, about values."

They both looked incredulous.

"What do you mean, values?" Mario Puzo said. "Like what's on sale at the supermarket?"

"No. Values in the culture, cultural values."

"A cultural values novel?" Mario Puzo said. "What do you think that would be?" he said to Robert Ludlum.

"Beats me."

"Hey, what are you eating?" Mario Puzo asked me.

"Peanut butter on whole wheat."

"What are you, a fruit?" he said.

"I just took what was in the refrigerator."

"You're never going to write a book with balls if you eat peanut butter on whole wheat."

"Mario is right," Robert Ludlum said. "If you want to write with gusto, masculinity has to be part of you."

"I'll buy a trenchcoat," I responded.

"A trenchcoat is a start," Robert Ludlum said.

"You almost finished with your book?" Mario Puzo asked. "How many more values do you need?"

"I'm about halfway there. I have about a hundred fifty typewritten pages. I figure I need another hundred and fifty or so more."

"It's a novella?" Robert Ludlum said.

"No, a novel."

"Three hundred typewritten pages?" Mario Puzo said, doing the arithmetic. "I've been thinking of trying the short form myself."

"Well, good luck with your book," Robert Ludlum said. "You should be finished working on it by the weekend."

"You should work on your diet next. Eat sissy, write sissy," Mario Puzo said as they started off.

"I'm going to get some Genoa salami and keep it in the house!" I shouted out to them.

"That's better," Mario Puzo said, and then, under his breath to Robert Ludlum he added, "He'll probably put cucumbers on it."

•   •   •

On the trip to Los Angeles my first couple of meetings with producers were unsuccessful. I don't know how these trends originated, but one of them also wanted to do a movie-of-the-week on Lyme disease. To clear my head I took a walk along Rodeo Drive and looked in the windows of the clothing stores. I was wearing a tweed jacket and slacks, which I had bought in New York. Somehow I never managed to buy any clothing when I was on the West Coast. I had these opportunities to "go a little California," but I couldn't bear the prices or the milieu of Rodeo Drive.

I set out after a while for Melrose Avenue, which had several good antique shops. As a result of my trips to the West Coast my children had a truly outstanding collection of Disney memorabilia, great Mickey Mouse watches, Donald Duck dishes; vintage items. Maybe one day they'll appreciate them as much as their father. My wife, a free-lance illustrator, didn't discourage me in this, and we kept the collection in a breakfront in the apartment. This time I found a good Mickey Mouse clock.

Returning to the Beverly Wilshire Hotel where I was staying, I ran into Joe Staples in the lobby, another New York scriptwriter out to line up work. Joe was in his forties, a tall, spindly man who wore bush jackets, dark shirts, and dungarees in New York, but as soon as he came to L.A. he worked in costume. He switched to pastel colors, sneakers, and a Dodgers baseball cap as a tailoring accent. I never seemed to get out of my tweeds. And it always felt cold to me out there except in the summer, Angelenos continually apologizing for the weather, "It really isn't like this all the time. Only when *you're* here, Paul."

Joe and I shook hands. He had a pinkish tone to his face and I knew the man had toasted himself under the sunlamps in New York to prepare for his trip.

"Whaddaya got out here?" he asked me.

Not an innocent question. In terms of competitiveness, Staples was the Tommy Lasorda of scriptwriters.

"Just fishing around," I said.

"I got a possible series. A TV movie for sure, signed and delivered, on Joe DiMaggio. Serious interest in a sitcom—I'd also produce on that. And a long shot on a miniseries." He came close and whispered in my ear. "On Greta Garbo."

"This is generous of you, Joe, to just say it out loud, sort of."

"They're talking to a lot of writers. I give that one to you."

"I'm out here for a few days. I don't have anything so specific."

"Who you seeing?"

"What's left? Cineflex. Ronnie Hill."

He took a small pad out of his pocket and made note of that in front of me.

"What else you got?"

"Joe, I got a Mickey Mouse clock is what I got."

"I gave you the Greta Garbo."

"Lyme disease is going around. Tod Martin and Bill Maxon are both dealing in it."

"Beautiful concept."

"Martin already loves my closing shot. The dog who passes the disease on to the family, roaming the grounds of the empty house."

"I'm going to get right on it! I owe you one, Paul." He set out for the phones then stopped and called out to me. "The closing shot, you think the dog should look *straight* at the camera as we freeze-frame?"

I was involved in Great Moments in the Arts here.

"Whatever you want to express, Joe."

. . .

I spoke to my wife and children in New York, ordered room service, read the newspapers, and made some notes for my next day's meetings. Before I went to sleep I watched part of the old "Thief of Bagdad," starring Sabu, on television. Overly identifying with the character, I saw myself surmounting perils, but not for a magnificent diamond. Sabu didn't know about perils; he should have tried a few years of free-lance life. My goal was a quiet room with the bills paid in advance so I could finish my novel. It would have made for quite a story conference if I pitched a remake along the lines of my fantasy: Okay, the genie is a producer. The Sabu part is a writer. The diamond is an amnesty from American Express.

. . .

The following morning I had a meeting with the head of Cineflex Productions, Whelan Briggs. He was a fitness maniac and we were scheduled for a jogging meeting. So successful was Briggs in television that he had inspired the very concept of the jogging meeting. Other producers were now out there running along with writers and agents. Since he had several shows on the air and always had a multitude of projects in development, a common sight in Beverly Hills was some unfortunate writer out from New York trudging along trying to sell Briggs on a project between gasps. I presumed the California writers accustomed to a more outdoorsy life could keep up with him. Once I let it slip that I ran around the reservoir in Central Park a couple of times about twice a week, and Briggs had me down as one of his jogging companions. He ran eight miles each day. I didn't mind doing some exercise when I was out there but my deal with him was that I ran only the last three miles.

Briggs was in his fifties, six feet three, broad-shouldered with a full head of wavy brown hair. I am forty-seven, five feet nine with light-brown hair and eyes, and of medium build—except perhaps to California fitness maniacs, to whom I am probably chubby.

"Gained a little weight have you, Paul?" he said to me without stopping, and we set out, Briggs in a jogging suit, I in a sweatshirt and shorts. "You should move out here. Have you trim in no time. And you'd be richer than Croesus, all the work you'd get."

"It's the nature of the work that counts, isn't it?"

"You're difficult, Paul. Do you know that? It's the word on you. Hard to get."

"Sounds good to me. If you were a writer, would you want the word on you to be that you were compromising?"

"Oh, I wouldn't *be* a writer."

"That's candid."

"I want you to come aboard for a sitcom. This could be a good change for you. It's about a teenager who wins the lottery. What happens in her family and her life. Write me some scripts. Be my story editor. If it goes, you'll live out here, get a house in Malibu. It'll be like winning the lottery yourself."

"I know it sounds too much in character, Whelan. But I don't want to do that kind of work."

"Three, four years, that's all you have to give it. Maybe five. You'll be in clover, and I bet you'll be up to eight miles a day, easy. Marathons. You'll be running goddamn marathons when you're through."

"I'm ready for a corn muffin."

"Paul—"

"No is my answer, Whelan. Sorry."

"Well, then I've got a rewrite for you. Won't be available for a few weeks. This you'll like—on Joe DiMaggio."

I stopped in my tracks.

"Don't stop. You can't stop. You stop and you'll tighten up," he said, still running in place.

"You're offering me the Joe DiMaggio script to rewrite? You just hired Joe Staples! How can you be firing a writer off a project and bringing in somebody else before he's even delivered his script?"

"Just looking ahead. You can come in later and quality it up."

"*Quality it up?* Is that English?"

"I'm covering myself on an important project," he said—as if that explained it.

"I'm walking on this. Literally."

I walked away from him. These people were Machiavellis in sweat suits. The man was already talking to the next writer on a project when he had just hired the first. I headed back to the hotel. I had only run a few blocks but I felt I had earned my corn muffin.

. . .

The incident prompted a phone call from my agent, Peter Raskin. He was one of the most successful agents in New York for television writers, a high-strung, diminutive man in his early forties whose principal emotional state was hysteria. Whelan Briggs had called Raskin's West Coast associate, who had called Raskin. Briggs was asking for a clarification. He did not want to give a major agent and a major writer the impression that he was double-dealing. He merely had anticipated a rewrite on Staples's script and thought I might be interested. According to Briggs, our meeting came to such an abrupt end that he never had the opportunity to present his full proposal to me. Would I meet Briggs for lunch that day? He was canceling his scheduled appointment to do so.

"Paul, he wants to make nice. Mend the fence," Raskin said.

"Who cares about this guy?"

"He's important. And he's important to me. Have lunch with him. Just take the meeting."

"Where am I going to take it? Are we supposed to eat running?"

"Do it for me, will you?"

"What is he proposing?"

A long pause from my agent followed.

"Peter, what aren't you telling me?"

"Just go and listen and tell him you're not interested and the circle is complete and everyone played out their parts and nobody's angry."

"What is the project he wants to discuss?"

"He'd like you to write a two-hour movie, *The Secret Loves of Benito Mussolini*."

"What!"

"He went to Italy and loved it and wants to do something Italian."

"Then let him take a cooking course."

"Paul, I implore you. I need a smooth working relationship with this guy."

Finally I relented as a favor to my agent. I was to meet Briggs at a trendy new Italian restaurant. We worked our way through on small talk, exchanging opinions on movies and television shows we had seen. At the end of the meal Briggs said:

"Mussolini is a fascinating character."

"You don't hear his name that often."

"History has passed him by a little, I'll grant that. But the substance is there for a memorable show. I can see it eventually on videocassettes, that kind of quality. Your kind of quality."

"It's just not my cup of espresso, Whelan."

"We'll send you to Italy for research."

"But then I still have to write it. And what I'd be writing is *The Secret Loves of Benito Mussolini*."

"Well, I tried to get you aboard," he said, playing out his part.

"I appreciate your taking the trouble. And so does my agent."

We shook hands, and as we were parting I said facetiously, "If it doesn't work out with anybody, you might try *The Secret Loves of Woodrow Wilson*."

"We'll stick with what we have," he said, taking my remark literally.

· · ·

My last meeting in L.A. was with Ronnie Hill. Ronnie and I had worked together on several projects, including a movie about an unemployed auto worker, for which I was given one of the Emmys. She was thirty-four, slender with long black hair, an aquiline face, hazel eyes. She was striking enough to have been an actress on one of the programs she produced. Ronnie had been in charge of daytime programming at NBC, then established her own production company and was column-item successful. At the moment, as reported in the columns, she was going with a real-estate man with holdings in California that were reputed to be about the size of New Jersey.

We met in her office, a large space with a huge black marble desk, the decor so elaborately electronic with television sets, sound equipment and exercise apparatus that it looked like a Sharper Image showroom.

"How's Sandy, the kids?" she asked.

"Everyone's good. Who is your latest, the Shah of northern California?"

"He does have a little money, yes."

"Are you in love?"

"I'm in—like. We're a good match. He has as many phones as I have."

Lights were blazing on her phone console. As a courtesy to me she had asked her secretary not to put any calls through.

"Paul, I have a nice project to offer. It's about a girl from a good family who gets in with a surfing crowd over a summer vacation and her boyfriend gets killed dealing drugs and she spots the killer and then the killer starts stalking her."

"Pan to the writer," I said. "He sits dully, his eyes glazing over. He has seen this movie before, and he wonders why the usually responsible producer is asking him."

"Because in somebody else's hands it will be cheap and exploitive and in your hands it will be intelligent and exploitive."

"I'll make you a counterproposal." I offered one of the ideas I intended to present to her. "A young girl refuses to say the Pledge of Allegiance in her classroom because she feels there is no liberty and justice for all. It becomes a major event, disrupting her family's lives. They're people who've never been challenged before in their principles. We get into how the girl is treated, how it gets played by the media, what goes on in her life and with the people around her."

"The Pledge of Allegiance. Too political," she said flatly.

"One thing about you, Ronnie, you don't waste time saying no."

"Neither do you."

"I got a million of 'em. Actually, I have one other I'd like to do. A black high-school basketball player gets a scholarship to college and in his freshman year rips up his knee, a devastating injury. His playing career is over. A boy who never paid much attention to school, just a ghetto kid who could play ball. What does he do next? The pressures are on him to cave in, drop out of school, go back to the streets."

"This is good. I just made a new deal with NBC. I'll put this in with it. Your agent can call my lawyer. We don't have to tarnish ourselves with money," she added wryly.

"Terrific!"

"It's serious television. And the ball playing can be very visual. I can see it all on the screen. Just one little thing—he can't be black."

"Ronnie, that's the starting point! That's what gives it a reason for being."

"You still get what you want if he's white. Make him poor-white, from a farm, or out in the boondocks. It's still important."

"But it's not the same story."

"We don't do public service programming."

"The National Basketball Association is not overstocked with ball-players from farms. This is a city story. You do it with a young black actor. Or you don't do it. Fine. Good day, Ronnie, nice to see you—"

"Because I respect you—" She buzzed her secretary to call the head of programming at NBC. When he was on the line, she said to him: "I've got a wonderful movie idea from Paul Brock. A black kid up from the ghetto, basketball star, goes to college, wrecks his knee freshman year. What happens next to him? Does he go back to the ghetto, stay in school? All done with Paul's taste and sensitivity."

She flipped a button on her phone enabling me to hear the other party on the line.

"You want to go with this as part of the deal?"

"Yes. It's quality television, it's visual. I love it."

"In terms of demographics, does he have to be black?"

"That was just a first draft of the idea," she said, instantaneously yielding.

I stood up, waved goodbye to her, and started out of the room. She motioned to me to stop.

"But if you make it white, it's not the same story," she said, quickly changing her position. "You have so many professional basketball players who are black and that's what gives it the validity. The energy comes from it being a city story about a black kid."

"Let's get a script," he said.

They concluded their conversation and Ronnie then came over to me, kissing me on the forehead.

"We've got a go."

"We barely made it."

"You mean that little byplay? It's the nature of the business. So when can we have it?"

"It writes itself."

· · ·

I gained what I went out there for, a commitment to write a script for a two-hour movie for television. With Ronnie Hill as the producer it would be made with good people. By any scriptwriter's standards this had been a successful trip, but I was unnerved by how close it came to being fruitless. What Ronnie referred to as "the nature of the business" was an attitude I had encountered far too many times.

· · ·

Walking back to the hotel I saw some people who were not in my business—Tom Wolfe, Stephen King, and James Michener. A multicolored hot air balloon was set up in front of a bookstore and they were standing in the gondola, waving to a crowd. Wolfe was wearing a luxurious white suit, King a flannel shirt and jeans, Michener a windbreaker and slacks with a John Deere cap on his head. They all looked to be in high spirits.

"Hello there!" I called out. "I also write."

"Oh? Do you live around here?" James Michener asked.

"I live in New York. I do television scripts, but I'm working on a novel," I was eager to add.

"They don't grow too many novels in California. You'd better get home," James Michener said.

I surveyed the balloon, the crowds.

"What's going on here?"

"We're going from bookstore to bookstore checking on the massive displays of our books," Stephen King said.

"And greeting our vast number of readers," Tom Wolfe added.

"And you're doing it by balloon?"

"It's great fun. You should try it sometime," James Michener said, waving as the balloon lifted off the ground.

"On your last books, did you submit the entire books, or just parts of the books, or outlines?" I yelled, eager for some how-to information.

"What's an outline?" I heard one of them saying as their balloon lifted up and floated sumptuously into the sky, the three of them waving to the public and the scriptwriters below.

2.

I CAME THROUGH the gate at Kennedy airport and my wife was waiting for me with our two boys, the children holding up a handmade poster saying, "Welcome Home, Daddy!" I made these trips to California fairly often and came and went on my own; nobody ever met me. But when I spoke to my wife on the phone and told her about the edgy quality of those meetings something in my voice must have registered. So she had brought the boys out to greet me. It was one of those moments when you realize that by some incredible piece of good luck you have married exactly the right person.

"This was wonderful to do."

"Hello, honey."

"How are you guys?"

"Mom said we can see the planes take off and land," Joey, our ten-year-old, said.

"Sure we can."

"Were you worried the plane would crash?" Sammy, the seven-year-old, asked.

"Somehow the plane crashing didn't make the cut on my worries," I said.

We went to the observation area for a while and then drove back to Manhattan. In the middle of the night, awash with sentimentality and feeling the need to reestablish for myself what was important in my life, I got out of bed and quietly walked around watching my people sleeping. Sandy had auburn hair that she usually wore in a ponytail, was five feet two, slender, with blue eyes and an expressive, sunny face. At forty, she still retained a young girl's vitality. She was so pretty she always attracted the interest of men on the street—men my age and younger, too. Yuppies working on their macho tried to make eye contact with her.

We had been married for twelve years. She had been engaged just out of college to a dentist, the mythical Roland Greenblatt, now quite successful, "a big dentist," as he was often referred to longingly by my in-laws, who never quite understood the economic vagaries of free-lance life—but then I'm not sure I did either.

Sandy was an illustrator for book jackets, magazine articles, children's books. She worked in watercolors principally, a radiant light inhabiting her work, several examples of which had been included in anthologies on commercial illustration. We seemed to have stretched the limits of sanity for a two-career marriage—two free-lancers. There were moments when both of us received good-sized checks—a beach house in Fire Island was testimony to that—and there were also moments when we both scrambled frantically to find work. The ebbs and flows of Sandy's profession had more to do with times of the year and professional circumstances, such as a new art director at a magazine or book publishing company. Mine were entangled in producers' whims, television executives' fears, actors' and directors' egos. At least Sandy worked at something different from what I did for a living. I often wondered what the anxiety level would have been like in our household if Sandy was in a more closely related profession. They would be checking me into Mount Sinai Hospital every few weeks with anxiety attacks.

A few relatives on my wife's side of the family had reddish hair, and Joey had red hair, blue eyes, freckles. A couple of years before we were approached by a woman in a playground in Central Park who worked for a casting agency and wanted to sign Joey. "He's got a great heartland look," she said. "He can do commercials." We didn't want to put him into that life and rejected the idea. Sammy had brown hair from my side of the family, and coal-black eyes. The same woman approached us and said, "Let me have the younger one. They're hiring ethnics now. He's got a great immigrant look."

"All we're trying to do is assimilate here," I said in declining.

Our apartment was in a building on West End Avenue and 79th Street in Manhattan. It was a sprawling, old-fashioned city apartment. I worked in what had once been called the maid's room in these older buildings. Sandy felt she had to be out of the house; too many demands would be made on her by the children, so she rented space in a brownstone office building in the neighborhood. I preferred writing in the apartment where I could have my work right there and I could act on any sudden inspirations. And working at home I always could count on good cookies for snacks. I figured Gore Vidal to snack on olives in his Italian villa. Joan Didion, an occasional carrot. Joyce Carol Oates, celery. Writing in an apartment with young children, I had Lorna Doones, Chips Ahoy, Pepperidge Farm Distinctive Tahitis, and Pecan Sandies.

On my return to New York from Los Angeles I learned that a much-rumored decision had been made by the landlord of the building, and a proposal was offered for the building to go co-op. I was not thrilled with the idea. I knew the advantages—an opportunity to buy our apartment at an insider's price and to have equity. On the other hand, we would have to come up with money, get a mortgage. A tenants' meeting was called, Sandy and I brought chairs into the lobby along with the other tenants. People argued the pros and cons of the issue, and I kept thinking, *Who needs this?* I just wanted to write the new script, get a few months ahead, and finish my novel.

The tenants' meeting was predictably shrill and contentious. Neighbors in the building I'd never talked to because I suspected I wouldn't like them turned out to be people I didn't like. After putting the children to bed Sandy and I, worn down from the night, sat slumped in the living room.

"We can always move to the West Coast where our children will become drug addicts," I said.

"We could move to Vermont and become vegetarians," she quipped.

"What are we doing wrong? Why do I want to scream?"

"Honey, there are people going to film schools studying how to be you."

"Thank you for that. There are people going to art schools studying to be you."

"Studying to be serious artists maybe."

"You *are* a serious artist."

"A serious commercial artist. But it's okay. I'll never be Hopper or Georgia O'Keeffe and I've made peace with that."

"And I've made peace, too," I said with mock-seriousness. "And if this building goes co-op I can always do *The Secret Loves of Benito Mussolini* and make peace with that."

"You're kidding."

"I passed on it."

"Someone's going to do it?"

"I guess Mussolini was a good kisser."

This was not a night for momentous decisions to be made. The co-op situation was certain to unspool over a period of months, Sandy was in the middle of an assignment to do a series of book jackets for a new paperback publishing house, and I had my project with Ronnie Hill. I had been to California to look for work and that was over and now I was back into real work and New York life.

· · ·

I had a meeting with my agent in his office after I finished working the next day. Peter Raskin was five feet five with a narrow, nearly gaunt face, long black hair, and brown eyes. Raskin, who had been representing me for ten years, specialized in getting good terms for his scriptwriter clients and feigning nervous breakdowns.

"You're going to hospitalize me yet. Is it true what I heard?"

"I pitched Ronnie Hill on the basketball movie and when she started to sell out before my very eyes I began to leave the room."

"Not that. You suggested to Whelan Briggs *The Secret Loves of Woodrow Wilson?*"

"I didn't think he was listening."

"It was reported back to me by someone who was sitting near you. He thought it was funny."

"See? It played for someone."

"Wait. What did you just say? You started to walk out of the room on Ronnie Hill?"

"You had to have been there."

"What do you want to do to us? I have you positioned as a

guy with high standards, but who's ultimately worth it. It's taken me years to get that reputation for you."

"Could I throw in that maybe my work had something to do with it?"

"Fabulous work, Paul. The best. But walking out of rooms! Calm down!" he shouted at me.

We settled into a discussion of the details of the deal with Ronnie Hill: delivery times, payments. The important factor in the terms Raskin had negotiated was that I would be paid in full whether or not NBC decided to air the program. It was never guaranteed in these deals that the script you wrote would actually be *produced*. One writer I knew from the Writers Guild offices, Bill Heaton, went to the south of France every summer with his most recent wife, had a house in Bucks County and an apartment in New York, was a wizard in sitcoms, conceiving ideas for them, writing them, rewriting them, and in six years never had one program reach the screen. This was a business where so much money was available to "develop" ideas and so little was produced that a person could make a living writing material the public never saw. I wondered how Bill Heaton managed to live with this, and one night we went out for a few beers and I asked him about it.

"The trick is," he told me, "you don't write shows, you write deals. You think of them as deals. Since you only write with a contract and you only write deals, then in a sense *everything* you write gets done." Generally, I was spared having to live with such circumlocutions of logic.

"So you'll sit in your nice room and stay home with your nice family and you'll write us a nice script," Peter Raskin counseled me. "How *is* the family?"

"We're fine."

"How dare you have a happy marriage in this day and age? It's hostile."

"I couldn't afford the upkeep on anything else."

"Keep it that way. No cutting up. Or you'll end up where all you can get, Mr. Quality, is quality National Geographics. You'll be off months on end with baboons."

He was very pleased with himself for his riposte.

"Baboons are available?" I teased.

"You're going to give me a nervous breakdown and then you won't have anybody to negotiate the terms for you and your baboons!" and he ushered me out the door.

.   .   .

Our beach house in Fire Island was in a family community, Fair Harbor, and we usually spent as much time as we could there in the summers and on good-weather weekends in the spring and fall. Sandy had a studio at the rear of the house and I worked in a room on the second floor. A few years before, I had written my first piece of serious fiction there. It was a short story, my initial entry into prose after all those scripts. I submitted it to *Esquire* and they bought it. The story was loosely based on an experience of mine in trying to maintain a friendship over the years with a high-school friend. Eventually we stopped meeting once every couple of years for lunch when it was obvious the boys who'd had something in common could no longer find a common ground as men. The final lunch—which was the title—formed the basis of the short story. Beneath the ordinary table conversation, both men are seething with feelings of regret and loss, and I'd tried to convey that if only they could express those feelings they might have a basis for a new relationship. But they could not.

I left the story for Sandy to read while I went off the island for a business meeting in Manhattan. I was returning on a Friday night on the "Daddy Boat," named for the fact that the wives and children on the island waited on the dock for the daddies to come in. Sandy and the boys greeted me with our cocker spaniel, Skippy, and we strolled back to the house, Sandy's arm in mine. I was very tense. Was I fooling myself to think I could write anything in sentences, something that filled up a page?

"I feel like I have this wonderful secret," Sandy said to me. "I read the loveliest story, honest and beautifully written, and I'm the only one in the world who knows what a terrific writer of prose you are, and are going to be."

.   .   .

Warm weather was predicted for the upcoming weekend and we organized ourselves to go out to Fire Island for a couple of days.

I wanted to look over my novel and I Xeroxed a copy of what I'd written up to that point. I planned to spend Saturday going through it. There were no surprises when I read it. The book was what I'd intended and I liked it very much, but it was maddening that I had only about half of it completed thus far. The basketball script would earn a block of time for me to work on it again. Saturday afternoon I shot baskets with my boys on a backboard and rim set up on the side of the house. We rested, leaning our backs against a fence, and my mind drifted.

"What's wrong, Daddy?" Joey asked.

"Nothing. Just thinking about the novel I'm writing."

"When will it be out?"

"I have to finish it first. Then it has to be published."

"You've been working on it a long time," Joey, my editor in residence, said.

"I work on it when I can. I'm doing a basketball movie next."

"When will it be on?" Sammy asked.

"I have to finish that first. Then it has to be produced. That doesn't always happen," I felt obliged to say.

"Daddy, are we rich?" Sammy asked.

"Well, your ma is good-looking. We're all right. There are people who are richer and a lot more who are poorer."

"When Daddy finishes his novel we'll be rich," Joey grandly explained to his younger brother.

"That's not necessarily true. Where did you get that from?"

"We went to the movies and you saw a man get into a big car and you knew who he was and you said he wrote novels."

"Oh, right."

We had been to the movies with the boys and passed a theater where they were having a screening and William Styron, whose face I recognized, entered a limousine. A novelist getting into a limo! A vivid image for someone with *part* of a novel done.

"We don't know what will happen when I finish it."

"If you don't finish it will we be homeless?" Sammy said.

"Don't worry about that. We'll always be fine. Mommy works and I do. We'll be fine."

. . .

The following morning before everyone awoke I strolled along the beach. I saw walking toward me an elegant woman in her seventies in a yellow dress, a yellow bonnet, carrying a parasol.

"Excuse me," she said. "Is it possible that you're Paul Brock?"

"Yes, I am."

"For goodness sake. I saw your picture in *Esquire* when they published the first of your three published short stories."

"You know about that?"

"I've begun to follow your work. So you can imagine my delight when my niece, who works for a photocopy store in Manhattan, said you brought in pages from a novel to make a copy of it. She said she peeked as she was making the copies. And what she could see was wonderful."

"It's still a work in progress," I said modestly.

"I can't wait to read it. Based on your previous writings I am certain it will be outstanding. Mr. Brock, may I be so bold as to ask if there is an economic strain attached to your being a writer?"

"It's cyclical. Right now, I'm trying to get enough ahead to finish that novel."

"You know, I have enjoyed your short stories every bit as much as writers far better known and, I trust, far better established monetarily."

"You're very kind. And what is your name, please?"

"Amanda DeWitt DuPont Carstairs Bernays. What a fortunate happenstance, to meet one of my favorite writers on a beach. Mr. Brock, I think it is an unhappy situation that people such as yourself must undergo financial stress. I would like to do something for you, in exchange for the reading pleasure you have given me. Do you own your own apartment, Mr. Brock?"

"No. As a matter of fact our building will probably go co-op and we'll have to come up with the money to buy it."

"I have plenty of apartments. I have a lovely three-bedroom on Madison Avenue in the Seventies, which just became vacant. Please accept it as a token. My accountant will work it out so you don't have to pay rent or carrying charges for the rest of your life."

"Really?"
"All I ask, Mr. Brock, is that you keep those pages coming!"

. . .

One of the best features about writing scripts was that I could become involved intensely with a subject for a fixed period of time, immerse myself in the project. Research was part of this, learning about something new. I didn't have to do much research for the basketball movie, but I thought I would still get some background information. One afternoon I put on my basketball sneakers, shorts, and a sweatshirt, carried a basketball under my arm, and headed for a schoolyard near Benjamin Franklin High School in East Harlem. When I finished college I taught English at Franklin for five years so I was fairly familiar with the terrain. I had been a passable schoolyard basketball player when I was a kid and I kept up my skills, to a certain extent. We had the backboard and rim on our beach house and I sometimes took the children to a local schoolyard to shoot baskets. They could barely reach the basket and became bored watching their father indulge himself, but I tried to keep my hand in. In a catastrophic season where we went 0 and 12, never losing by less than 20 points, the Writers Guild fielded a basketball team in a corporate night league and I played along with a few other middle-aged dreamers. I could throw a ball through a hoop, however, and I had done it in my life. Not to overstate this, my skills were to basketball, I think, better than George Plimpton's were to hockey.

. . .

In the schoolyard six people were playing a half-court game on one basket. They were black and ranged in age from seventeen to their early twenties. Respectful of their turf, I shot baskets by myself at the other basket. After a while a few other ball-players showed up to watch their half-court game.
"Hey, Pops," someone called out to me.
"Pops?" I said, wincing.
"We need the basket. We're gonna play full court."
"I'd like to play."
"We got our teams."

"Then I've got next."

"He's got next," one of them said derisively.

They played one game and then another. I was informed it wasn't "next" yet. Finally, they let me on the court when they didn't have an even number of players. I never received a pass. A few times I picked up a stray ball and once I scored an easy layup. After that game, people came and went, sometimes I was permitted to play, sometimes I just watched.

"What are you doing around here?" one of the better players asked me. His name was Duke. He was the one who called me "Pops." In his late teens, he was six feet two and muscular. One time in the game when I was playing defense, he totally ignored me to dunk the ball right over me. It gave the impression of Michael Jordan flying over a Sumo wrestler.

"I'm writing a movie for TV."

"Oh, yeah," one of the other players said. "You gonna put us in it?"

"I just write it."

"What's it about?" Duke said.

I tried out the plot line and then I asked what they thought would happen to a ball-player like that, who came out of a neighborhood like theirs and got hurt. I had a crowd of eight schoolyard ball-players standing there and they were split; half thought he would go back to his neighborhood and "get messed up," as one of them put it, half said he would stay in school.

"Anybody around here play varsity ball?" I asked.

"I do," Duke said. "For Clinton."

"And there's Mason," someone volunteered.

"Yeah, Mason. He ain't been here last few days. He plays for Manhattan."

"Does he come around?"

"Maybe Saturday."

"Well, I appreciate the help. See you guys."

"Okay, Pops," Duke said.

I had to straighten out that "Pops" appellation. We were fellow ball-players now, in the very loosest sense of the term.

" 'Pops' I take to be an older man," I said instructively. "Not someone who can get out on the court and—get out on the court."

"If you say so, Pops," Duke said.

I went back for several days. The word got around that a writer had been talking to people and when I came by that didn't get me any more court time. I had to wait into overtime for that. But I was able to talk to the schoolyard ball-players, try out the plot, ask their opinions. Mason was there on Saturday. Six feet four, wide shoulders, he was a powerful player with a great shooting touch. Whatever I was doing, compared to Mason and Duke, it wasn't basketball; it was some other game entirely. I posed the question again in a break between games. Mason spoke thoughtfully. "The guy busts up his knee. Does he still keep his scholarship if he stays in school? Even if he's not on a team?"

"I'd write it that he would."

"So he'd stay in school, man. It's coming to him, right?"

"Right, man," Duke said. "I'd stay, too, Pops."

"Of course, you know what you got in your movie if he stays in school? A fairy tale," Mason said, breaking into a big grin. "I'm just kidding, Pops. I'd stick it out, if I could. With heavy tutoring," smiling again. He was enjoying needling me.

"Seriously," I said to Mason.

"Seriously. You'd like to think you could make it through," he said, not kidding at all.

I played in another game before I left and may have achieved the slightest bit of acceptance because on one play in the game, Mason passed off to me—it was a true rarity for me to receive a pass in these games—and as he did, he set a pick so I could get a shot off, which I actually made. Afterward I said goodbye to them and thanked everyone for their help.

"So long, Pops," Duke said and gave me a high five.

"Hope you're a better writer than you are a ball-player," Mason said cheerfully, grinning broadly. "See you around. Write it good."

. . .

The agreement with Ronnie Hill called for me to deliver a first draft of the script in six weeks. Then we would meet and discuss the script and she had the contractual right to ask me for a couple of sets of revisions. My usual method of working was to show a draft to my wife and then to my agent. I listened, took notes, and if I agreed with their responses, made adjustments before I showed the script officially. My agent was so connected to the goal of selling the script and moving on to the next project that he read principally to decide if the script was showable—the broad picture: It works. It doesn't work. Show it the way it is. Spend more time on it. Sandy, on the other hand, was very specific. She had an intuitive sense about construction of a script, where things went wrong, what was working. Some writers might give a script to a mate and hear, "It's wonderful, darling. Let's make love, you're so terrific." A little fantasy there, but actually in the long run I was better off the way it was with Sandy, who was quite capable of saying, "In act two when Fred doesn't seem concerned with Diana any longer, his distance seems to be important information about his character. But it's really because you don't know what to do about him. Sorry, but you're not there yet." None of this was ever presented in a superior tone, but if I wasn't there yet, Sandy was going to tell me.

I showed the first draft of the basketball script to her after working on it for over a month. She read it on a Saturday at Fire Island while I took the kids to the beach for a few hours.

"I love it," she said. "It's everything you wanted it to be. I love the kid, and when he ruins his knee, that's heartbreaking, and you're rooting for him all along to stay in school, and not get pulled down into the subculture. I really love it."

"No complaints about anything?"

"Well, maybe just the ending."

"*Only* the ending? Apart from that, how was the play, Mrs. Lincoln?"

"It's a cliché to see him going back to school in the fall as the story ends. And you know he's got three more years still to go, so there's no sense of completion. What if you took it a little farther out in time?"

"And what else?"

"Nothing else. It's something to be proud of."

I worked on the ending and changed it to a scene where a ballplayer in a college game is driving in for a layup, trips, and twists his knee. It seems like a flashback of the injury to the main character. But as the camera pulls back, we see the person injured is not the main character. The ball-player, not seriously injured, is helped to his feet by the coach of the team. The coach is the main character. He has made it through.

Sandy was very pleased with the script, as was my agent, but I wanted the opinion of the people who would be closer to the material. This was probably the first time anyone ever gave script approval to guys in a schoolyard, but I took my script uptown to check it out with the players. I went there on a Saturday. Duke and Mason and several of the others were shooting around, and I gathered them together and read parts of it, guys leaning on the fence, standing around. I was soundly sassed for some of the language: "That's white bread, man." But basically I received passing grades. When they started shooting around after the "reading," Duke said to me, "You want a game, Pops?" I played a last game there. I didn't suddenly become Larry Bird and dazzle them, but I didn't have a coronary either, and left with some form of acceptance, a few high and low fives.

I made a few changes in language to make some of the dialogue more streetwise, and submitted the script to Ronnie Hill, who called the next day, ecstatic. It was "award-winning," "my best ever," and she was sending along some notes for the "teensy-weensiest" revisions. They turned out to be inconsequential—the producer's need to be actively involved, some name changes, a change of location for a scene, a few lines dropped. I sent the script back with the revisions and I was done. The check arrived and I had enough money in the bank to buy about three months to work on my novel.

The title of the book was *Upward Mobility*. I had been writing it for over two years in the intervals between scripts. I rewrote constantly as I went along and I think I worked rather slowly, certainly more deliberately than on scripts with their fixed delivery dates. This was my novel and I wanted to get it right. It concerned a New York couple who meet in the 1960s and while dating go through a period of social protest, marching and petitioning against the war and for civil rights. By the 1990s they have settled into staid middle-class life. They have two children in private schools. The man is a lawyer in the legal department of a real-estate corporation. The woman is a marketing consultant for department stores. They are in a dead end in their marriage, emotionally, sexually. Their only vitality as an entity concerns the raising of their children. Their energy individually goes into their careers. I had finished ten chapters and I judged that I needed another ten to complete the book.

The remainder of the novel would follow the couple's attempt to rediscover the past and their lost passion, by participating in a march in Washington to support the homeless. As the march unwinds they learn that homelessness is a more complex issue than they thought, and insufficient for them to attach themselves to, that they must begin to re-create their relationship from within.

The novel was the dark side of my own marriage and those of others I knew about. Nothing in my own life was specifically the same as the experience of the characters, however with a difference of a few degrees we could have been those people. I used elements from my life, my marriage, reinterpreted. My literary model, my aspiration really, was the Maples stories of John Updike, and I intended *Upward Mobility* to be a sort of Jewish Maples. I knew that I lacked Updike's elegance of language, but I was working at capturing his specificity.

. . .

I was flattered to receive a phone call from a fiction editor at *Esquire* checking in with me asking if I had written any other short stories recently. I said I was working full-time on a novel—it was a great feeling to be able to say that—and he asked if any part of it might be suitable for the magazine. I sent the first ten chapters in and he selected the first chapter for publication. This was extraordinarily encouraging, to get a part of my novel-in-progress into *Esquire*. It was also intimidating. The rest of the book had better be good.

. . .

Just when I was feeling my most tentative about the novel, I received a phone call at home from John Updike and Philip Roth, both on the line.

"Mr. Brock," John Updike said to me, "I've got to talk to you about that fiction you sent in to *Esquire*. I was over there and happened to see it. Outstanding."

"Really?"

"The craft is there, but what excites me about your work is the honesty. So much fiction today is oblique, overly mannered. But the truth of your characters explodes off the page."

"You called to tell me this?"

"We've spent over an hour tracking you down," Philip Roth said. "And at our hourly rate, kiddo, that's not chopped liver."

"I can't tell you what a call like this means to me."

"What I really want to say to you is—did you ever think of writing a novel?" John Updike said. "A reader wants more of the essence of you."

"I *am* writing a novel! I've been working on it for the last couple of years. What you read was the first chapter."

"This is fantastic news," Philip Roth said. "Look, I have a place in Connecticut and a place in England. I have plenty of room. If it will help you to get the book done, come stay with me. I might be there, I might not. But I think it's important for you to get the work out."

"Philip Roth is setting up my own personal writer's colony?"

"Or if you prefer, come up to the Cape," John Updike said. "I'll be happy to put you up, we'll sit around, talk fiction. Something about your work reminds me of the Maples stories, by the way."

"It does?"

"If you don't mind," John Updike said, "I'm working on something of my own and I'd really be interested in your comments. I'll send you some pages."

"Ditto, buddy," Philip Roth added.

"Wow!" I said to my new pen pals.

.   .   .

A strike against producers and studios was called by the Writers Guild. The writers believed that whenever management felt their profits were decreased in an area, management looked to renegotiate to the writers' disadvantage. This had happened with the videocassette market and was happening again with foreign sales of television shows. Some people were off writing the plays, original screenplays and novels they always meant to work on. For me it meant I could continue to write my book undisturbed. No one could try to tempt me away from the novel with a fantastic offer, once in a lifetime, the *real* Evita Peron; I was offered that before the strike by Whelan Briggs. I surmised Briggs was trying to write off a recent trip to South America.

With the strike in place it meant you were not permitted to even talk to a producer or television executive about a project or work on a script in progress or rewrite a script you had done. I was thoroughly involved in the novel when I received a phone call from Tod Martin.

"Paul, what are you up to?"

"Writing a novel."

"A novel, that's good. I like a novel now and then."

"How did Lyme disease work out? Did you find a cure?"

"I'm not calling about that, you understand. With the strike on we both know we can't talk about anything like that."

"You're calling just to say hello and find out how I am?"

"That's right," he said eagerly. "Just to find out how you are."

"I'm good."

"I'm good, too, but I could be better. Paul, supposing an apple needed polishing, but there was a strike of the apple polishers. But there wasn't a strike, say, of the apple producer-directors, and supposing somebody who needed this apple polished asked someone who usually is an apple polisher if he could become an apple producer-director this one time, and in the course of his work, do the polishing of the apple."

"You've bought a farm, Tod?"

"No! Supposing the apple was like a *script*," he said impatiently. How could I be so dense that I didn't get it?

"Oh, it's not an apple."

"It is, but it's not. And supposing the apple polisher who was asked to be the apple producer-director didn't usually do that kind of work, but was helped with all the technical parts so he wasn't actually the producer-director."

"But was called in really so he could polish the apple."

"Yes! Exactly," he said, relieved that we were talking about the same apples.

"And this was a devious way of getting around the strike by

bringing in the apple polisher and calling him something else.''

"I wouldn't say devious.''

"Would you say this conversation was direct?''

"Does it help if I tell you other apple polishers are doing it?''

"I don't know about that. I am sure other apple farmers are offering it.''

"Top dollar.''

"Supposing the apple polisher was polishing not an apple but an orange. An orange he had been working on for a while. He couldn't go near polishing the apple. And do you know why? Because it's a question of apples and oranges.''

I left him with that. But even though I flatly turned down his attempt at a back-door way of getting a writer to do a rewrite during a strike, still I felt uncomfortable about the exchange, about this being the field I worked in.

· · ·

When the strike was over, agents, writers, and producers were scrambling around to sign deals, put together packages.

"What do you mean you won't take any work?'' Peter Raskin said to me over the phone.

"I'm almost finished with this book. I don't want to be side-tracked.''

"Pots of gold are sitting out there. The projects, there are so many of them, it's like air traffic congestion.''

"I am simply not available.''

"I'm out of my chair. If you were with me in my office you would see me, out of my chair.''

"Arms flapping.''

"And they will be as I go out the window. The only man ever to die simultaneously from a fall and a nervous breakdown.''

"Peter, just say no.''

· · ·

Ronnie Hill's secretary called me from California. Ronnie was coming into New York and wanted to have lunch with me at the Russian Tea Room. My immediate concern was that she would ask me to do more work on the basketball script before it went into production, on request of a director or an actor. I was waiting for her at the table when she arrived. She kissed about a half-dozen people en route to me, the restaurant filled at lunchtime with the usual show-business types. We spent the first part of the lunch discussing the strike and its aftermath. She asked what my plans were and I told her I was finishing a novel.

"I'd like you to spare a little time, if you could," she said.

"I was afraid of that."

"Paul, I don't know how to tell you this. The network is uncomfortable about making this a black ball-player. The market research on those kinds of shows is just not what we'd like it to be."

"This is a story, not a toothpaste commercial."

"I know all that. But to put a black kid at the center of this, it's just not going to work. So he's white. And he's from Indiana. That way we can pick up some of the ambience of Indiana basketball, and aside from that, it's exactly as you wrote it."

"*Aside from that?*"

"Be flexible, Paul."

"You're one of the good guys. How can you be saying this?"

"It's the only way they'll make it."

"No way!" I said, my voice rising.

"Take it easy, Paul. This is the Russian Tea Room. We want to come back."

"He's a ghetto kid! That's what the story comes out of. That's what makes it work!"

"I don't know about that. The conflict can be about whether he has to go back to live on the farm for the rest of his life."

"It isn't the same. Emotionally, in every way, you'd be distorting it."

"What I would be doing is getting it on. Now I wanted to meet with you to ask you to do the rewrite. It's your script; you know how to fix it so the integrity is retained."

"What integrity?"

"I don't want to do it without you. But I will if I have to."

"I wonder what the guys from the schoolyard would be thinking if they were here now."

"We're not making this for guys from the schoolyard."

"It's black. Ronnie, have you lost your way? Don't you know the difference between black and white anymore?"

"Don't you know the difference between a go project and something that sits in a drawer?"

"It can be made the way it was written—if you make it."

"But we don't want to. I'll put it bluntly. Are you in or out?"

"I'm out. But what I want most of all is to be out of this goddamn business. Take my name off the script," I said as I bolted out of the restaurant, which was humming with sweet talk and sweet deals.

. . .

I worked on the novel, driven. Finally, it was done. Sandy read it and said it was wonderful.

"That isn't us, is it? What you think we could become?" she asked.

"The fears of us, the nightmare of us, but not really us."

"Well, I think a lot of people are going to see themselves in the characters; how you get caught up in—stuff. Like you say, upward mobility, and the core of yourselves gets lost."

"It's fiction," I said, and I took her in my arms.

"I'm very proud of you. You finished your novel."

. . .

I gave the book to Peter Raskin. He was so excited after he read it he was threatening a nervous breakdown out of happiness. As a television agent, he was concerned about his ability to place the book properly with a publisher and said he wanted to go into association with a literary agent whom he knew. I met her a few days later in Peter's office.

Martha Sipes was a stocky brunette with long black hair, well tailored, a composed woman in her fifties.

"Your book is lovely," she said. "When I heard you were a television writer I expected the usual, a novel that reads like a script. You know, fast dialogue, rat-a-tat-tat. The detail, the unfolding of events, the march as a leitmotif in the second half, it's all very well balanced."

"What are you saying, you didn't like the dialogue?" I joked.

"The dialogue is fine. The narrative line is the surprise."

She thought the best approach would be to auction it to publishers. First novels, she said, tended to be overlooked or downgraded by publishers as just that—first novels where the author doesn't have a reputation. But by auctioning it off, they would be making a major announcement, a first novel of uncommon interest.

. . .

I had lived in New York all my life and had never taken a horse-and-buggy ride through Central Park. At every point during my years in the city it had always seemed an unjustifiable extravagance. This was the time. I had finished my novel and someone who was not a member of my family had said it was lovely. On the next Saturday morning I gathered Sandy and the boys and we went to the Plaza for breakfast—another extravagance our family had never enjoyed. The sight of my children picking at their eggs at those prices would certainly have unnerved me on any other day. Nearby was a family of four also eating breakfast at those prices. When the father signed for the check, I said to Sandy "You think he just finished his novel?"

Then we hired a horse and buggy and the driver took us through the park.

"This is fun," Joey said. "It's like a pony ride."

With the dead-on accuracy of a child, Sammy added, "The horse smells."

"That's what makes it authentic," Sandy said.

"William Styron can have his limo," I said, luxuriating in the experience.

. . .

The auction was concluded and I sat in the office with Peter and Martha Sipes. The highest bidder was a new company, Greystone Books. They bid $20,000 for my novel. They were not making a first printing guarantee until the trade reviews came in but were talking in the area of about fifteen thousand.

"My wife designs book jackets," I said to the agents. "She picks up publishing talk. And when we were discussing it, she said publishing is a business of self-fulfilling prophecies. And unless you get a really big advance and a big first printing and big advertising budget, your book isn't going anywhere."

"That's not always the case," Martha responded.

"I did some research. I went through back copies of *Publishers Weekly*. The books that get promoted in the first place are usually the ones that sell. Isn't that so?"

"By and large. But four houses bid on it. That's very flattering to the book."

"It will be published, Paul. Your first novel published off the bat," Peter Raskin said.

"And there's a chance for a paperback sale and a movie sale. Of course, that's not guaranteed," she was quick to add. "And the book won't be published for another eight or nine months and the paperback money is usually deferred past publication."

"This is not winning the lottery, is it?" I said.

"When I talked to editors," she said, "the overall feeling was that the book wasn't sexy enough."

"You mean sexy as in sex?"

"In terms of marketing. It's interesting, moving, well written. But what they said is—it's not a thriller or a romance or a roman à clef. It's simply a lovely book on a contemporary theme, and that may not be enough for a first novel to be a breakaway."

. . .

I thanked them, saying I needed to absorb the news. The reality was with two children in school and with their orthodontia bills and with rent and our overall expenses, and even with both of us working, the advance wouldn't last but a few months. The book would probably be published respectfully, but it wouldn't launch me into a career as a working novelist. Work would still mean television work. I thought I had found a way to write myself out of that world, but I hadn't; I was trapped.

I left Peter Raskin's office and walked along Park Avenue and thought of the scene in *Raiders of the Lost Ark* when the Harrison Ford character is chased by the huge boulder. The boulder behind me was drawn in animation, a round, gummy mass, and stuck in it was Whelan Briggs and Tod Martin and Ronnie Hill, their heads protruding, their arms brandishing typewritten pages; the Lyme disease dog was in there, and Joe DiMaggio, and Benito Mussolini. The gummy boulder kept rolling after me about to suck me up into itself, and I ran as fast as I could.

I started to run along Park Avenue full speed, as if I were a cartoon character looking to defy gravity, running, trying to run right out of my script.

3.

THE POSTGAME FESTIVITIES were muted. The chilled champagne was unopened. Sandy came home from the studio, we sat in the kitchen and I reported the results of the auction.

"They were all within the same range on money. It's like it had a preordained level."

"But four publishers, that's very impressive," she said.

"Maybe I should publish it myself. Syndicate it, like they do with race horses. Sell shares. You can have pages one through thirty. Sixty through ninety is available. I don't know. I should talk to Mel. He might have some ideas."

"I think we should open the champagne and celebrate what you've accomplished. You've written a wonderful book."

"I can't believe I'll have to go back into the TV business. I was getting so negative that they were going to bar me from the Russian Tea Room."

· · ·

The Mel I referred to was Mel Steiner. He was a show-business entrepreneur whose firm, Steiner Varieties, was referred to in articles as one of the most successful management firms in the business. He managed performers, served as a booking agent, negotiated recording contracts, produced national and international concert tours.

Every few weeks Mel and I met for breakfast. He also appeared at our apartment for dinner now and again. He came to our place whenever he was seeing someone he wanted to show that he was a regular kind of guy, that he knew people who were just plain folks. In his silk suits and silk shirts, Mel appeared with women in wild hairdos, punk fashion designers, singers in rock bands. Sandy and I talked about the arts, politics, exuding domesticity, and after Mel and his dates left we felt as if we had just been visited at a senior citizens' colony.

I called Mel's office, his secretary said he was in a meeting and might not be able to get back to me; he was leaving right after the meeting for Europe.

"How long will he be away?"

"Three weeks."

"That long?"

"Let me break in and tell him it's you. You're one of the people I'm allowed to do that with."

He was on the line immediately.

"Paul, how did the auction go?" he asked.

"The book was sold, but it wasn't great. I hoped you'd have some suggestions about my entire life."

"Come over right now. I'll finish up my meeting and we'll talk."

I took a cab to his office, which was located on a high floor of a building on Seventh Avenue and 55th Street. The reception area was lined with framed eight-by-ten glossy photographs of show-business personalities Mel represented. The furnishings were plush with thick carpeting, blond wood paneling, recessed lighting, luxurious leather couches and chairs—but on the walls were all those framed eight-by-ten glossies. It was as though a crazed decorator had loaded that fancy decor into a Broadway delicatessen.

From speakers behind the receptionist came the voice of the "New Julio Iglesias," as Mel had merchandised him. He was Manuelo Regas, known as "Manuelo"—as in his latest hit album, *Manuelo*. Mel's secretary, Freda Kloss, a conservatively dressed woman in her fifties, came out to lead me into Mel's office. Mel worked in a plush beige room with a sound system, a piano, the disciplined work of a designer upended by walls of pictures of Mel with show-business personalities, awards, gold records, framed letters, Mel's delicatessen decor intruding.

Mel Steiner was six feet one, broad-shouldered, trim. His face was narrow with brooding eyes. He had a habit of squinting when you talked, which gave him the appearance of continual impatience with you. He *was* impatient. Mel lived in two time periods simultaneously—the present and the future. Whatever you said he was factoring against the implications for the future. He was wearing a custom-made suit with a silk shirt open at the neck revealing a diamond-studded gold chain. The chain had been given to him by Liberace, which approximately indicated its tastefulness.

Mel was on the phone as I entered, completing a conversation.

"The language lessons are part of it, darling. You speak better English, you earn more money." He finished the conversation and rose and shook my hand. "A new act. Good voice, heavy accent. I'm thinking of billing her as the Czechoslovakian Barbra Streisand. So what happened with the auction, what were the terms?"

"Greystone Books offered twenty thousand. A fifteen thousand first printing. The word on the book is that it's not 'sexy' enough for marketing. It's not a genre novel or anything like that. It's *merely* lovely writing."

He squinted at me, analyzing what I had said. He motioned for me to wait a moment and buzzed his secretary.

"Freda, get Marvin on the line." Mel turned to me. "My lawyer's been doing some work in publishing lately. Let's see what he says."

When the man was on the phone, Mel told him:

"I've got an Emmy award—winning writer, Paul Brock. Wrote some short stories that were in *Esquire*. Great stuff. His first novel auctioned off, goes to Greystone Books for twenty thousand. Fifteen thousand first printing. What are the book's chances in the marketplace? No, I'm talking sales. I see. From the movie, *Once in a Blue Moon*. Thanks."

Mel put down the phone and turned to me.

"He said you could come away with a literary success. But with those kinds of numbers, it's sure to be outmuscled by bigger books."

"What if I published the book myself, syndicated it like you would with a race horse? I sell shares in it and that goes to finance the printing and the advertising."

"Freda, get Marvin again."

Mel asked him:

"Marvin, what if he publishes the book himself, sells shares in it like for a race horse? Right, right. Thanks."

He turned back to me.

"A long shot. Imaginative, but it might seem like you couldn't get it published on its own. Look, let me read it. You got a copy for me?"

"Yes."

"Let me read it and I'll think about it when I'm away. In the meantime, don't make any deals."

"Mel, this book has got to get me out of TV. I feel like a punch-drunk fighter and I'm mumbling, *Don't let me go back in the ring*."

He worked my shoulders with his hands the way a trainer would for a fighter. "Don't worry about a thing, champ. I'm in your corner."

. . .

Mel and I met in 1963 when we were both working as busboys during the summer at a Catskills hotel, the Pineview, formerly Swensky's. My father was the house photographer at the hotel. He took pictures of guests at the dining room tables, in the nightclub, at the dance contests, and the pictures were available for purchase in key-ring viewers or in "I Had Fun at the Pineview" souvenir folders. This was my father's summer work. During the rest of the year he operated the Marvin Brock Photography Studio on Bainbridge Avenue in the Bronx for weddings, bar mitzvahs, confirmations. My mother was the receptionist, bookkeeper, and business manager for his studio. The Bronx was beginning to change then, areas were becoming blighted, the catering halls where "functions" were held had been going out of business. The summer move to the Pineview was his way of diversifying. My father had artistic aspirations to landscape photography, which he displayed in his store window and in a glass case in the hotel lobby. Occasionally one would be bought for $10, which thrilled him as if he had sold a poem.

He was a wiry man of five feet seven, birdlike in the frantic quality of his movements, always rushing in little steps, unsmiling. Got to get the work out. Money has to be made. While working in the dining room I saw him trying to get people to pose, doing his little patter. He was sometimes insulted, ignored. This was not the way I wanted to see my father. My mother, Bea Brock, a slender brunette of five feet four, had a permanently pinched expression on her face. She had the overview. While he scurried about with details, she surveyed the customers, the books—and what she saw was not inspiring. She expressed herself best through the flamboyant sunglasses she wore, with large colorful frames, a suggestion of possibilities. If we had money, I could be glamorous, a Hedy Lamarr.

During the summer, my parents lived in a small house off the grounds of the Pineview. When I took the job our agreement for my own independence was that we would not fraternize. I was staying in the busboys' cabin, which had an unforgettable acrid smell of mildew and unwashed clothes. Mel slept in the nearby bed, but we had little to do with each other at first. He was not unfriendly; he was largely preoccupied, often talking on the pay phone outside the kitchen, negotiating. I thought he might have been a bookie.

· · ·

On Saturday night of the July 4th weekend, the big gala holiday show was staged in the Pineview Crystal Ballroom. On the bill, announced on the dinner menus, was Fred Wilp and his Amazing Singing Dogs; Marty Traum, comedian, star of stage, TV, and radio; and direct from the Copacabana, song stylist Janice Scott, the "Why Was I Born?" girl. The room seated over three hundred and was filled to capacity. The emcee and social director, Bobby Cole, permitted a few of the staff members to watch the show from a backstage area and I was there, along with Mel and a couple of others. On this night Cole had received a call that Marty Traum was running late at a hotel nearby where he was the opening act and would be delayed coming to the Pineview. While Cole waited to start the show, people in the audience were stamping their feet and clapping their hands impatiently. Finally, Cole introduced Fred Wilp and his Amazing Singing Dogs. Wilp, a scarecrow of a man, six feet seven, led out three German shepherds, whom he introduced as "Patty, Maxene, and LaVerne." He then played on his accordion while the dogs howled. They did not alter pitch at all, they just howled, stopping and starting on cue—which was apparently the amazing part. While Fred played such songs as "Finiculi, Finicula" on the accordion they "sang," sounding like nothing more than howling dogs.

The comic still hadn't arrived, and Cole, who functioned as the producer of the show, pressed into service the hotel magician, Benny the Great. He ran a magic shop in the lobby of the hotel and was a regular on the middle-of-the-week bills in the smaller casino room where the Israeli dance teams appeared. Benny was suddenly summoned from his room and was still making clothing adjustments to his tuxedo. He came out on stage to do his magic act. In Benny's haste, his rabbit evidently was not given the proper motivation and bit Benny's hand as he tried to remove it from his hat. The spring did not work for the doves in Benny's Appearing and Disappearing Doves routine and the doves wouldn't disappear. Beginning to panic, Benny tried to do a card trick and dropped all his cards. Cole gestured wildly for Benny to get off the stage, and he was given a musical exit by the house band to the tune of "It's Magic."

The strains of "Why Was I Born?" played, and out came Janice Scott. A buxom blonde in her thirties, she was running a precarious will-she-or-won't-she-pop-out-of-her-gold-gown side routine. She commenced a shrill rendition of her theme song but before she could complete it a loud blast of barking was heard. On stage in full flight came Benny the Great's rabbit, pursued by Patty, Maxene, and LaVerne, pursued by Benny the Great, pursued by Fred Wilp. The rabbit ran between Janice Scott's legs—and she began to question, no doubt, why she was there. She screamed, the dogs barreled past her, knocking her off her feet, the rabbit got out into the audience, the dogs following, running amok. Women were shrieking, the dogs were barking, guests were scrambling out of the ballroom, and the band tried to cover by playing "The Star-Spangled Banner"—hoping for what? That the rabbit and the dogs would suddenly come to attention? Benny was colliding with people, trying to get his rabbit before the dogs did, and the dogs, in pursuit, were stopping to eat abandoned food on the tables. Benny finally captured his terrified rabbit in an outer corridor, Wilp got his dogs under control, and the staff members present were told to clean up the debris. Cole called out, "It's dance time!" The band started to play a mambo and the remaining guests took the suggestion and moved on to the next activity.

By the time I went back to the cabin Mel was in bed with the lights out. I thought about the gala and burst into laughter. I heard Mel in his bed making a similar sound.

"Some show," I said.

He didn't answer. I realized he wasn't laughing at all; he was crying. I went over to him.

"What's wrong?" I asked. He shook his head, sobbing in his pillow. "What is it?"

He turned to me and in the next instant our friendship was sealed. The hotel photographer's son knew what he felt.

"Benny the Great. He's my father."

. . .

We began to spend time together, hanging out on our days off, going on double dates. I learned that in his negotiations on the phone Mel was conducting an overheated social life. The previous summer when I was a counselor at Camp Orani, in a blaze of under-the-stars glory, Rhoda Peltz and I had consummated "actual" behind home plate of the baseball field. Since then I had compiled an almost unfathomable number of scoreless innings. Much of my post-Rhoda time in the city had been spent cultivating the favors of Ellen Moskowitz, a sultry vixen from N.Y.U. whom I slept with every weekend, but only in my fantasies. Despite spending vast fortunes to date and feed her, the most I was favored with was "bare shoulder."

Mel would lurk near the hotel check-in counter trying to get a jump on the new arrivals. He managed an inside track with the Goldner girls from Brooklyn College. He took the older sister, Carol, a sophomore, and I paired off with Mona, a freshman. To impress them Mel and I serenaded them with doo-wop songs under the moonlight. I would have tried anything. Eventually, blissfully, Mona Goldner and I vanished into the woods.

At the end of the summer Mel and I promised that we would stay in touch with each other. He lived near Pelham Parkway in the Bronx, a few minutes away by bus from my apartment near Fordham Road. One evening he came over for dinner and my mother cooked her brisket, which had the tenderness of the shoe in *The Gold Rush*.

"Delicious," Mel said. "Just like my mother's cooking."

"What do you plan to do after City College?" my mother asked.

"I'm going to be a millionaire," he answered bluntly.

"In what?" she said, taking a follow-up question.

"In whatever it takes."

My mother nodded approvingly, indicating that was the correct answer and my father and I should take note.

After dinner Mel and I strolled through the neighborhood and I showed him my father's place of business.

"This is a real dinosaur of an operation, isn't it?" he said. "Those are nice," as he noted the landscapes in the window.

"He has a shelf of photography books. He sits looking at those books and you don't know what he's thinking. Meantime, he takes pictures at Robert Shlossman's bar mitzvah, if he's lucky enough to get it."

The following weekend I visited Mel's apartment for dinner. Both our mothers came from the Gold Rush School of Cooking.

"Delicious," I said, borrowing from Mel. "Just like my mother cooks."

Mel's mother, Bertha Steiner, was a tallish, thin woman, a head taller than Benny the Great, her hair pulled back in a severe bun. She was solemn, studying me. Benny was a portly man with sad, tired eyes. Not a lively conversationalist, he concentrated on his tenacious pot roast.

"What are you taking at Hunter?" Mel's mother asked me.

"Liberal arts," I said. "English major, history minor."

"What do you do with that?"

"I don't know yet."

She seemed content with my answer, perhaps assured that this new friend was no threat to get ahead of her son. Mel's mother was a dressmaker who worked in their apartment. Part of his parents' bedroom was given over to her sewing machine and a rack of women's clothing. The apartment was small and dark, similar to ours. Throughout were cartons with "Benny the Great" labels on them. Mel's father operated a mail-order business from their home, selling magic tricks by placing small ads in comic books.

"Want to see a trick?" Benny said to me over dessert, canned fruit salad.

"He doesn't want to see a trick," his wife said angrily.

"Let the boy speak for himself."

Benny was so eager. He hadn't spoken much at dinner. This seemed to be the only way he was able to communicate.

"I'd like to see a trick."

"Good," he said, his face brightening. "This is our latest feature. The Disappearing Nickel." He took out a small box, placed a nickel in it, turned it around, and the nickel was gone.

"Wonderful," I said.

"Thank you."

He seemed very pleased. Mel was looking down at his uneaten dessert; his mother had already left the table. After dinner we took a walk through Mel's neighborhood.

"I'm sorry about my father," he said.

"He was trying to be friendly."

"He's very good at entertaining children."

"He's a very quiet, nice man."

"The mail-order business is so nuts. He doesn't make anything out of it. I give him ideas. Do a 'Magic Trick of the Month Club,' I say. He won't listen to me."

We walked around the neighborhood for a while, went for pizza on Arthur Avenue, then stopped on Pelham Parkway where we leaned against a car and sang pop songs. I had confessed to Mel that I sang in the chorus in high school and he said the genes were in his family, that his father actually started out to be a singer in vaudeville. Our singing eventually became a routine; we sang to girls on dates, thinking we were charming.

During the year that followed Mel began to look to me as an "intellectual." He took suggestions on books to read so he could be smarter—which really seemed to be about appearing smarter to girls. He wanted to attract "classier personnel," as he expressed

it. With me in the lead when we went on our double dates sometimes we saw foreign films or bought balcony seats for plays. I, in
turn, looked to Mel for his energy and braggadocio.

"No more working dining rooms," he announced one night.
"This summer we're going to make big money. I've got a plan for
us."

It had become unthinkable that whatever plan Mel was conceiving would not include me too, just as I would have included
him. We each understood a secret about one another. Both our
fathers had somehow become lost in the culture, and we saw the
terror in our mothers' eyes that we, their sons, might turn out to
be just like our fathers.

4.

IN THE SUMMER OF 1964, when we were entering our senior year of college, the pop music field was dynamic. On the airwaves you could hear rock, folk, folk-rock, traditional pop singers, jazz sambas. Mel wanted to take our fooling-around singing and turn us into a duo.

"We're not professionals," I said to him when he suggested it. "We're two guys who sing leaning against cars."

"Pure, raw talent."

"Nobody will hire us."

"Did Fred Wilp and his Amazing Singing Dogs get work? We'll put together an act."

"We're not even good enough to be amateurs."

"We just have to be good enough to play the Mountains. And here's the brilliant part."

"Yes, I'd like to hear brilliance. Because what I'm hearing is insanity."

"We don't play big rooms. We avoid the nightclubs. We don't pretend to be Steve Lawrence and Eydie Gorme."

"I'll say."

"We play the middle-of-the-week shows, small rooms. I can't believe how brilliant this is. We *aspire* to be second-rate!"

"We won't even be that."

"All we have to do is pass. We can pick up a whole summer of second-rate bookings on second-rate bills."

"The kings of mediocrity."

"We *are* going to need a name, but the name should be good. You're an English major. Come up with something."

We started practicing on the weekends to see where it would lead and we listened to pop music when we were together, making notes. We joked that if we ever succeeded in having the act we could bill ourselves as the "White Everly Brothers"—assuming that in the circles we would be playing nobody would know that the Everly Brothers were already white.

Mel suggested we include original material with the standard songs.

"We'll have sort of an American Edith Piaf medley."

"We're going to sing Edith Piaf?"

"No, you're going to write some words, like out of our own experience—about dating and girls. We'll make up some music and we'll weave it in. The audience will think they're getting their money's worth."

I wrote some lyrics for songs about dating in the Bronx, about the rituals, about girls who only wanted to marry doctors. That one I called "The Undoctor of Love." We wrote singsong music for my lyrics, hummed it into a tape recorder, and these songs became part of our material, which ran for twenty-five minutes. Mel announced that we were second-rate enough and that we were going to see his Uncle Bob. This was Benny's brother, a studio musician who played saxophone.

"He used to play with the big bands. He's like an elder statesman now, but he's smart. He's heard a lot of singers."

"Then it won't take us long to be found out."

. . .

We visited Uncle Bob on a Saturday morning in his apartment on Riverside Drive. Bob Steiner was a distinguished-looking grey-haired man in his sixties with a slender build, wearing a sports shirt, pressed slacks, shined loafers. I might have been less nervous if the man had turned out to be seedy. His wife, Aunt Dora, was present—a petite woman in her sixties with a sweet angelic face. On a table in the living room was an array of photographs—a young Bob and his saxophone with Glenn Miller, Woody Herman, Tommy Dorsey, Dora as a band singer in front of a microphone.

Apparently we were not giving the impression of being ready for the rough-and-tumble of show business because Aunt Dora served us milk and cookies.

"What is this about, Mel?" Bob asked.

"I need your help, Uncle Bob. Paul and I are going to have an act, a singing team for the Mountains this summer. And we need some simple arrangements."

"Are there many teams in the Mountains with two boy singers?"

"It'll make us unique," Mel said.

"We call ourselves the Journeymen," I offered.

"We do a musical journey through the world of pop music," Mel said. "We start out with your Beatles medley, then your folk medley, then your bossa nova medley, then your doo-wop medley, our own original Edith Piaf—type songs about dating in the Bronx—" Uncle Bob breathed heavily. "—and we end with the big Israeli medley, 'Tzena, Tzena,' hand-clapping, the works."

Aunt Dora excused herself on that note. Uncle Bob sat stoically.

"A musical journey. That's why we call ourselves the Journeymen," I explained.

"You want arrangements? Do you have any idea how expensive that would be?"

"Some simple piano charts," Mel responded. "The house bands can fake it behind us. They do it all the time. But with a set of arrangements for piano, it won't seem like we're off the street."

"You are off the street."

"Listen to our act. And while you're listening imagine how much better we'd be with a piano and a band behind us," Mel told him.

"I'm all ears."

We launched into the result of our hours of rehearsal, singing lustily, doing a few little dance movements à la Motown, which I had argued against, but which Mel said gave us visual appeal. When we got down to the Israeli medley where we clapped our hands, and which was supposed to inspire the audience to clap their hands and send us off with a big round of applause, Uncle Bob kept his arms folded. We ended with big smiles and waited for his reaction.

"You guys are terrible."

He had confirmed my worst fears. I turned to Mel and said:

"I knew it. We're terrible *and* we're crazy."

"How terrible?" Mel asked his uncle.

"Pretty terrible. You planning to do something else with your lives?"

"This is only for the summer. So we don't have to work in dining room jobs."

"Well, I suppose I've heard worse."

"He's heard worse!"

Mel was exultant.

"That is not high praise," I said.

"Uncle Bob, think of us on the level of Fred Wilp and his Amazing Singing Dogs. On that level, don't you think we could play midweek dates in some places?"

"Maybe."

"A definite maybe," Mel said to me. "And he's in the business."

"How are you going to get bookings?" Bob asked.

"We're going to take our arrangements, hire a piano player and audition for Joe Bosso, who's going to book us as a bona fide second-rate act."

"Is he?"

"Please, Uncle Bob. Some simple piano arrangements."

"All right, give me a tape of what you have."

"It's right here," Mel said, giving him the material.

"This is going to take a few weeks. I may not do it myself. I may just get a guy to do it as a favor. To tell you the truth, I don't want to have to play the tape and listen to you over and over."

. . .

Uncle Bob gave us piano arrangements with musical bridges between songs to tie our medleys together. It looked wonderful, although neither of us could read it. Mel copied names of audition pianists from a trade paper and we went to an apartment on Eighth Avenue for our appointment with Stella Bradley, at $15 an hour, Mel's best buy. She was a small woman of about seventy with badly dyed blond hair, who lived in an apartment cluttered with music and theater souvenirs. She looked over our material and was critical that we hadn't included any theater songs. Mel told her we were "pop stylists." We went through the songs while she accompanied us. To my ears we sounded worse with a piano.

After two hours of rehearsal with Miss Bradley, Mel deemed us ready to audition. Also $30 was the limit we were prepared to spend on this part of the deal. Mel made an appointment to see Joe Bosso, who had known Mel's father for years and was a major booking agent for the Mountains. We met Miss Bradley a few days later in the lobby of the Brill Building and went up to the office of the Bosso Agency. Joe Bosso, a large, balding man in his forties, was in his shirtsleeves, wearing suspenders, holding a cigar, which he used to punctuate his sentences. He spoke in a gruff voice, a constantly frowning man. Mel and I, nineteen years old, with a bleached blond accompanist nearly four times our age were not going to erase the frown.

"You're all three of you, the package?" Bosso asked.

"Miss Bradley is accompanying us for the day," Mel answered.

She handed Bosso her business card, which he dropped on his desk.

"All right, Mel. Let's hear."

"We have our own special arrangements," Mel said, selling.

Bosso gestured impatiently with the cigar for us to start. Miss Bradley took her position at a piano in the office and we faced Bosso. Mel began:

"Presenting a wonderful new singing team here to take you on a musical journey through the world of song: the Journeymen!"

We did the act, each of us losing our place a few times along the journey, attempting to gloss over the mistakes with a smile. Smiling was one of our main features. We smiled throughout. Bosso did not. When we were finished, he chewed on his cigar.

"Can we discuss this?" he said and Miss Bradley, a veteran, knew the cue and departed. Bosso seemed to be frowning even more and I didn't take it as a good sign.

"Mel, you're in college, no?"

"I am. For business."

"So go into business. What do you want this for?"

"Mr. Bosso, last summer, Paul and I worked as busboys and we made about eight hundred dollars each for the whole summer. We figured we can do as well with an act."

"The Journeymen. You should call yourselves the Meshuggeners."

"My strategy is we don't play big rooms," Mel said. "We don't pretend to be anything but filler. We go on before the Israeli dance team in the middle of the week. To round out the bill."

"Did anyone ever tell you guys you could sing? Mel, you're awful. What's your name?"

"Paul."

"Paul, you're not as awful. Together—you're awful."

"We auditioned for my Uncle Bob."

"This I'm interested to hear. A man who played for Jo Stafford and the Pied Pipers."

"He gave us the piano arrangements. That's what he thought."

"That's what he gave you. He's your uncle. That's not saying what he thought."

"He said he'd heard worse. Mr. Bosso, admit it. Have you ever heard worse?"

"I have to admit I have. But have I ever booked worse? A mob guy had a singer. He told me book him or he'd bust my knees. He was worse."

"So there's a precedent," Mel said, undeterred.

"The Journeymen!" Bosso said, wincing.

"You don't want to send us back to dining rooms. We'll give a good twenty-five minutes."

"You graduate next year?"

"Yes."

"One summer. Then you get yourself a job. You, too. Next year I don't want to see you showing up in here with a girl as the next Peter, Paul, and Mary. I'll book you at two hundred dollars a show. I take twenty-five percent. You pay your own expenses. Don't complain to me about bookings. Don't be late for a show. Don't call me unless you decide to retire, an event you should begin making plans for right now."

. . .

I think it is fair to say that historically we have a place as one of the worst acts ever to appear in the Mountains. Not that we were *the* worst. That summer we were no worse than the Wanda and Tony dance team we preceded on several bills, who had their own particular medley—ballroom dances and frequent stepping on each other's feet. Nor do I believe we were worse than Fred Wilp and his Amazing Singing Dogs "Together Again!" We played second-rate bills at second-rate hotels, and some second-rate bills midweek at first-rate hotels. What we were was noisy and smiling. We averaged almost two performances a week over the summer. After expenses we cleared about $1,600 a man, so we doubled our busboy income. A few places booked us a second time, so it is possible to argue that we improved as time went on. Principally, we were cheap entertainment. We met a few girls, guests at the hotels, and managed some sexual activities, but you really had to wonder about the taste and intelligence of any girls willing to be groupies to a group like ours.

One time we played the Pineview, a midweek engagement in the casino. We were second in billing. Wanda and Tony were the headliners, the opening act was Albert and Friends, a juggler-dog act. Albert, who might have been eighty, had two poodles and as the house band played Sousa marches, he and the dogs whirled red, white, and blue hoops on their noses. Our finale was no more tasteful. We had worked on the big "Tzena, Tzena" finish and now had large oak tag cards with the words, which we held up for the audience to sing along. Our parents were back at the Pineview for the summer and after the show we adjourned to the hotel coffee shop.

"You actually got up there?" my mother said.

"You've been doing this all over the Mountains and getting paid?" my father commented.

They were merely perplexed. By contrast, Mel's mother was depressed. Her fears had come crashing down on her. Her son, the soon-to-be college graduate, was in the same world as Benny the Great.

"How much farther do you boys plan to take this?" she asked.

"Ma, a simple congratulations is in order here. We made more money than we did last summer and we had more fun."

"It *was* more fun. And we've gotten better," I said. "We started out terrible and now we're—"

"Peppy." Benny, who had not spoken, finished the thought. "A peppy little act."

"Thank you, Mr. Steiner. We're peppy and we've moved up to mediocre."

. . .

At the end of the summer we were at Ricker's Hotel and Cabins, a small, shabby place down the road from Grossinger's. The entertainment was so bad that for their big Saturday night show Albert and his poodles opened for us and *we* were the headliners. We performed in a room that accommodated about sixty people sitting on folding chairs. This was an "older crowd." Several appeared to have fallen asleep before we came out on stage, and nothing we did—not even the hand-clapping at the end—managed to wake them. A storm had been raging in the area for hours and after the show we lingered in the lobby waiting for a break in the weather so we could get to Mel's jalopy and go back to the city. The hotel manager called us into his office. Someone from Grossinger's was on the line. Their entertainment in the big nightclub was Señor Wences, preceded by the Sabra Dancers. The Sabras were coming by van, but they had been delayed in the storm and were forty miles away. The audience was seated for the show, management couldn't delay the start much longer and they had been calling around to hotels in the area to find someone, anyone who could go on as the opening act in the next few minutes. They were even willing to take us. Without thinking long enough to panic, we agreed. We raced to the car, drove over to Grossinger's and, still wet from the rain, stood backstage peering out at the crowd.

"There are more people here than at Yankee Stadium," I said to Mel in a not-very-inspired tone of voice.

"Don't speak. Or we'll lose our nerve."

"What nerve?"

Grossinger's was proud to present, for a Grossinger's debut, surprise guests—the very wonderful Journeymen.

I have no idea what we sounded like. Our main goal was to

get to the end. We got to the end. The cards with the words on them, soggy from the rain, were held up, the "Tzena, Tzena" was done, the hand-clapping was heard, and we were off. The stage manager for the show, an officious man in his thirties in a seersucker suit, came rushing up to us.

"The Sabras aren't ready," he said. "And we want to hold Señor Wences for the end. Go back out. Do a few encores."

"We can't," I said.

"You have to. I've got a full house out there."

"We don't have any encores," Mel told him.

"What do you mean, you don't have any encores?"

"It never came up," I said.

"Go out there. Fake it," and he pushed us back on stage.

We stood dumbstruck before the audience. Lacking anything else to do, we motioned to the band and started our act all over again from the beginning, like a child who memorizes something and can't start it in the middle. We did the complete act that we had just done, the full twenty-five minutes down to the end, cards and all. From the little I could make out, people were sitting there with their mouths practically hanging open. I'm sure some of the bubbas who were not too good in the memory area were having a lot of trouble—*Didn't we just hear all that?* The hand-clapping and singing on "Tzena, Tzena" didn't work this time. We were probably one of the few acts ever to perform in the Mountains who went off stage to dead silence. The summer had ended and we were out of show business.

5.

MISS EPSTEIN, a cantankerous Socialist, laid entire industries before me in little booklets: "Your Career in Journalism," "Your Career in Advertising," "Your Career in the Burgeoning Field of Library Science." Before my graduation from college I was completely rudderless and sought the advice of my assigned guidance counselor. A tall woman in her late fifties with an intense face and unkempt grey hair, she wore black exclusively and favored large pendants.

"Brock, it's all about class. They don't want to hear that around this place, a city school. But when you graduate, you're going to be competing with Ivy Leaguers, private college graduates. You're already in a hole."

"Very inspiring, Miss Epstein."

"An English major. You don't go into a place of business and see a bunch of English majors sitting there. You have to do something with an English major. What did you like best about school?"

"Reading books."

"In the Capitalist system you are not honored for reading books. Ah, do whatever you want. Go ahead and read. Maybe you'll marry a rich girl who also reads."

"This is guidance counseling, Miss Epstein?"

"In America it's all about class, I'm telling you." She looked around conspiratorially. "The key to it is this. You have to do something in your life that overrides class."

"In the meantime—"

"In the meantime, you could process the waste products of

the Capitalist system—advertising, public relations. They're conducted in English."

I was shaky about my ability to function in the business world. If Mel, the business major I knew best, was a role model, I certainly lacked his aggressiveness.

"What else do you have?" I asked.

"All right, I'll give you the ticket. Take some education courses. You'll get a job. A male English teacher. They'll love you. So, your life is settled."

. . .

Mel and I took long walks talking about the future, which seemed to be commencing immediately. A heart murmur would keep him out of the Army. He decided to work for Joe Bosso, who offered him a job booking talent on cruise ships. Bosso told him, "If you could sell me that cockamamy act of yours, you can book anything."

I went into the Army for six months in the Army Reserve and then attended weekly meetings once a week for several years to do what was called "fulfilling your military obligation." When I finished active duty I took several education courses to improve my résumé and looked for work as a teacher. Two elementary schools in the South Bronx called me regularly to fill in as a substitute. This was the height of the Civil Rights Movement and I felt a great deal of support from the news headlines about teaching inner-city kids. Eventually, I worked my way along the line to teaching English at Benjamin Franklin High School. My mother was not overjoyed with my chosen profession; other mothers' children had bolted past me economically, but she settled into an explanation for her peers. "My son teaches poor children. He helps people, like a rabbi."

. . .

I was living in a small apartment in the East Village while Mel was in a much larger place on the upper West Side, dating aspiring performers. He would invite me to parties, and some of my attempts at competing socially with high-powered young lawyers, doctors, executives—I, a schoolteacher—were ludicrous. I wrote a satiric piece on the subject and it was published in the *Realist*, an underground publication. An editor at *Playboy* saw the piece, called and asked if I would submit something on dating for *Playboy*, and it, too, was published. My mother finally had something to work with; she made copies of the articles, laminated and framed them and put them in her foyer where her friends could see them. She also carried copies in her pocketbook in case she met someone on the street. "My son, the English teacher, who's like a rabbi. He's also a published writer," she told people.

. . .

Mel decided to leave Joe Bosso's office and work at the William Morris Agency in Los Angeles. For his going-away party he had the idea of inviting every girl he had ever dated in New York. He also invited some men he had been friendly with, but the women were the main reason for the party. Twenty women showed up, and several brought husbands and boyfriends. Some of the women made little toasts recalling their relationships with Mel. He made a speech, teasingly inviting everyone to mingle and get married to someone in the apartment since it obviously hadn't worked out with him.

Mel's women tended to be flamboyant, several were professionally beautiful-looking, models, performers. I was drawn to looking at one woman in particular who sat quietly to the side, seemingly amused by the proceedings. She was in her mid-twenties, slender with a beautiful face, her auburn hair in a ponytail. The way she sat, distant and poised, gave her an elegance unique in the room.

"I'm Paul Brock," I said to her. "I'm an old friend of Mel's."

"Sandy Green. Obviously, I went out with Mel since those are the terms for being here."

"I don't remember him mentioning you."

"Oh? I was the one he actually married. No, I went out with him a couple of years ago. It lasted about a minute. Or maybe a few minutes longer than that."

"What prompted you to come here tonight?" I asked, looking for any kind of information about her.

"I was free. It's an unusual idea for a party."

"How long did you say you went out together?"

"Are you going to ask if we slept together? We'll let that go."

. . .

I took Mel's advice about mingling at the party and marrying someone there, and I married her. During our courtship Sandy and I dutifully marched for civil rights and against the war in Vietnam. We set up tables on street corners and solicited signatures for petitions—all of which I used as material for the novel. On the question of how long Sandy and Mel went out together, there was a period of about five months or so when Mel was doing a fair amount of traveling, and we lost touch. My guess is that Sandy fit into that period, but she was always noncommittal about their involvement, and so was Mel. The general agreement among all of us was to let the matter pass into history, and it did.

. . .

Sandy's parents lived in Huntington, Long Island. Sandy's father, Milt, was a CPA with the coldest blue eyes in accounting. Life was a balance sheet and with my teacher's salary I was on the debit side. Sandy had been engaged once to the son of their neighbors but had broken off with him three months before the wedding— the very wonderful Roland Greenblatt, dentist. Sandy's mother, Belle, a stocky redhead, worked as a travel agent. She had the coldest brown eyes in travel. Although I came into the picture years after the breakup with the dentist-prince, they held me responsible for their daughter not marrying a man who was one of Belle's best clients and who traveled lavishly on tooth and gum money.

On occasional weekends during the summers Sandy and I went to the Pineview. My father was still working there. He had a weariness about him, from age or from recognition that he would never win the gold key ring on the carousel. With the Bronx blighted, he had opened a storefront in Yonkers and scratched for business. He still took his landscape photographs, which Sandy and I thought were quite beautiful and which helped him maintain his dignity.

. . .

After working for a while at William Morris, Mel opened his own office in Los Angeles. He came to New York for a show he was producing at the Westbury Music Fair. He was creating festivals, mostly for Las Vegas floor shows—a Brazilian Festival, a Japanese Festival. He sent us pictures of these garish events. He appeared at our apartment looking like a Mel Festival himself, with a silk suit and silk shirt open at the neck. He hired a car and we went out to Westbury for his latest extravaganza, a Hawaiian Festival. Through a combination of radio advertising, newspaper ads, tie-ins with travel agents, and giveaways of trips to Hawaii, he managed to fill the auditorium. After hula dancers, sword swallowers, and Hawaiian variety performers, the highlight of the evening was the entire troupe depicting the history of Hawaii in song and story, ending with a filmed volcano erupting under the stars and stripes.

"Well?" Mel said afterward.

"Volcanic," Sandy answered.

"Paul?"

"The audience seemed to like it."

"And you? Give it to me straight."

"It's like Busby Berkeley produced it after he had too many mai-tais."

"Right! He was my inspiration. That's who I told them to copy."

"That's what you got."

"You thought it was really bad? Don't spare me. Be honest."

"Really bad."

"That's great," he said. "This show isn't for you. If you liked it, I'd be worried," and he beamed, completely delighted that I thought his show was dreadful.

· · ·

I wrote an article for the *New York Times Sunday Magazine* about my experiences teaching in a city high school. After it was published I received a call from a television producer, William Carlson, who has long since retired. Carlson was one of the grand old men among television producers. He had read my piece and he wanted me to write a television documentary on inner-city schools. He had other projects, too, which he thought I could work on. When I said that I didn't have any experience in television work, he told me he could see from the way I used dialogue in the *Times* piece that I could do this kind of writing. He offered to work with me and teach me how to be a television writer. I had begun to be restless with teaching; probably I was getting burned out and didn't realize it. But leaving a paying job for free-lance life when my wife, an illustrator, wasn't on salary either was precarious.

I met with Carlson on several occasions. He screened programs for me. He showed me why scripts were well crafted and why they weren't. In addition to producing documentaries, his production company was beginning to create movies for television and he thought I might be able to work in that area, as well. Before I said yes to doing the script for Carlson, Sandy, my parents, and I were all at my in-laws' home for a barbecue. My father-in-law was questioning me about how much I made on the *Times Magazine* article, if I broke it down by the hour.

"You don't think of it in those terms," I said.

"What are your long-term goals, stated objectively?"

"I'm not asking for your daughter's hand. I'm already married to her."

"We're not telling you how to run your life, but if you ever consider having a family, you might spend some time on your income projections."

I excused myself to talk to an ally in Sandy's family—her cousin, Don, an affable man, an electronics engineer at RCA, who was kind to me and had called immediately to congratulate me when the *Times* piece had appeared.

"They're on my case here. They'll never forgive me for the dentist who got away."

"I knew that guy. He loved to talk about teeth. I'm an engineer. I'm supposed to be dull. But he was *dull*."

Don had played football at Lehigh and was working on a postfootball career belly. When we passed Sandy's mother, who was serving people from a buffet table, she loaded food onto Don's plate. He received mounds of baked beans, cole slaw, macaroni salad, leaving barely enough room for his hamburger. My portion from her was an insult, a pathetic little serving. Granted, Don was a blood relative and of ample girth; but still, you give equal servings, don't you, in a family? You don't announce your contempt through the agency of baked beans. I wanted to say, like Major de Coverley in *Catch-22*, "Gimme eat."

It would have been more poetic if my epiphany came while responding to a wonderful piece of writing. But instead it was the baked beans, the cole slaw, the macaroni salad—or the absence thereof. Looking at my sorry plate, the disdain with which my in-laws held me, it came to me that I might as well commit myself to being a writer. My current profession couldn't even get me a decent plate at a family barbecue. I had their disapproval anyway.

"I'm going to do it," I said to Sandy. "I'm going to leave at the end of the semester and do the script."

"You'll be great. That's terrific."

"That means no job."

"We'll manage."

"What's this?" my mother said, eavesdropping.

"I'm going to stop teaching and become a writer for television. I'm going to do a documentary about schools."

"You're going to leave the teaching?" she said.

"It's what I want to do."

My father, who had joined the conversation, considered this.

"It's like if I could just do my landscapes all the time because it's what I wanted to do," he said. "I wish you all the luck in the world."

"Thank you, Dad."

"We don't have much cash, but if you get short—" he said.

"We'll show them," my mother said. She meant Sandy's parents, not the world at large.

Then I walked over to my mother-in-law and actually said it: "Gimme eat!"

"What?"

"Gimme," and I brandished my plate. "I want the kind of portion you'd give to Rod Serling. Gimme Rod Serling's portion."

"Did you have too much beer?"

"There's beer? I didn't get any beer. Gimme beer."

"Is there something the matter here?" my father-in-law said, coming over to us.

"Just this. Your daughter is now married to a full-time writer. I'm leaving my job to write. And if anybody ever asks you what your son-in-law does for a living, you'll have to say, 'He's a free-lance writer.' Writer, free-lance. Not dentist. Now, gimme!"

Her hand went to her mouth. He stared at me. Mechanically, she gave me a proper portion. One could interpret the fear in their expressions in either of two ways: They were reacting to the wildness in my face. Or they were simply responding to the basic information received, that their daughter's husband had been transformed into a free-lancer before their very eyes. I think the latter.

6.

A HUGE FLORAL bouquet in the shape of a horseshoe arrived at the apartment, the kind you would see festooning a Derby winner. It was sent by Mel with a note, "The best novel I ever read." Not a man for understatement.

He was back in New York and asked me to meet him for lunch at his office. Mel seemed to need reaffirmation through me of his unpretentious origins. When we met for breakfast it was at ordinary coffee shops, and for our lunches we usually ordered sandwiches and ate them in his office, or in warm weather we sat in Central Park. This was fine with me. I wouldn't have allowed Mel to always pick up the check, and I wasn't eager to swap $200 lunch tabs with him.

"The book is great. I totally loved it," he said.

"This is very sweet. Of course, the last novel you read was probably *Catcher in the Rye*, which you read, as I recall, at my recommendation. And you were looking to make out from it."

"True. I don't read many novels. I bet I could make out from this one. Imagine how impressed someone would be that I know the author."

Suddenly, a man appeared from Mel's private bathroom, wiping his hands on a towel. He was in his early thirties, slim with a full head of curly black hair, high cheekbones, pale green eyes. It was Manuelo.

"I found the trouble. Goddamn washer," he said. He didn't

expect to see me sitting there and stopped in his tracks. "I'm Miguel," he said clumsily.

"Aren't you Manuelo?"

"Miguel!" he insisted. He started toward the door, angrily depositing the towel on Mel's desk, speaking under his breath in Spanish. I understand a little Spanish from my teaching days; he was saying, "There's nobody there, then there's somebody there."

"That *was* Manuelo," I said to Mel. "A plumber doesn't drop a towel on a rich man's desk. Plus I recognized him. Plus he spoke English, which I was a little surprised to hear."

Manuelo had recently appeared on "Manuelo!"—an HBO special that was followed by an interview taped in Venezuela. He spoke only Spanish in the interview and was present with an English interpreter. Manuelo, who had just left the room, came back in and, without a word, walked into the bathroom to retrieve a white sports jacket he had forgotten. On leaving he glared at Mel.

"That man is not from building maintenance," I said.

Mel looked like he would have preferred not to get into the subject.

"It was Manuelo. He's very compulsive. He was in my bathroom, he saw a leaky faucet, and when I told him nobody could fix it, he felt challenged. He was in there so long I forgot about him."

"Why would an international singing star be challenged by a leaky faucet?"

Slowly, a little smile appeared.

"You can't tell a soul."

"Go on."

"Manuelo, star of stage, recordings, and videos, the singing sensation from Venezuela, is from 116th Street." He could no longer contain his little smile and smiled broadly. "Manuelo was my super. He came into my apartment one day to fix the toilet and he was singing. And I said to myself, *This guy has a good voice.* So I signed up my super and I made him a star. We changed his hair, made him lose weight, shaped him up. Gave him Spanish lessons."

"Why Spanish lessons? He's Hispanic."

"We cleaned up his diction. And he was told, never speak

English. You'll give yourself away. After all, what kind of glamour is there in a Puerto Rican super from 116th Street? Women the world over are not going to fall in love with that story, so we gave him another story."

"And like an alcoholic going off the wagon, every once in a while he goes into a bathroom and fixes toilets?"

"Like I say, he's compulsive. Now you mustn't tell anybody."

"He was supposed to be from a well-to-do family, an estate, wolfhounds."

"Rented. Rented estate, rented wolfhounds."

"There is a sleaze factor here, Mel."

"Granted, it's a little Barnum. But nobody is hurt by it. And this *is* show business. Actors have been changing their names for as long as anybody can remember. So we changed a little more than that."

"What about the people who lived in the building? Don't they recognize him?"

"They wouldn't believe it's him."

"I've been having trouble with my kitchen faucet. Will Manuelo make house calls?"

Mel had his driver and Jaguar waiting outside the building. We went to Central Park and ate sandwiches on a bench—unpretentiously, but for the anomaly of having a chauffeur waiting outside for us. Mel removed a few sheets of paper from his jacket pocket and went over material with me that he had requested about the publishing industry, the number of books published, sales figures of publishers, sales by types of books, authors, first novelists, best-selling writers.

"They're silly to get a book like yours and not powerhouse it. But they're afraid. They haven't had a book from you before. They want to see where it fits in, how it goes. From what I can tell, in publishing too much is left to chance."

"So what do you think?"

"Beats me."

"All this paperwork and I get a 'beats me.' "

"I'm not sure what to do yet. What I do know is you have to reduce the element of chance. I wouldn't put up with chancy stuff in *my* field. You got a few minutes? I'll show you."

Mel said he was scheduled for a session in a studio. His driver took us to a building in the Fifties. In the studio were musicians, technicians, and about sixty women in their teens and early twenties wearing punk clothes, all with red hair. They were seated holding sheet music. Some of their hair was streaked with red, dark roots showing; some were wearing ill-fitting red wigs.

"I'm putting together a new group," Mel said and motioned for me to sit on a folding chair to the side. He positioned himself in the middle of the room. Before him was a rock band consisting of three guitarists, a percussionist, keyboard player, drummer, and a section with two trumpets and a saxophone. The rock band played a rhythmic, driving accompaniment, and in groups of four the girls sang a song called "Hot Property."

> We're hot property, but not your property.
> So hands off unless we tell you,
> And then hands on and more, don't stop and more,
> Hands on, don't stop and more and more.

Lyrically, musically it put my teeth on edge, but Mel was deep in thought as the women appeared before him in a passing parade of singing redheads. They wore paste-on labels with numbers and Mel made notes on a clipboard.

"Most of these kids are professional performers," he told me, "and I'm going to put the group together just the way you'd cast a show. I control the casting and the result. Nothing's left to chance."

We went into the engineer's booth and Mel listened to several takes of the singers. He gave an assistant the numbers for sixteen performers. All the rest were dismissed. Mel seated himself in the center again, and the sixteen went through the song once more in groups of four. He appeared to be displeased. I didn't see how he had, as he claimed, reduced the element of chance. But as he sat there thinking, with the singers, musicians, and technicians watching him think, I realized that whatever the result, *he* was the one who formulated it.

Finally, he rose, smiled, and said:

"Presto! We want all of you."

People were astonished. The women congratulated each other, not quite believing.

"I thought I'd have this new group and four singers seemed about right," he said to me. "But we're going to do it with all sixteen."

He gathered the singers into two rows. "I want you to think of yourselves as a bunch of cooped-up hot cats who've been in a cell or something for a week and you're let out on stage and you're just exploding with energy and sex. Just erupt. Sing the song, children."

The change from four to sixteen was extraordinary. A pack of feral young women had been unleashed musically. Mel was calm, he smiled benignly. The effect was as he imagined it would be. In that one instant he had taken an idea that didn't seem to be working and converted it into what became Hot Cats. Visually, they were like no other group—sixteen wild-looking punk redheads—and Mel did it. Within six months Hot Cats would have the top-selling album in the country. As for me, I still would have been sitting back there trying to figure out if number seven sounded better than number twelve.

· · ·

Peter Raskin and Martha Sipes called, both on the line, very impatient for an answer to give Greystone Books. Mel wanted a little more time to work out details of a notion he was thinking of for me, and I said they would have to find a way to hold Greystone off for a while longer.

Mel asked me to come to his office; he had worked out the plan.

"Here's what I did. I hired consultants, I talked to investment bankers. Basically, the numbers on book publishing are good enough. But the fifteen thousand first printing projected for your book isn't so great. So what I decided to do was go into the business."

"What do you mean?"

"I'll show you."

He led me to the elevators and we went to the floor below. The elevator door opened on a reception area where a blonde in her twenties was seated. Behind her on the wall in raised letters were the words "Steiner Publications."

"This is Mavis. Mr. Paul Brock."

"A pleasure to meet you, sir."

"Mel, what's going on here?"

"Big things."

We walked down a corridor with several offices on either side. Mel knocked on a door and we entered. A woman in her forties wearing horn-rimmed glasses was seated behind a desk.

"Barbara Moss—Paul Brock. Barbara is our editor-in-chief. She's had important jobs in publishing."

"Well, I'm editor-in-chief, but so far there's no one to be chief of."

"Why don't you explain it to Paul?" Mel said to her.

"We'd like to do about a dozen titles a year to start," she said. "All original, hardcover books. We're looking for a mixture of fiction and nonfiction. Of course, with Mel having so many show-business clients, we intend to do our share of books by and about his clients."

"The beauty part is that I was able to finance this on my track record," Mel told me. "And why have someone else publish a book on one of my people when I can? This way I own the candy and the candy store."

Barbara Moss told me they were making an arrangement with a distributor to get the books into retail outlets. Mel would be taking an overall view of the operation. She would oversee the editorial side. Eventually, they would also be involved in publishing paperback editions. Mel brought his new sales manager into the office, Tom Riggs, a trim, balding man in his forties who had been with Doubleday. The respectability of these people was undeniable. I was speechless, doing a great deal of nodding. Mel had an idea and suddenly he had offices, personnel. He said he wanted to make it comfortable for his clients to write books, or to collaborate with professional authors. They showed me furnished offices which were to be work areas for authors and an authors' lounge.

"I'm going to leave you alone with Barbara and she'll fill you in," Mel said, for the first time breaking into a smile, and he left with Tom Riggs.

"We love your book," Barbara Moss said. "It's touching, it's important, and just the kind of title we think should launch our fiction list. We'd like to offer an advance of one hundred thousand dollars, and based on the kind of strong reaction we expect from the chains and independents, we'll go in with a first printing of around a hundred thousand, and an advertising budget of about a hundred thousand."

I was numb. On some level I could understand the logic for Mel of owning a book publishing firm. There was a good market for books by show-business personalities and he had successful performers on his roster. But I also knew that Mel would never have considered this but for trying to help me. And the terms! With one sweep of his hand Mel was freeing me from my demons.

"Is this really taking place? This isn't a 'Twilight Zone' episode?"

"It's a pleasure to have this book."

I shook hands with her and left the office, returning to Mel's floor.

"You've come to congratulate me on my new venture?"

"Mel, what you're doing for me—"

"This is just good business. Sign the contract. Use one of the offices. That's what they're here for."

"Mel—"

"Shh. Why don't you start a new book? You're a novelist now."

. . .

I went immediately to Sandy's studio to tell her the news.

"I can't believe it. Is the money out of his own pocket?"

"No, he has outside financing."

"Well, he's darn lucky to get you," she said, smiling, both of us knowing it was out of a storybook. I *was* Sabu and Mel was my genie. "What would you like, little master?"

. . .

Mel insisted on taking us out to dinner at Lutèce to celebrate the purchase of *Upward Mobility*. He brought his latest girlfriend, a tall, slender, high-cheekboned model in her twenties, Samantha Reilly.

I raised a glass to him. "This may be the kindest gesture in the history of Western civilization. Or the craziest. Probably both."

"My husband thanks you, my children thank you, and I thank you," Sandy added. "That may not be exactly right."

"This is why I love New York," Samantha said. "Imagine a city where you can get a book published, or spareribs twenty-four hours a day."

"I think they move more spareribs," I said.

"I'm going to write it all down, the experiences I've had here, the people I've known, and I'm putting it in a book, which is going to be mostly about the modeling business and me, which I'm going to write myself. And guess what? Steiner Publishing is going to do it!"

If every woman Mel dated was going to get a book out of it, this was not going to be much of a publishing house.

"Do you have a title?" Sandy asked her.

"I was thinking of song titles—you know, songs I've made love to over the years. But that wouldn't have much to do with modeling. Barbara Moss, she's very smart, she says it should concentrate on the modeling business. So I was thinking of *Do Me, Do Me One More Time: My Story in the Modeling Business.*"

"Catchy," I said.

"Mel, is this the direction your publishing house is going in?" Sandy asked archly.

"In addition to signing Paul, we just arranged to republish a collection of early short stories by Tennessee Williams, so I wouldn't say we're going to be lacking in the prestige area."

"That's impressive," Sandy said, looking at me.

"I know the early stories. That does make me feel better."

"*Why Don't We Do It in The Road? Me and Modeling,*" Samantha Reilly said, operating on her own wavelength.

. . .

Barbara Moss told me publication would be a few months away; the company had to solidify the distribution aspects, and the preparation of the book for publishing would take a while—having it copy-edited, designing the inside of the book and the book jacket. I asked that Sandy do the book jacket and Barbara agreed to that.

"I'm going to do all your books now," Sandy said. "Think of yourself as my client."

"I better start working on another one, before everybody changes their minds."

. . .

My customary work schedule was to write five days a week, taking the weekends off to spend them with Sandy and the boys. On Mondays a rotating cast from a cleaning service came to clean the place and it was noisy in the apartment. On Fridays a sitter didn't arrive until 4:30 and I was often distracted by the children. I wondered if it made sense for me to take advantage of the furnished authors' offices at Steiner Publications on Mondays and Fridays. I decided to try it, taking a laptop computer downtown with me, and I began making notes for a new novel. I walked home from midtown, bouncing in my stride. *Hey, everybody, I'm an author.* Nobody called you an "author" in the television business. You were "the writer." You were an employee.

The work space for authors was down the hall from where Barbara Moss and Tom Riggs had their offices. The room I occupied was spartan but comfortable and on a high floor it was wonderfully quiet. I felt comfortable enough there to bring in my own package of Pecan Sandies, which I left in a refrigerator in the lounge.

One afternoon I was in the lounge sipping tea when Samantha Reilly walked in.

"Hi!"

"Hello, Samantha."

"I've been working on my book. It's so marvelous to actually be doing this where the wanderings of your brain can be converted into words that people will ultimately read in a book before they go to sleep. After making love. On Sundays when they might be lonely. In their private moments in the bathroom."

"Never quite thought of it that way, Samantha."

She took me by the arm and led me to her office. Taped to the walls and all over her desk were scraps of paper from notepads, envelopes, little scraps, large scraps, a mad display of pieces of paper with scribbling on them.

"This is your book?"

"It doesn't really have a form yet. Eventually, I'll tie it all together and type it up. Sex is important in a book, isn't it? I mean, I've slept with a lot of guys, which is part of my New York experience, so don't you think that should be in it?"

I remembered having heard Abe Burrows reminiscing about George S. Kaufman. Burrows was thinking of using a moving platform in a play and asked advice from Kaufman who had used one the season before. Kaufman responded, "A moving platform is fine, Abe. But what do you want to say on it?" And that's how I chose to answer Samantha.

"A book is fine, Samantha. But what do you want to say on it?"

. . .

I now knew the next novel I wanted to write. The book came out of a sense of unfinished business on my basketball script. It was to be the story of a scriptwriter who begins to hang around a schoolyard in Harlem to research a script he is writing. As he does his research, in part by trying to play ball with the schoolyard players, he is drawn into the life of the ball-players and the local community. He becomes close to one of the ball-players, a boy of promise in both basketball and academics. The writer becomes a kind of mentor to the boy. But the realities of inner-city life intrude and the conflict lies in whether or not the youngster is able to escape his environment and in how much the writer—white, an outsider—can actually accomplish. I saw it as a serious book about city life, race, social class, but with a comic side to it in the writer's attempts to fit in.

I was part of a writers' project and we made visits to adult literacy groups in inner-city libraries, so I had some experience in trying to relate to people who came from a different background. Then, too, I had lived in New York all my life; I had a feeling for the city, and there was my own little foray into the schoolyard on the basketball script. I was going to use the same approach as with *Upward Mobility,* taking what I knew and moving it over a few degrees, hoping for accuracy. With the confidence, perhaps the arrogance, of having completed my first novel, I thought that on this one I wouldn't be trying to measure up to Updike. I felt I was exactly the person to write this book.

. . .

My work pattern was established; on Mondays and Fridays when it would be noisiest at home, I wrote in the office at Steiner Publications. The rest of the week I worked in the apartment. I met Mel for our occasional breakfasts, and one morning I learned that he was no longer going out with Samantha. He deemed her "too scatterbrained."

"If she's so scatterbrained, why is she writing a book for you?"

"Content. Sex, drugs, manipulation of beautiful women. What more can you ask for?"

"You could end up in it as one of her lovers," I teased.

"I hadn't thought of that. This is an important lesson for me," he said with conviction. "If I'm going to be a publisher, I can't sleep with the authors."

I learned from Samantha that her relationship with Mel was not going to find its way into the book.

"Barbara and I worked out that the book is about my life in New York in modeling and Mel comes after I stopped modeling so he's not going to be in it because you have to have integrity about these things if you're a writer."

Samantha insisted on my seeing the latest stage of her book. She had transferred her various scraps of paper to bond paper now taped all over the room, which for her amounted to a second draft.

. . .

I was at the Steiner offices taking a break in the lounge, chatting with Samantha when appearing in the room, wearing white slacks, white loafers, and a white silk sports shirt was Manuelo.

"Hello, there," Samantha said. Manuelo fixed me with the famous Manuelo eyes. "This is Paul."

"We've met," I said and we shook hands.

"I know you know about me and how I speak English. Mel told me you are friends a long time. But it's between us, Mel's people." He turned to Samantha. "You are writing a book. You don't put that I speak English in your book."

"Not to worry," she said, her editorial integrity in order. "You come in postmodeling."

"I have a book myself. The story of the life of Manuelo."

"Manuelo, can I ask you something, colleague to colleague? How can you write the story of your life when your life was made up?"

"It is not the story of how I become Manuelo. Is the story of how I *am* Manuelo. What clothes I wear. The music I like. What I think of women. What I consider beautiful. What I eat, drink, how I exercise. What I think of different cities of the world. What makes me happy. What makes me sad."

"It sounds wonderful," Samantha said. "Do you have a ghost writer or are you making it up yourself?"

"Myself," he said indignantly. "I show you." We went to his office. These rooms were furnished with a desk, typing chair, and easy chair. Manuelo's office also contained a tape recorder for his writing and a wall mirror for him to look at himself.

"For a woman to be beautiful," he demonstrated, talking into his tape recorder, "she must be beautiful inside. But if inside, how do we see her on the outside? She must turn herself inside out. Women who can do this are beautiful women." He turned to us and smiled. "Good writing, no?"

"You're speaking in English," I said. "You're not supposed to speak English."

"They will take it from the tape. Translate into Spanish. Then translate back into English."

"I should have known," I said.

"Two weeks I'm working," Manuelo said. "I am halfway done with the book."

"Two weeks! After two weeks I'd still be looking out the window."

"You use a tape recorder?" Manuelo asked me.

"A computer."

"The new little tape recorders, minis. Very good. Stick it in your pocket, pull it out. You can write anywhere."

"This is so neat, writers talking shop," Samantha said. "Don't you just love being a writer? In some ways writing about your life is better than living it.''

"Well, you get to edit,'' I said.

. . .

On every new project I experienced an initial period of apprehension. If someone were to look over my shoulder while I was writing, they would see chaos. A compulsive rewriter, I type on the computer, print the pages out and then scribble all over the pages before retyping onto the screen. With the first pages of the new novel, I couldn't tell whether the material I had in front of me was absolutely fine or the work of someone deranged.

. . .

I was working at home when Judith Krantz, Jackie Collins, and Barbara Cartland came sweeping into my room wearing identical red ballroom gowns, looking like the literary Supremes. They picked up my pages and passed them around, browsing through the material.

"Is it a blockbuster?'' Judith Krantz said.

"I can't tell you,'' I responded.

"What do you mean, you can't tell me? You don't know if it's a blockbuster before you begin?''

"How could I possibly know? I start with a vision—''

"*Vision?*'' Jackie Collins said. "What are you, an optometrist? You don't get blockbusters with vision. You get them with plot.''

"And romance,'' Barbara Cartland added. "Is there romance in it?''

"The main character is married.''

"Who does he have his affairs with?'' Judith Krantz asked.

"Nobody.''

"What kind of book is this? There's no sex?''

"Not overtly. The boy he gets involved with has a girlfriend.''

"He gets involved with a boy? This is promising,'' Jackie Collins said.

"Involved emotionally, as a friend. The boy's a street kid and this fellow lives in another world.''

"You have a street kid in your novel? It sounds very urban,''

Barbara Cartland commented with perfect diction, saying "urban" as if it were a dirty word.

"My God," Judith Krantz said. "This room and this apartment! How do you work in a city apartment house that's not even a penthouse?"

"This is not a penthouse sort of book," I said.

"Who are you writing for, the poor?" Judith Krantz said.

"Do you have the miniseries lined up?" Jackie Collins asked.

"No, and I'm sure it doesn't have the right demographics for a miniseries."

"He doesn't have a blockbuster mentality, he has doubts about what he's working on, *and* he doesn't have the miniseries lined up," Judith Krantz said.

"Not only that, he scrawls all over the page," Barbara Cartland said, holding up a page of mine as if it were a smelly fish.

"Let's go, girls," Jackie Collins said. "We're obviously dealing with a troubled person," and they swept haughtily out of the room, leaving me alone with the start of my novel and my marked-up pages.

. . .

Samantha Reilly invited me in to see the latest phase of her book. The text was typed out and she had added photographs with captions, everything taped to the walls.

"Sometimes it's so frustrating," she said. "It's like you have this picture of what you want to say and how you want to say it, and it's always just out of reach and you never say it as wonderfully as you want to in your mind."

"I know exactly what you mean, Samantha."

If the definition of a writer is someone who writes, then Samantha Reilly was becoming a writer. She came in every day and worked. Looking at the pages on her wall I could see that Samantha wrote the way she spoke; her reminiscences were random, uneven. But within the material were excellent passages. Her working title was now *A Life in New York,* and the voice of the writer was very distinctive to me.

I had a conversation with Barbara Moss and spoke in general terms about the book I had started. She was encouraging about the idea and raised the question of whether I and my agent would be soliciting an advance. I didn't see how I could live with Mel's bankrolling my activities any more than he already had and I suggested we wait until I had something tangible to show. As I was leaving I asked about Samantha's book, which I knew she had completed and submitted in a carton.

"Frankly, there's no form to it. It's too quirky. It's just not publishable."

I was devastated for Samantha. I knew I was identifying with her, that the word "quirky" upset me, that Barbara Moss represented every television executive who didn't like a script or a proposal of mine because it didn't conform, because it was "quirky." Beyond that I thought Samantha had a clear, authentic voice.

"Would you have an objection if I went over her material?" I asked Barbara.

"Why would you want to?"

"Because I liked what she showed me. What did you think of the writing, purely as writing?"

"What I read I liked. But I was so put off by the lack of shape I stopped reading, and I'm sure that would be any reader's response, too."

Now I was really worked up. Barbara hadn't bothered to read it all. I did. It occurred to me as I went through it that the form was the form. They should have been publishing the book just the way it was, the photos, the written passages interspersed, as if it were a free-flowing diary of a life in New York. I spent the next day finding some internal rhythms to the material, moving sections around, numbering the order. I went into Barbara's office with it and told her I believed there was something special to Samantha's material. I asked that she keep an open mind and go over it again. To her credit she said that she would.

A few days later she knocked on my door at Steiner. "Paul, I wanted to tell you we're going to publish Samantha's book. I can see it working the way you laid it out. I don't know how many copies we can sell. But we'll publish it."

"Fantastic!"

A while later, Samantha came into my office, glowing.

"I'm going to be a published author! Barbara Moss said she

doesn't know how many copies she can sell, but the writing is very fine and I deserve my turn and she said you helped and I'm so grateful."

She kissed me on the cheek and was so happy she nearly went dancing out the door. It was the next best thing to having it happen to me.

. . .

Samantha must have mentioned something to Manuelo about my helping with her book because he came to my office one day and shyly asked if I would listen to his latest writing. He was so tentative about what he was working on and needful of approval that I couldn't decline. He began leaving notes for me under the door every Monday asking if he could see me, and when I took a break or finished for the day I would go in to Manuelo, who would play me his work in progress. I made suggestions, usually for clarity when what he had done was incoherent.

The book was much as he had described. Part one was "My Favorites," attitudes and fashions he liked in women and in himself. Part two, "My Dislikes," drugs, loud parties, dishonest women, leaky faucets. (An unguarded moment there.) Part three, "My Favorite Performances." The performances he was referring to were *his*. Part four, "My Wishes for My Fans," inspirational words about people trying for their full potential. Part five, "My Wishes for the Planet Earth," about keeping the air and the waters clear. The last two parts were rather sweet, the sentimental worldview of a man who, not long before, was unknown and fixing apartments.

. . .

Manuelo: The Book was rushed into print and published a few months later. The publication party was held in the main ballroom of the Plaza Hotel, six hundred guests present. Sandy and I stood in a special VIP section behind a velvet rope. We could see Mel coordinating the proceedings wearing a tuxedo and carrying a walkie-talkie, a millionaire security guard. The event featured a special personal appearance by Manuelo backed by a full orchestra as he sang from his latest album, *More Manuelo*. In a dramatic first, Manuelo sang a song in English, more accented than his regular speech. The title of the song was "The Writer," and the lyrics were roughly:

> I was a singer, a singer of songs of love.
> Now I'm also a writer, telling you my feelings.
> But song or book, being open with your emotions
> Is the answer and I open my heart to you.

Stephen Sondheim was not imperiled.

A new video was released for television, Manuelo singing "The Writer," promoting *Manuelo: The Book*. The book, liberally illustrated with photographs of himself with beautiful women, in the recording studio, comic-mugging for the camera, in serious moments, was basically the Compleat Manuelo. The merchandising included posters and life-sized standup displays of Manuelo. In a Mel Steiner gambit, the album was available in bookstores and the book was available in record stores. The most pungent line of the appearance of *Manuelo: The Book* was the one that appeared across the bottom of the displays: "English Language Edition."

It became the number one nonfiction bestseller.

7.

A FRONT-PAGE article appeared in *USA Today,* "Show Biz King Adds Another Diamond to His Crown," which reported on the new publishing company. The best-selling Manuelo book was high-lighted in the piece and *Upward Mobility* was mentioned promi-nently with laudatory remarks about it by Mel and Barbara Moss. On an inside page I was shown in a head shot, "Paul Brock, Steiner Author." The article continued with a rundown of the Mel Steiner hit parade. Manuelo on a European tour. Hot Cats on a national tour. B-Tuff, a black rap group with a hit album. Wanda, Mel's Madonna, a frizzy-haired blonde with a smash hit record and video, "I Want You Inside Me," the song banned by many radio stations. And a college campus tour by Delta Jack Green, an ancient black blues singer.

"I been dead and back so many times, I thinks I'm in heaven and heaven's where you plays the blues," Delta Jack said in the article. The quote had been in a publicity release I saw prepared by Steiner Public Relations, a subsidiary of Mel's that publicized his clients. And it was used by Jay Leno when he introduced Delta Jack for an appearance on the "Tonight Show." However, Delta Jack never said any such thing. Mel fabricated the quote and gave it to his staff for release. "He *would* have said it, if he thought of it," Mel explained to me.

. . .

I left the *USA Today* article on a table in the foyer of our apartment so that both sets of parents, who were coming for dinner, could see the piece. My mother immediately seized my copy, probably to laminate it. My father-in-law asked, "If you broke it down, how much do you think you make an hour for a book like that?" Leaving the article for them to see was courting their approval and it was a miscalculation. The mood in the room was all about when I would appear in interviews on television.

"He's months away from publication and nobody knows how a book is going to be received," Sandy said, attempting to ward them off.

"Imagine," my mother said. "He used to write for television, and now he's going to be *on* it," no doubt trying out a line she was going to use with her peers.

While I worked on the new novel, the publication process moved forward for *Upward Mobility*. The book was given over to a copy-editor and we met in an office at Steiner to discuss her queries. "I'm not paid to say this," she told me when we were finished. "It's a fine book. Congratulations."

. . .

I was floating through my days, uniformly cheerful. For a person to be uniformly cheerful who has worked for years through the vagaries of free-lance life—that was cheerful. Sandy had been busy with the artwork for the book jacket and I went to her studio to see her rendering; a couple faced each other with strained expressions on their faces, above their heads in an arc, rendered in a nearly psychedelic fashion, were scenes from the 1960s. "Not only does it capture the book, not only is it a gorgeous design, but my very wife did it. It tells me how lucky am."

"You only wrote the book," she said. "In my business we have to find out what the publisher thinks."

Of course, they loved the artwork. Mel was going to Europe for a few weeks and saw it before he left. He sent Sandy a dozen roses with a note saying, "I would tell the author to marry you, if he hadn't already."

. . .

On a high, launched in my new profession, untouched by bills, I glided into the Steiner office for a meeting with Barbara Moss and Tom Riggs, and settled into a chair to await the next wonderful news that was coming my way. Four seconds. That is how long it took me to know something ominous was in the air. My antenna for determining this was developed over years of script conferences. I listened to Barbara tell me how excited people were about Sandy's cover, that they wanted to make it into a poster that could be displayed in bookstores, that they would like Sandy to do other work for them, and I was thinking—let's get to the bad news. She turned matters over to Tom Riggs who said:

"Paul, we're having some problems with the book. We thought we could muscle our way into the marketplace, big first printing, et cetera. But the buyers at the chains and the wholesalers, they're reluctant to take on so many copies from an unknown writer."

"We can get about twenty thousand copies distributed across the country, and that's truly excellent for a first novel," Barbara Moss said. "However, it's not anywhere near what was promised to you or what Mel was expecting."

"Does Mel know about this?"

"I spoke to him a while ago," Tom Riggs answered. "He was in Europe on the run."

"You have a number one bestseller. Doesn't that give you some clout with bookstores?"

"We hoped. But they're looking at your book, your name, as a separate issue."

"What you shouldn't lose sight of," Barbara Moss counseled me, "is that people really do appreciate the book, and when the reviews come in for us, as I expect they will, we can have the ammunition to move on it."

"We just can't bully our way into bookstores," Tom Riggs said. "I had meetings with the wholesalers. Books by name authors dominate these days and there isn't much room anymore for authors who aren't well known."

"We felt obliged to be honest with you," Barbara Moss said. "I was talking in terms of a hundred thousand first printing. It's just not in our power to deliver on anything like that. We're very sorry."

. . .

I thanked them for their candor and left. When Sandy came home from the studio I told her about the meeting. She was thoughtful and didn't say anything for a while. She spoke slowly, as if she were choosing her words carefully.

"This has got to be disappointing. But it doesn't change the book you wrote. It's still wonderful."

"Can I quote you to yourself? Didn't you say this is a business of self-fulfilling prophecies?"

"True. Unfortunately, you've been thinking you were going to have a big book. But will you take 'critically acclaimed'?"

"Is that for sure?"

"*I'm* sure."

"My mother will have a major event out of this. But if the book doesn't pay its own way I can't go back and ask Mel to overpay me again on the next book. All we have then is vanity publishing."

She didn't answer because there was no answer for it. I wasn't going to be liberated from my previous career if I couldn't even pay my way in my new one.

"Maybe Mel will think of something when he comes back," she said.

"So I'm waiting for Godot."

. . .

I got cozy with the children and we watched a Charlie Brown movie on the television.

"Did you like it?" Sandy asked the boys when it was over.

"We did. Daddy didn't," Sammy said.

"I did."

"You didn't laugh so much."

"Daddy's a little sad. He had some disappointing news today," Sandy said.

"What happened?" Joey asked.

"He thought his book was going to be a big, big book. And

they told him that it wouldn't be so big, after all. But he has to remember it's still a wonderful book, and he's a wonderful daddy."

"Not so wonderful if I can't laugh at Charlie Brown," I said, making a preposterous face, pulling my mouth down with my fingers, which made them giggle.

. . .

I took a walk after the children went to sleep and, perched on the wall that runs along Central Park, I saw Snoopy. He was seated at his typewriter. I nodded, he nodded back. I came over to peek at the page in his machine. He had written: "It was a dark and stormy night."

"Working on your novel?" I said.

"I'm having a little trouble getting started," he answered. He spoke in a growly sort of voice.

"I've never seen you around here before," I said to him.

"I was in New York on business. I thought I'd get a little work in."

"I'm a writer. I just finished a novel and I've begun another."

"I envy you. I have writer's block."

"Maybe you should start somewhere else instead of the beginning. I do that sometimes when I'm stuck. I pick out what's going to be a good part and I write that, just to get going."

"Maybe I will. Thanks. Is your book in the stores? I'd like to read it."

"Not yet."

"And your name?"

"Paul Brock."

"Snoopy," and he extended his paw.

"I feel I know you," I said. "I have your towels."

"Look, I'm not getting anywhere tonight. Do you have a copy of your book? I'd like to read it."

"Sure. Are you going to be here?"

"This is my spot."

I rushed home, got a copy of the manuscript, and brought it back to him.

"I'll have it read pretty quickly. I took a speed-reading course for dogs. I can read fast, run fast, sniff fast. I can't write fast," he added.

I waved goodbye and returned to the apartment. Early in the morning I went back to the park. Snoopy was working at his typewriter.

"Hi. You inspired me. I loved your book."

"You did?"

"I admire that you finished the book. That really is an achievement to me, being as how I'm an unpublished beagle."

"Well, thank you for your thoughts. It helps my morale right now."

"I want to give you something."

He typed a few words and then gave me the sheet of paper. It said, "I loved it. The perfect book to read on a dark and stormy night. Snoopy."

That was very kind of him. But it wasn't a quote I could actually use.

. . .

I was attempting to concentrate on the new novel, working at home, when the doorbell rang. Mel was standing there in a new Italian suit.

"They're crazy. That's what I have to tell you. I just got off the plane and came straight here to tell you they're crazy. The bookstore people are crazy. My people are crazy. Your book is going to be a blockbuster."

"Would you like to come in and sit down?"

"I don't sit. I didn't get where I am by sitting. Moving forward is what I do. Do you know what a trip I had? Do you know how successful Europe was for me? I had three groups circulating, selling out. And I hear from New York, what? A first printing of twenty thousand copies?"

"That's what they tell me."

"Crazy. My point in all of this was—you don't leave anything to chance. And I won't, you'll see. I'm going to the office, I'm going to take care of a few things and I'm coming back here for you in my new Rolls-Royce. A guy with a Rolls has to be smart. Then we're going to get in the car, drive up to the Bronx, have a pizza on Arthur Avenue like in the old days, and we're going to focus on the good part, that you wrote a great book, and I'm going to publish it, and it's going to be a blockbuster, and they're crazy."

. . .

On our way uptown I said to Mel, "The music from *Aïda* should be playing as you return to the Bronx in a chauffeured Rolls." We arrived at the Belmont section. Dion and the Belmonts had been from this area and it was there that Mel and I had gone for pizza when we were kids. By the 1990s it was a modified version of what we remembered, but still in business were a few Italian restaurants, food stores, cafes, bakeries. We went into a restaurant that had a bar and started off with vodka and tonics.

"Now what are we going to do about the book? It's too bad you never took drugs," Mel said, unseriously. "We could get a lot of mileage out of you renouncing your habit."

"Too bad I'm not dead. We could get a lot of mileage out of publishing it posthumously."

. . .

Neither of us had any workable ideas and eventually the conversation drifted, Mel talking about his European trip. After the vodka and tonics, we ordered pizza and beer, then Mel insisted we celebrate his successful trip and my book with champagne. We left; I was very wobbly and we thought it would be good to walk off the alcohol. We decided to stroll along Mosholu Parkway like we used to when we were kids. The Rolls dropped us there, we walked a while and leaned against a car as we had done in another era. Suddenly, Mel said, "And now, presenting the Journeymen!" and he started to sing one of our songs.

"Mel, someone is going to look out a window and yell, 'You guys still trying to make it? Give it up!' "

I started to sing with him. We remembered some of the songs, missed some, then came to the Edith Piaf section and sang the lyrics I had written for "The Undoctor of Love," which included:

Oh, I'm not a doctor,
And the girls want a doctor.
I could stand on my head, I could make works of art,
But the terrible part
Is they just want a doctor.
It's their cultural dream
To be Mrs. M.D.
Where is that leaving me?
All alone as can be.
The Undoctor of love.

We fell to the ground in a laughing, boozy heap.

"We had something then, you know," Mel said.

"Insanity."

"To take that kind of music and do songs about dating—that was so great."

I launched into a reprise of the "The Undoctor of Love." Mel joined me and, lacking an audience, we applauded ourselves.

"Nobody was doing anything like it," he declared. "Comedy songs that said something. We were unique. We could've run with it."

"How many years can you sing about teenage dating? As we got older we would have moved with the times."

"Right," he said with the affable agreement of a man who has had too much to drink.

"I can write. I would have written about what concerned us next," I said, slurring my words.

"Absolutely. You would have kept us up-to-date. We would have been terrific."

"We could have done it, Charlie. We could have been contenders."

We helped each other up and made our way arm in arm back to the Rolls, where his driver was waiting.

"All those house bands," he said. "Too bad we never heard it with a big sound. It would've been even funnier."

"Even funnier," I said, slumping into the back seat. Woozy, I closed my eyes as the car headed back to Manhattan. After a few minutes I looked over at Mel to see if he had fallen asleep. He was thinking about something, his eyes squinting in concentration. He picked up his car phone and dialed a number.

"Henry? It's Mel. You free? I need sixteen pieces in an hour. With strings. Right." He hung up the phone.

"What are you doing?" I asked.

"Taking care of some business."

"You're going to work now? Jesus, I couldn't keep these hours." And I drifted into sleep.

．．．

"Rise and shine."

Mel was tapping me on the shoulder. I looked outside and we were not at my house; we were in front of the building where Mel's offices were located.

"What's going on?"

"I need you for something."

"I've got to get to bed. I already have a hangover and it's not even tomorrow."

He took me by the arm and led me, rubber-legged, into the building. We went to the floor above his office, where Steiner Varieties had a recording studio. We entered the studio and I blinked at the bright lights and the scene before me. An orchestra was there, sixteen musicians, technicians were on the floor, an engineer was in the booth. A man in his forties approached us, slightly built, about five feet six wearing sneakers, jeans, and a dress shirt with the sleeves rolled up.

"Henry Ross. Paul Brock. Henry's been in England a while. I convinced him to come back and work for my organization."

I remembered his name. Henry Ross had been one of the leading pop music producers during the sixties.

"Paul is going to sing a song," Mel told him. "The concept is, he'll write songs like the one he's going to do now, but about adult issues, and we build an act around him. I'd like to have everybody play it by ear so we can hear it with full orchestra."

"What?" I said.

"You're going to sing 'The Undoctor of Love.' They'll fill in behind you."

"Mel!"

"What's the problem? You remember the song."

"Could we have a little conference?"

I went outside the studio into the corridor with him.

"You want me to sing 'The Undoctor of Love' in front of all those people? You're drunk!"

"So are you."

"You were half the team. You sing it."

I headed down the corridor and he grabbed my arm.

"This is a little experiment."

"Sixteen musicians is not little. And violins! 'The Undoctor of Love' with violins? That's not even appropriate."

"The idea came from you. You said you could have written songs about what we were into next. Well, I want to hear how it would sound if you sang that kind of song with a full arrangement."

"Why?"

"Because if it works the way I think it could, you can write those songs, comic songs about where you are now, a family man, kids, bills. And we can put together an act and an album and you can be a star and people will buy your books in vast quantities."

"You are so incredibly nuts only your wealth keeps you from being institutionalized."

"Books by celebrities sell. So let's make you a celebrity."

"It's absurd!"

"Just sing it once so I can get a feeling about it."

"Those musicians will be throwing up. And I'm the one who should be doing that."

"Those musicians were hired by me to play for you. Now will you satisfy my curiosity?"

"No."

"Do this for an old friend."

"Absolutely not."

"What is it going to cost you to indulge me? You're drunk anyway. Come on, Paul, please!"

I surely must have been drunk because I said:

"I will sing it once and then we can all throw up."

We went back inside. A technician positioned a microphone in front of me. I was standing turned away from the orchestra, not wanting to make eye contact with the musicians. Henry Ross gave me a cue and I started to sing "The Undoctor of Love" a capella. Mel asked me to do it again with the orchestra playing and they filled in behind me, Henry Ross signaling for sections of the orchestra to accompany me. By the time I was finished with the song the full orchestra was playing.

"Great!" Mel said. "We have you on a track. Henry can noodle with the arrangement and we can put it all together. Get a good night's sleep and start thinking of song ideas."

"I can't do this," I protested.

"If a melody comes to you while you're writing the lyrics, fine. Hum it into a tape recorder. Henry can clean it up or he can write the melodies."

"I said I can't do this!"

"You *are* a writer."

"I can't have an act. I am a person in my forties who has not sung since I was a kid, and barely then."

Undaunted, Mel said to Henry:

"What if we sprinkle in some standards like Willie Nelson sang on the *Star Dust* album?"

"It's possible."

"I'm not Willie Nelson!"

"And Willie Nelson doesn't write novels." Mel put his arm around me and led me out of the studio. "You're going to be a contender, after all."

. . .

Mel told his driver to take me home. I slept a dream-riddled sleep that night. When I was awakened in the morning by a ringing phone for a split second I wasn't sure if I had dreamed that entire episode in the studio. Mel was on the phone to confirm I had not.

"Wake up. Big doings. We took your track, mixed it together with an arrangement Henry worked out, and it sounded great."

"Are you still drinking?"

"I want you in the studio one sharp. I want to try out that idea of doing standards."

"Should I send an ambulance for you? Or just have the Rolls take you in for observation?"

"Paul, I'm going to make you a star. People are going to be scrambling to buy your books. Forget twenty thousand copies. Forget a hundred. A five hundred thousand first printing. How does that sound to you? Now what do you like to sing for your own enjoyment? What do you sing in the shower?"

"This is a classic good news—bad news story. The good news is a man says he's going to give you a five hundred thousand first printing. The bad news is he's insane."

"One sharp."

A half-hour later Henry Ross called. He wanted to do an arrangement and needed to know what song I would like to sing. Crazy people kept calling me.

"You're going to have all those musicians there again? Forget it."

"You know how persistent Mel is. If you don't do it, he'll probably send us all over to you. Mel told me I'm supposed to say something to you that apparently has some significance. Five hundred thousand first printing."

"Sometimes in the shower I sing 'I Get a Kick out of You.' "

"Perfect. See you later."

I went to the studio at one; Mel and Henry were there with the musicians. The first time I was drunk and singing a song nobody knew. Here I was supposed to be singing one of the great songs in the pop lexicon.

"This is going to be fun," Henry offered.

"In the way that horror movies are."

Henry cued the orchestra, the brass came in, the strings, the electronic section, and then I entered. Grinding my way through in nervousness I delivered what had to be one of the worst renditions of any song ever, including from drunks on sidewalks.

Mel and Henry took me out of the studio and we went into the men's room where Mel suggested, in terms redolent of Professor Higgins coaching Eliza Doolittle, that it was a great song and I was capable of singing it. Henry said he was an experienced musician and according to what he had heard before, he knew I could do it. I seriously questioned the mental health of this operation. A man was telling me that based on my rendition of "The Undoctor of Love" I could do a good job on "I Get a Kick out of You."

Henry insisted I was merely nervous and he had me sing the song in the men's room. I went out again and tried not to look at the musicians and to think of myself as singing in the shower instead, but I messed up the words. On the next take one of the musicians missed an entrance and I wondered if that was thrown in for me, the way a juggler drops a plate to make it look like a harder trick: Don't be nervous, Paul. Even the pros can make a mistake here. We did it three times more. Compared with the way I started I sensed I might possibly have been getting better as we went along. At the conclusion Henry and Mel both complimented me, saying it was excellent.

. . .

Into the studio making a surprise appearance came Erica Jong, Gloria Steinem, and Erma Bombeck. They were wearing red polka-dot dresses and their hair was made up 1940s-style so that they looked like the Andrews Sisters.

"We're your new backup group," Erica Jong said.

"We call ourselves the Publishettes," Gloria Steinem announced.

"Eventually what we'd like to do, after backing you up for a while, is go out on our own," Erma Bombeck said.

"We'll back you up, but frankly we heard that 'Undoctor of Love' song and we think it's sexist beyond belief," Erica Jong commented.

"You have to realize it was written years ago. Before my consciousness was raised."

"Let's do a standard," Erma Bombeck suggested. "Why don't we do 'I Could Write a Book'?" She turned to the orchestra and said, "Hit it!"

With yours truly doing the lead vocal and the Publishettes backing me, we did an up-tempo, scintillating version of the song. Cleaning people, security guards came in to hear us. We were great.

"I've heard a lot of writers sing in bars and at parties," Gloria Steinem said. "You are definitely up there with the top vocalists among writers."

"Is that fiction or nonfiction?" I asked.

"Of everybody," Erma Bombeck declared.

"Anytime you want us to back you up, just whistle," Erica Jong offered. Then in unison they said, "You know how to whistle, don't you? You just pucker up your lips and blow." And they went off to a sparkling buck and wing.

· · ·

Mel gave me a cassette tape of the edited version of "The Undoctor of Love," the best take of "I Get a Kick out of You," and an inspirational speech. I had the talent to write and perform the material. This was the business he knew. He would take care of promoting me and he would hype me into stardom. He was guaranteeing stardom.

· · ·

Probably remembering something I read once in a magazine, like "How to Achieve a Long-Standing Marriage," I repressed the urge to explode with the news of my day and asked Sandy how her day went. She saw through this and said, "Fine. Tell me what's happening with you."

"Mel has decided I can become a star in his stable of stars."

"Darling, you're that now," she responded, not yet to the point of understanding.

"He means a singing star."

"As in singing?"

"As in singing with a sixteen-piece orchestra with strings."

"*My* honey, who sings 'I Get a Kick out of You' in the shower?"

"That could be one of the standards he's thinking of including."

"I know you boys sang together once, but my impression was that you weren't very good."

"We weren't."

"So?"

"Mel insists I can carry a tune well enough and he's brought in Henry Ross." When I saw she didn't know the name, I explained. "He's an arranger and record producer. He thinks I can sing well enough, too, but he's being paid to say that. They want to create an act, an album."

"You're going to get up in front of people and sing 'I Get a Kick out of You'?"

"And songs I would write. Comic songs, Mel says, about family life, kids, bills."

"I always thought you had to be a little off to do what Mel does."

"He says if I go ahead with this he guarantees stardom. The first printing of the new novel will be five hundred thousand."

"Do you have some zeroes in the wrong place?"

"The idea of making me a show-business personality and then using that to promote my novels is a new, unexplored level of craziness. On the other hand, this is a man who can promote anything."

"Darling, you are not Manuelo."

"It defies logic. Manuelo is not Manuelo."

I inserted the cassette into our tape player.

"This is what we recorded today."

Apprehensively, she listened to the tape, frowning in concentration. When it was over she rewound it and listened again.

"It's unreal," she said, finally. "With the orchestra and the arrangement, I might not have known it was you. He wants you to do songs like that, 'The Undoctor of Love'?"

"Updated versions."

We looked at each other with confusion.

"Does he have any ulterior motives?" Sandy said.

"Meaning what?"

"Would he want to make a fool of you?"

"That's a very odd train of thought. Is there some background here I should know about, such as between Mel and you?"

"I'm merely raising the question. You trust that he's being totally straight with you?"

"Of course. What are you suggesting?"

"I just wonder if there's something else going on here. What if you don't go for this deal of his? Will he still publish the book the same way?"

"I'll ask him."

I reached Mel later in the evening and confronted him. He embarked on a long, tangled discourse. He originally said he would publish a one hundred thousand first printing before he understood the nuances of the publishing field, and although we were the closest of friends, this was business, and the correct business thing to do was for me to accept Major Stardom, and that was what he was talking about—*Major* Stardom—and I shouldn't even be considering an alternative.

"So you won't publish it aggressively if I say no to your scheme."

"It's not a scheme. You say 'scheme' and it sounds as if there's some risk involved. This is a guaranteed situation."

"I hear you, Mel. You won't do much with the book."

"It doesn't have to come to that. Let's just proceed."

"Sandy was raising questions, an odd tone to her voice. Is there something relevant you want to tell me about the two of you?"

"This has nothing to do with Sandy. It's about you. And what I can do for you. Look, I know how to do this. I do these things even for people I *don't* love."

I reported back to Sandy the exchange with Mel.

"He says he loves you, but he won't publish the book in a big way unless you go along with him."

"Well, he says it's business."

"Of course. He's hardly an artist."

"The book will probably disappear and I'll be back in television meetings. *Got that little indulgence out of your system, Paul?* Another TV scriptwriter who merely wrote a book on the side."

"How can he 'guarantee' it? How can he say such a thing?"

"A five hundred thousand first printing. A lot of writers would sing for that."

"All those years of waiting for my parents to accept you. If you do this, how are we possibly going to explain you now?"

"If I'm a star, they'll love it."

"I'm sure you're right."

. . .

Mel asked me to come to his office and we ordered sandwiches for lunch.

"Paul? Have you made up your mind?"

"It's a very complicated situation."

"It isn't at all. It's eminently do-able. You write comic songs with a point of view. Think of it as writing a little revue. And we blend in a few other songs, that's all."

"That's all? I'm not a professional singer!"

"We don't say you are. You're everyone who ever sang in a shower and had a fantasy of what it would be like to sing with an orchestra. You're telling the audience, *I'm just like you and isn't this fun?* You don't take your singing seriously. You're just having a great time and you're inviting the audience to share it with you."

"I say to you I'm not a singer and you say my amateurism is a plus?"

"That's right. I just shot down your best argument, didn't I?"

"How can this possibly work?"

"It can't fail. Knowing that is how I make my living. Incidentally, I take fifteen percent. Is it a go?"

"No."

"Paul, what sells in our culture is names, celebrity-ness. There's a whole machinery for cranking out stars. People who aren't all that different from the next person make it with the right packaging, the right finesse. You think every big star is demonstrably, definitively better than the person who doesn't make it? Don't be naive. It's in the merchandising."

"But I'm a writer, not a performer."

"And nobody knows who you are. We use one to sell the other. Look at all the celebrities who write books today that sell like crazy; novels even, and they sell—because the authors are brand names."

"What kind of author can I possibly be if I consent to this? This has got to affect who I am, what I write."

"Why? Is your voice as an author so timid? You're going to be thrown off so easily by some freedom? Because that's what you're getting here. I'm giving you a built-in audience for your books, people who'll be eager to read you. That should be goddamn liberating. You can write exactly what you want, knowing there's a huge audience for it. Books that are review-proof. That are going to be publishing events. What author would turn it down?"

"An act?"

"What isn't an act today? Authors go on book tours. Scientists go on 'Nightline.' The machinery keeps working, Paul. A few years ago nobody ever heard of Madonna. Well, that's where you are, outside the machinery. But you can get in on the inside. You can use it. It's there to be used. You're talented. But you're unknown. So get yourself known. Have fun with this act and from now on you'll write exactly what you want to write and people will read it. This is a no-lose situation. There's nothing wrong with being a celebrity-author. If Ernest Hemingway were alive today and he had a new book coming out he'd be on the 'Today Show' plugging it. And he'd go into the makeup room, too, so he could look his best."

"He wouldn't have sung songs."

"Carl Sandburg did. He cut a folk song album, for chrissake. If Carl Sandburg were alive today, he might have his own television show."

He walked from behind his desk to put his arm around me.

"Updike, Bellow. They give interviews to push their books. *You* can't because nobody knows you, nobody cares. They will now. Freedom to write what you want. A huge audience for your writing. What's to say no to here? Think about it a little more, if you have to. But Paul, I'm talking major status as a brand-name author—and a five hundred thousand first printing."

. . .

Over the next few nights Sandy and I went to sleep exhausted from talking about it. I couldn't bring myself to say yes. But to say no was to go back to paying the bills with work I couldn't bear any longer. I had seen scriptwriters who stayed too long at the game, getting old and bitter, complaining about young writers moving up behind them. I didn't want to live that way. I was like the character in my own book, looking back to a time when you were supposed to "do your own thing." What I wanted to do was write for me, not for them; to not be for hire anymore.

. . .

While walking in midtown I stopped to sit in a little park on East 53rd Street. Seated at the next table reading a newspaper was Saul

Bellow. He looked distinguished, elegant in a grey suit, white shirt, and tie. I smiled in his direction and he smiled back.

"I'm a colleague, in a sense," I said to him.

"Yes?"

"I've written my first novel. Not published yet. Up to now I've written for television—Paul Brock. I'm sure you've never heard of me."

"There are so many writers. If we asked the people in this park, many would never have heard of me."

"I admire you, sir, the consistent quality of your writing throughout your career, the dignity with which you've conducted your professional life."

"Thank you."

"There's something I'd like to ask you, given your moral standing and your reputation. Someone is offering me a chance for my first novel to have a five hundred thousand first printing."

"Is that so?"

"But I have to sing."

"Sing?"

"Be a performer and write songs, comic songs."

"You would write the songs?"

"Yes. They'd be observations about life."

"If you're a writer you should be able to write observations, about life, it would seem to me. Can you sing?"

"Well enough, I'm told. The idea is not for me to be a great singer, just to be able to do the songs. But I don't know if I should say yes to this. Will my reputation as a novelist be tarnished?"

"I don't believe you should concern yourself with reputation. The main thing is internal, you as a writer and the quality of what you write."

"I see."

"If you accept this, it seems to me you will simply become a writer with a large first printing. Very large."

"And you don't think my moral standing as a novelist would be affected?"

"By your singing songs that you write? What would that have to do with the quality of your novels? So long as you write the novels you wish to write and do the best job of which you're capable, I don't see how that can be anything but moral."

"Right. I appreciate your taking the trouble to talk to me. This has been very helpful."

"Not at all. You'll sing songs, you say? I've never been asked to do that. I might have enjoyed it. To get up on a stage and have a good time performing."

He contemplated this for a moment, then suddenly Saul Bellow burst into song, singing "Walkin' My Baby Back Home."

He did the first chorus, then I joined in with him, singing along with Saul Bellow. We did a nice up-tempo job on the song, snapping our fingers and really getting into it. Several people in the park applauded us at the end.

· · ·

I called Mel from a phone booth.

"A first printing of five hundred thousand?"

"Five hundred thousand."

"I'll do it."

"No problem," he said.

8.

MEL CAME TO our apartment on a Saturday morning to examine my clothing, of all things. Tailoring had never been one of my major concerns. When I chose my clothing each day I was guided by two considerations—whether it was clean and whether it was soft. For everyday wear I favored well-worn jeans or chinos, soft plaid shirts or T-shirts, sneakers, a Banana Republic bush jacket, a down jacket in winter, a Giants football hat for the rain. When I needed to dress for a meeting or an evening out, I usually wore a tweed jacket I bought at Paul Stuart or a navy blazer from Brooks Brothers. I may not have been sending the strongest message to my sons. Some of their friends' fathers wore shirts and ties every day to work. But I chose my clothes for comfort. I wasn't about to get dressed up to go to another room in the apartment. I felt it was already enough that I didn't stay in my pajamas all day. On days when I went down to the Steiner offices I didn't get dressed up either. I just didn't care very much about appearances. When I needed to look properly dressed, I had my basic outfits.

Mel was no one to judge me, he in his glitzy clothes. You wouldn't see either of us in *GQ*. But there he was, wearing a loud checkered jacket, looking me over as I stood before him in chinos, a sweatshirt, and old loafers.

"You need an image. And it has to be total," he told me. "That's what I did with Manuelo. He doesn't set foot outside his bedroom without being in 'his' clothes. And we have to do the same for you."

Under Mel's franchising a line of "Manuelowear" had been introduced, silk shirts worn open at the neck with matching to-readorlike slacks, in which I would have looked like a mariachi player.

"You want me to wear a Manuelo ensemble?" I asked.

"You have to look successful. You can't go around in jeans and an old bush jacket."

"It worked for Hemingway," I said.

"Because it was his look. You need your own, consistent look."

"Paul dresses like that pretty consistently," Sandy said.

"It's too free-lance looking. You want to make a fashion statement."

"When I woke up this morning do you think I said, *Today, I want to make a fashion statement?*"

"Let's see what you've got in your closets."

We went into the bedroom and he looked through, making *tsk-tsk* sounds.

"Where are all the suits, the jackets?"

"That's it."

"Put this on," and he handed me my blazer.

"I think he looks cute," Sandy said, not taking this too seriously.

Mel did not respond; he was studying me. He removed the blazer and handed me the sports jacket.

"I feel like my kids would feel. Do I have to get dressed up?"

He walked around me and appraised how I looked in the jacket.

"This is not bad," he said. "Nice. Tweedy."

"A guy who wears a Liberace chain is judging me."

"You're going to be established as a singer *and* a novelist. We don't want to let the novelist part get lost. We should go for a university look. You'll always wear tweed jackets, good slacks, dress shirts, striped ties. You don't want to look Manuelo. You don't want to look Broadway. You want to look tweedy, on stage and off. It's perfect."

"Do you notice how closed-off this is? He gives you an idea and then he gives you the reaction to his own idea," I said to Sandy.

Mel said we had to leave immediately for Paul Stuart and buy me a new wardrobe. The money for it would be drawn against my performer's earnings, Mel assuming there would be earnings. We arranged for a sitter to stay with the children for a few hours and we went downtown in Mel's Rolls. We entered the store, Mel asked for a salesman, and a well-dressed man in his thirties introduced himself as Derek.

"Derek, this is Mr. Brock. He wants everything."

"Everything?"

"Consider that he has just arrived from another planet and does not own a stitch of clothing, but for the clothes he is wearing, which we will discard."

Poor Derek was having difficulty breathing after a while from his commissions. Back at the apartment Mel gathered together my old clothing to make sure it was purged. We were going to give it to charity, but I held on to my bush jacket, a sweatshirt, and chinos.

"Forbidden!" he said. "This has to be a total image."

"Like hell. These are my oldies but goldies."

"I think, in a sense, it's his teddy bear," Sandy suggested.

"You wear these only in the neighborhood. If I ever catch you downtown wearing anything other than good threads, you're going to get it. Don't make me hire private detectives."

· · ·

My first public appearance trying out my new clothing was when I took the boys to school Monday morning, and was wearing new suede shoes, twill slacks, a Shetland sweater, sports shirt, and a tweed sports jacket. I intended to start working on the songs for the act when I went back to the apartment, and I felt completely overdressed. I wanted to get back into my old sweatshirt and chinos to write. I would be changing outfits so often that *I* would be another Liberace.

· · ·

I kissed the children goodbye at the school entrance and walked along West End Avenue toward the apartment. Reading a newspaper, sitting on the stoop of a brownstone, was J. D. Salinger.

"Good morning," I said. "Excuse my intrusion, but I know who you are. My name is Paul Brock."

"Oh, Paul Brock. *Esquire.* Good pieces."

"J. D. Salinger read my pieces?"

"Just because I haven't been publishing doesn't mean I haven't been reading."

He was wearing khaki slacks, a plaid shirt, and cardigan sweater. He gestured for me to sit down next to him and I did.

"I'm sure you've heard this so many times," I said to him. "You were so influential. That unique, wonderful voice. I was intoxicated reading you. I probably thought of being a writer because of you."

"I appreciate it."

"So what are you working on?" I asked casually.

"This and that. Yourself?"

"I just finished a novel. And now I'm going to do a musical project, write comic songs and perform them."

"That sounds interesting. But why are you all dressed up?"

"It's part of my new life-style for being a public person. I have to look presentable."

"Is that important these days, what a writer looks like?"

"Apparently. I'm going to keep some old clothes for when I'm writing."

"For your gestalt? And you're going to write songs?"

"They'd be about contemporary subjects. I've been thinking about it and I'm going to make them like humorous essays."

"Can I give you a little advice?"

"Oh, my God, *yes.*"

"Even though you're writing songs and not prose, they have to be first-rate."

"Absolutely."

"Once you have your voice, and I assume you do, there's nothing you write—fiction, nonfiction, or songs—that shouldn't contain that voice in its essence."

"I'll definitely follow your advice. But could I ask you something? What is it like to know that on the day anything you write appeared—anything at all, a short story, a novel—there would be lines of people around the block waiting to read it?"

"That has nothing to do with writing, does it?"

"Can we expect anything new from you?"

"You never know."

"Why did you stop publishing?"

"That has nothing to do with writing either."

He rose to leave. I shook his hand heartily.

"It was wonderful to meet you."

"Are you in the phone book?" he asked.

"Yes, I am."

"Sometime when I'm in town, we'll have lunch," J. D. Salinger said to me. He moved on, unnoticed along the street. He turned and called out. "Good luck with your songs and your clothes."

• • •

When I opened my closet and saw the new things I owned it was slightly disorienting, as if I were in the wrong apartment. I met Mel for breakfast wearing a $375 sports jacket for our $1.79 eggs. Mel suggested that I compile a list of songs I liked, that it would be better if the standards I sang were favorites of mine, his version of truth in packaging. We said goodbye, his driver was going to take him to the office, I was headed uptown.

"Where are you going?" Mel said sharply.

"The subway."

"You can't go in the subway anymore. Stars don't take the subway."

"Have checks started arriving without my knowledge?"

"You take taxis, you hire cars. I'll give you the name of a car service. Your stars, your Willie Nelsons, your Manuelos, they don't take public transportation."

"For now, I'll walk," and I started on my way. "Don't worry. More people will see me in my clothes."

"Joe, call a car for him," he said to the chauffeur, who used a phone in the Rolls and, from a car, called a car.

• • •

Writing songs began with the same sensation I experienced beginning any new project: Facing the Blank Screen. I sat before the computer, with a tape recorder nearby in case any music occurred to me while I was writing the lyrics. I realized I didn't know how much material I needed, so I called Mel to ask him.

"Generally, what are we aiming for in terms of minutes?"

"An hour and ten."

"I beg your pardon?"

"I don't think we want an opening act. You wouldn't want a comic intruding on the comic songs. Or a singer intruding on your singing. I figure it would be just you. So that's how much you need."

"I can't hold a stage that long. I can't write that much material."

"That's why it's good to have you doing standards along with your witty, wonderful songs. Figure about three minutes a song. You need about ten originals and ten standards."

"An hour and ten minutes is impossible."

"Once you get going you'll be coming to me for more time. The Grateful Dead does three-hour concerts."

"They have over twenty years of music to draw on."

"And you have the rich musical heritage of the pop song and your own unique talent to draw on."

"Mel—"

"Stop talking. Get working. If you have trouble we'll get the material written for you."

"Sometimes people who write a musical, and this is like a minimusical, take years to do it."

"Is this writer's block or something?"

"Writer's terror. Remember the old radio show 'Escape'? I'm in it. You are going along and someone says, *Write ten comic songs.* If you do, you will be a star. If you cannot, you will be obscure. Will you ascend to the promontory? Will you descend to the abyss?"

"What are you *talking* about? Sometimes I think writers are nuts. All that sitting alone in rooms makes you nuts. Start writing and if you can't do it, we'll send out for it."

. . .

If Lenny Bruce were alive he could have rewritten the routine about the comic who bombs at the Palladium. I was going to set a show-biz record for bombing, one hour and ten minutes' worth, bombing beyond any act ever, even ours.

I went to record stores to buy albums by people who used comedy in music—Allan Sherman, Tom Lehrer, Noel Coward; also shows that had comedy songs, like *Fiorello!* and *Annie Get Your Gun.* If I were going to make a bombing fool of myself at least I would begin where every writer can start—with research. "You mean to tell us," a reporter was going to ask me one day, "that what we saw out there was *researched?*"

The anchor for me was to keep focusing on this as a kind of musical or revue that I was writing. That helped me organize my thoughts. The subject matter was contemporary life as seen through the eyes of a married man with two kids. Within that context many things could be material for songs. I started to accumulate ideas. I took the boys for sneakers one day. At today's prices children's sneakers cost up to $80 a pair. A child needs a couple of pairs of sneakers, as well as snow shoes and dress shoes—and this was the genesis of my first lyric, "Children's Shoes Blues."

The wearers of said shoes were at the dinner table. Sandy asked how the work was going and I told her I had begun writing.

"Are you writing a new book?" Joey asked.

"I was. But I set it aside for a while. I'm doing something different. I'm writing some songs."

"What kind of songs?" he said.

"Funny ones, I hope."

He thought about that for a moment, so seriously that he stopped eating.

"How can you write funny songs?" Joey said.

"Someone has to write them."

"But you're not funny."

Now *I* stopped eating.

"I don't know about that," I said. "There's usually some humor in my work, in which case you can say the shoes on your feet were earned, in part, by my humor."

"Is Daddy funny?" he asked his younger brother.

"No," came the definitive reply.

"Your father has an excellent sense of humor," Sandy said.

The children looked perplexed and I realized they were not criticizing me; rather, they were concerned. They knew their father earned his living from writing and they were simply worried. I was reminded of the moment in *A Thousand Clowns* when the kid says to Chuckles the Chipmunk, "You are not funny. Funnier than you is even Stuart Slossman, my friend who is eleven and puts walnuts in his mouth and makes noises . . . "

"Well, I'm going to be as funny as I can and write these songs."

"You're not as funny as Kermit the Frog," Sammy declared.

"I just have to be as funny as Judith Krantz," was my rebuttal. They had stone faces. "I bet I could make you laugh right now."

"Go on," Joey said.

"Moose breath," I said. I almost had them, a slight smile appearing on each little face. But they did not laugh. "Chicken lips." Still nothing. That had always been my best shot. Chicken lips always made them laugh. "The songs will be funny," I said. "Amusing," I added, retreating.

"Who is going to sing them?" Joey asked.

"I am."

They were really solemn now.

"But, Daddy," Joey said. "You can't sing."

. . .

I wrote a lyric, "Chicken Lips," based on our conversation, about the passing of time with your children, how as they get older they don't think you're as funny. I hummed an Aznavour kind of melody into the tape recorder to go along with it. The chorus was:

> Oh, chicken lips, oh, chicken lips
> Bring back the chicken lips of our youth
> Oh, chicken lips, oh, chicken lips
> Through chicken lips we spoke essential truth

I was still playing with the melody, singing it different ways into the tape recorder. I took a break from work and treated myself to a pastrami sandwich at the Stage Delicatessen. I noticed that seated across the table from me was Jackie Mason.

"Mister, you were humming," he said. "You don't know the difference between humming and eating?"

"Sorry. I was working on a song."

"And I'm working on my lunch."

"I'll be quiet."

"If you could write a song as good as your sandwich, you'd have something. Is the song as good as the sandwich?"

"I don't know. I'm really a novelist."

"You hum your novels?"

"What I'm doing now is a different kind of project. Where I take observations about life and turn them into songs."

"You mean you observe a person having a heart attack and you write a song about it? A song is, *I love you*. A song is not, *When will the ambulance be here?*"

"I'd use Piaf-Aznavour kind of melodies, passionate, soulful. But the lyrics would be about everyday concerns. And that's the joke."

"That's a joke?"

"I mean joke in the juxtaposition of the lyrics and the music."

"Juxtaposition? This is something to do with sex?"

"Comments about life. Like whatever happened to the girls you dated when you were young. And the song might be called 'Cynthia Rosenbloom.' "

"It's a comedy act. Well, you never know. I'll tell you a story. Years ago, when I was working in the Mountains I saw a couple of kids and they did a little act. One song I'll never forget. It was called 'The Undoctor of Love.' Just like you're telling me, a fancy melody for a funny lyric."

"That was me! I wrote 'The Undoctor of Love'!"

"You wrote 'The Undoctor of Love'? Mister, you had something. And you're going to do that kind of thing now, but more grown-up?"

"Exactly."

"Good for you! I'm sitting with a guy who hums and eats, but he's also a talent. What was this song you were humming?"

"It's about how I used to get my kids to laugh by saying 'chicken lips,' and now as they get older, they don't laugh anymore."

"It's a deep song. Deep and funny. That's all right. It couldn't kill you. Waiter! I'll have the check for him, too," he called out.

"Thank you. A pleasure to meet you."

"Chicken lips. You could also try chicken *hips*. A song about what it's like to make it with a chicken. Do you worry if the chicken is more experienced than you? Afterward does the chicken lay you an egg, so in the morning you'll have a nice breakfast?"

He took the check and left, humming "The Undoctor of Love."

    • • •

Over the next few weeks I worked on the songs, still focusing on the concept that this was a musical revue with myself in the lead. To "Chicken Lips" and "Children's Shoes Blues" I added "Cynthia Rosenbloom," the song about a family man who wonders whatever happened to his old girlfriends. A nervous tango called "Paying the Bills." "Sports Heroes," about rooting for pouty young athletes making enormous amounts of money. "Taxes" was a big ballad. "Where's Star Dust?" was a lament about the quality of today's pop music. Then I went through all our records and picked out several standards I liked. I timed my performance and it came to just under an hour without musical accompaniment.

I performed my act for Sandy in the living room. She had a smile on her face throughout—too much of a smile I thought.

"Very interesting," she said when I was finished.

"You don't refer to comedy as 'interesting.'"

"I think you did a great job with all those new songs. Really great. But to hear someone sing without any accompaniment and to hear it for the first time, you have to absorb it."

"It's a disaster."

"I didn't say that. I'm responding honestly. But it requires an adjustment for me to make. My husband is standing there singing without music."

I decided I definitely needed more rehearsal time before I made a presentation to Mel. I spent most of my working hours over the next few days performing in front of a full-length mirror in my bedroom. Looking at myself singing these comic conceits and then audaciously interposing them with the works of the Gershwins, Berlin, Porter, Rodgers and Hart, there were moments I had the feeling that I was conceiving the worst act in the history of show business. When I was a child a talking dog once appeared on a radio talent show and growled something that sounded like "I wanna hamburger." The saving moment for me would be when

Mel abandoned this idea because he realized the talking dog was a class act compared to mine.

.   .   .

Wearing tweeds from my new wardrobe I arrived at Mel's office to appear, live, in front of Mel and Henry Ross.

"I'm really excited about this," Mel greeted me.

"How do you want to handle it?" Henry asked. "Do you want an orchestra?"

They would have assembled an entire group of musicians for me.

"I'll just sing."

"Anything you want," Mel said as he and Henry sat on the couch in the office and I stood before them.

"I've written ten songs and I picked out ten standards. I didn't know whether to have a running commentary, so I decided to keep it simple. Leave the jokes, if you will, to the songs."

"Good call," Mel said.

"So—here we go."

I started with "Taxes," then "Cynthia Rosenbloom," followed by my first standard, "A Foggy Day in London Town." They applauded each song as I continued to the end, "Chicken Lips." Mel embraced me at the conclusion, Henry Ross shook my hand with both of his.

"Outstanding!" Mel said.

"Terrific work," Henry added.

Mel didn't say anything further; he was pacing the room. His eyes were squinting, his face serious. I sat in a chair and watched him pace. Then he said:

"The standards stink. You don't have a good enough voice to carry standards. At first I thought the audience would go for somebody who's just like them singing these songs, but it doesn't work. And it breaks the continuity. We scrap the standards. The heart of the act is the material you wrote. That's good and you don't have to be a great singer for that—which, let's face it, you're not. What we need are ten more original songs."

"And some help on the music," Henry volunteered.

"Right. A lot of your melodies stink, too. Face it, Paul, the premises, the lyrics are what's best here, and that's what we'll work with. All in all, I couldn't be happier. It's a very promising beginning."

Mel had gone right to the essence of my own doubts, that as a singer I couldn't carry the standards and my original melodies were weak. Suddenly, by telling me what I knew to be terrible *was* terrible, this had become very real. I was not being rescued from this idea. The man was serious about it.

9.

I DIDN'T HAVE TO concern myself for the moment with performing. I felt liberated. I was a writer again. Without the standards I had a unified concept; the material was taking shape as a middle-class song cycle. I wrote a lyric called "Lost in the Middle," about how overlooked by politicians, advertisers, and Hollywood is the middle class. "Me and My Car" was about how the expense of buying and running a car makes it one of your most important relationships. "Bourgeois Bopping" was a mock rap song about the difficulty of running a household while trying to keep up with trends.

I continued along that line, taking observations about middle-class life and turning them into lyrics. In our neighborhood were several second-rate Chinese restaurants largely frequented by yuppies on the singles scene. The yuppies, with no tradition of eating good Chinese food in New York, filled these places because either they didn't know better or they didn't care. What did this tell us about the future, about these younger people to whom my generation was passing the torch? I wrote a song dealing with these feelings, called "Yuppies Don't Know Chinese Food."

After another couple of months I had the new songs and once again I made a presentation of the material to Sandy in the living room. She was very enthusiastic this time and said the songs were amusing and fun. Mel suggested that before I perform it for him I work out the music with Henry Ross. Henry had taken over an office in the building where the Steiner studio space was located. I stood before him and sang the songs in the order I thought was most effective. Henry smiled, laughed, he applauded after each song. When I was finished he said it was outstanding, adding after a discreet interval: "The music could use some help. But we were expecting that, weren't we?"

Over the next three weeks I went to his office each day as Henry worked at the piano and shaped my attempts into genuine music. Melody lines were modified, expanded, or discarded, and finally arranged for piano accompaniment. Next I had to learn the newly adjusted melodies. Henry played the material, recording it for me on a cassette, which I studied at home. He worked with me for a week of rehearsals and then he deemed me ready to perform for Mel.

We went to Mel's office for the presentation. Henry explained to Mel that a decision was made to have a range of musical influences and rhythms, rather than limit the sound. As he told this to Mel, Henry anxiously cleared his throat and I felt him deferring to Mel's power. My presentation had become Henry's. We were collaborators, in a sense, and *he* was nervous.

We began, Henry accompanying me on the piano in Mel's office. I had to stop now and then for water and my voice cracked a few times. Throughout, Henry maintained a bouncy, antic performance, smiling, perky. Mel did not see fit to encourage the singer with smiles. He had on his game face. He watched with deep, penetrating eyes, studying me. I was convinced I had bombed. Then at the conclusion Mel leaped to his feet, hugging me.

"Fantastic!" he said. "It's everything I hoped it would be. Beautifully written, Paul. Great job, Henry. We'll do it big. These lyrics against a full background. We'll get a musical joke out of big."

Mel returned to the chair at his desk, put his feet up and went into the Steiner retreat, thinking.

"The songs are great," he said. "The one problem I can see, Paul, is your instrument."

"I don't play an instrument." I quickly added, beginning to panic, "I can't *learn* an instrument."

"I mean *you*. You as the instrument. Your voice breaks, you can't sing for an hour without taking breaks. How do you expect to command a stage? Your instrument is shit."

"Mel, your old friend, Paul here."

"Don't 'old friend' me. This is business. What kind of exercise do you do?"

"You know. I run about three miles a couple of times a week."

"You're in lousy shape. What if you have to do a performance a few nights in a row? And stand up straight. You stand there like a shlump."

"But I'm dressed well."

"Henry, you work on the arrangements. I'll work on his instrument. Paul, the shape you're in, you'd be hospitalized in two nights. And with laryngitis so bad you'd be doing your performances in longhand."

. . .

I returned to the apartment with a tape Henry had made of my presentation to Mel and played it for Sandy and the children that night.

"It's hard to believe," Sandy said. "It really sounds professional, like someone who isn't my husband. It's just kind of hard to grasp."

"I'll take that as high praise."

Joey offered that it was "very good." I don't know if Sandy coached them, but Sammy also said I was "very good." A part of me was feeling that I should hold it right there. I had a nice memento of this little project, a party tape I could play for family and friends. Then I would hear the voice of unreason reminding me that we were talking about a five hundred thousand first printing. If he could make a super into a singer he could take a writer and turn him into a "writer-singer," placing me in the most favorable editorial category.

. . .

Mel wanted me to meet him for breakfast the following morning and we went to a coffee shop on Eighth Avenue in the Forties, both of us ordering pancakes, Mel watching me eat with interest.

"What is it?" I asked.

"The condemned man ate a hearty meal. Goodbye pancakes, hello wheat germ. That could be one of your songs. You know, as you get older, you can do songs about getting older. And as your kids get older, you can do songs about that. You're totally open-ended. As an act, you can go on forever."

"I just want to get through this next period and get back to my novel."

"I'm realizing how valuable you are. The built-in continuity. You can be the 'I Love Lucy' of performing artists."

He wouldn't tell me why we were going there, but had the driver take us to a loft building on Broadway and 18th Street. We went up in the elevator, Mel rang a bell, and the door was opened by a small Oriental man in a white robe. He bowed to Mel and motioned for us to enter. We were standing in a gym, mats on the floor, a trampoline to the side.

"This is Mr. Chin. Paul Brock."

"Pleased to meet. Come office."

He led us to an office where we sat in white deck chairs. On the walls was a collection of show-business pictures, Mr. Chin and a small Oriental woman posing with various people—the Italian diva Anna Scavallo and several of Mel's clients, including Manuelo.

"Mr. Brock is my friend," Mel explained. "He is going to be a star."

"You are writer, no?"

"Yes. How do you know that?"

"I am, in reality, Charlie Chan. No, just making joke. I know you are writer by the size of your behind. Too big for your shoulders. A man who sits too much."

"That's our problem here. We've got to get him in shape for a one-hour act."

"Please to stand."

Reluctantly I stood and he walked around me, surveying my behind and my front. Then he grabbed a fold of skin at my waistline.

"Mr. Brock, for shame."

"Mel, I don't like this."

"You're in no shape to be a performer," Mel said. "Manuelo had a gut out to New Jersey, and Chin and his wife, they transformed him."

"I call wife." He pressed a button on the intercom.

"These people are fabulous. And this is part of the deal," Mel said insistently.

Chin's wife entered the room, a petite Oriental woman in a white robe. She bowed to Mel.

"This new client. Mr. Brock, this my wife."

She appraised me. No Oriental inscrutability there. She looked at me with disdain, focusing on my rear and my waistline.

"We have to do a Manuelo on him," Mel said. "He'll have to sing for one hour."

"Speak!" she said to me.

"I'd like to thank the people behind me for this Grammy. My manager, Mel Steiner, my producer, Henry Ross."

"Stop. All in nose. Disgusting," she pronounced. "To gym, now!"

She pushed me to the door and we went to the gym, where I had first entered. She positioned me in the center of the floor.

"Sing loud note," she demanded.

"Mel, isn't this the point where you intervene and say, *All right, we've had enough?*"

"Let's understand this. I consider Mr. and Mrs. Chin brilliant at preparing the instrument. We can't proceed without them."

I sang from "Johnny One-Note," "Ahhhhhhhhhhh."

"Louder!" Mrs. Chin yelled.

"*Ahhhhhhhhhhhh.*" I stopped, out of both note and breath.

"That was your note?" Mrs. Chin said. And she pretended to collapse with chagrin, falling to the floor. Mr. Chin laughed and Mrs. Chin laughed also, getting back on her feet.

"Funny, no?" Mr. Chin said. "See, we not only good workers, we funny."

"Is this obscure Oriental humor?" I asked.

"No voice control. No power. You sing like you speak. In nose," Mrs. Chin said. "We have much work to do."

"And when you finished, you have control over body," Mr. Chin said.

"On that, I leave you to one another," Mel announced.

"Mel, don't. They come from a culture that turns out people who can play volleyball for twenty-four consecutive hours."

"And they're going to get you in shape. Work with them. *It's required!*"

He bowed, they bowed back.

"You not in good shape yourself," Mr. Chin said to Mel.

"I'm not the singer." And he left.

Chin handed me a clipboard and pen.

"First you fill out list."

I followed printed instructions to list everything I had eaten the previous day—meals, snacks, drinks. They looked at my answers and it seemed to confirm their expectations.

"You know what they say in computers. 'Garbage in, garbage out.' " Mr. Chin grabbed my fleshy fold again. "You eat garbage, you get garbage."

"Each day you must give three hours. At end of six weeks you have attitude and body for rest of life," Mrs. Chin said. "We start." She opened a door to a stairway. "You run down stairs, then run up. No stopping."

"I'll take the elevator, thank you."

"No stopping."

"This is the eighth floor. I can't run up eight flights of stairs."

"I think can't run *down* eight flights of stairs," Mr. Chin said.

"Mr. Steiner said work with us is required," Mrs. Chin pointed out.

I headed down the stairs. A little tightness in the knees I wasn't thrilled about. I jogged my few miles a week. I was in passable shape. Then I started up. I got to the third floor when I could feel the strain in my legs and chest. I stopped running and walked up. Like gnats the Chins were flitting around me.

"Up! Not walking, running up!" Mrs. Chin shouted.

"Like this," Mr. Chin told me and they ran up the stairs, looking down at me, yelling, "Up, up!" running down to me, hectoring me, "Up! Run!"

I managed two more flights and I gave out.

"The idea is not for me to expire before I do my act."

"Manuelo would be upstairs having orange juice by now," Mr. Chin said.

"You bad boy," Mrs. Chin informed me. "You go down. Start from bottom again."

"Yes, I go down. But at the bottom, I go home."

I went down the stairs. They followed along with me, yelling: "You fat boy! You loser!"

When I reached the bottom I called up to them: "Since you already have me down as Porky the Pig, th-th-that's all folks."

I walked along Broadway practically mumbling to myself about the absurdity, that Mel expected me to train with these robed maniacs. I was not going to be an Olympic gymnast, a world-class Ping-Pong player. What did running up a flight of stairs have to do with singing? The diva Anna Scavallo, who was immense, couldn't run up a flight of stairs. I dialed information from a street phone, asked for the Chins' number, and called. Mr. Chin answered.

"Anna Scavallo doesn't run up your goddamned stairs!"

"You wrong. She come to New York, she run up our stairs. Two things she do in New York. She go to Bergdorf Goodman and she come to us to train and run up our stairs. Be here eight in morning. Bring exercise clothes." And he hung up.

. . .

Granted, I could see a connection between being in good physical condition and being able to withstand the rigors of performing in public. But I thought I was in good enough shape. I was conducting an internal monologue with myself on this subject when I saw Clint Eastwood and Cher on a street corner, trying to hail a cab. They were wearing stunning cowboy clothes. Clint Eastwood noticed me, turned, and said, "Say, aren't you Norman Mailer?"

"No! I am a writer, though. Paul Brock."

"Oh, right," Cher said. "I saw your picture in *Esquire*. The reason Clint mistook you for Norman Mailer is the close physical resemblance."

"Norman Mailer—and I think he'd be willing to admit this— has a bit of a belly now. He really doesn't look anything like me, and vice versa."

"I think you look quite alike," Clint Eastwood said. "And I know types. I direct movies."

"I don't look anything like Norman Mailer!"

"No offense intended," he told me. "You're just both roly-polies."

"Compared to Californians, New Yorkers are totally sedentary," Cher commented to Clint Eastwood.

"And the food they eat. That bologna and pastreemee," Clint Eastwood remarked.

"It's pronounced *baloney* and *pastrami*," I said.

"As you wish."

"In any case, I couldn't compare myself to you people."

"We're almost painfully thin to look at, aren't we?" Cher said.

"I'd say—lean," was my response.

"Mr. Brock," Cher told me. "I'd be attracted to a man who writes well. But seeing you, so soft and roly-poly, I'd never sleep with you. Think of that. If you ever entertained a fantasy that I might sleep with you, the answer is—no. You're too New York pastrami."

"I wouldn't sleep with him either," Clint Eastwood commented, and they both had a lean laugh over that. "But I might call you sometime. If I'm casting a western and I need a roly-poly undertaker."

"Could I ask you—what do you think of running up and down flights of stairs for exercise?"

"Oh, that is *so* New York," Cher commented. "But whatever works for you. Keep writing."

"And keep eating," Clint Eastwood added for his own amusement.

They had given up trying to get a cab. Two mounted policemen came along. Clint Eastwood and Cher exchanged words with them and borrowed their horses, riding off into the canyons of the city, looking painfully thin and gorgeous.

· · ·

I told Sandy about the Chins that night, hoping to hear a ringing indictment of the need for such a rigorous physical fitness program. Instead she said that if Mel thought this was "required," he must have a reason. Teasingly, she took her thumb and forefinger and gently squeezed me above the waistline, pointing out that I *was* developing little love handles.

"Did you read the article about it?"

"I did not."

"It's very common for men as they get older. Weight gets redistributed."

"This is not what I want to hear. Insane Chinese people are ready to work me over."

"Mel isn't going to put you at risk. And you're an investment now."

I called Mel at home with an elegant argument—If the premise was for me to speak for ordinary people then it was antithetical for me to be trained to lean hardness. I was struggling not to fall into the hands of the diabolical Chins. Mel said that sitting at a computer was not adequate training for performing. Manuelo had been reconstructed by the Chins out of beer and junk food into a person who was comfortably playing to capacity audiences in Los Angeles, and I should be at the gym the following morning as instructed.

                        . . .

I found out from Mel's secretary that Manuelo was staying at the Beverly Hills Hotel, and placed a call to him. I was going to check the Chins' references. Later on Manuelo called me back.

"Amigo!"

"How is it going out there?"

"Beautiful."

"Manuelo, I don't know if you heard anything about this, but I'm being promoted as a singing star by our Mel."

"You can sing?"

"Enough to get by. I've written some songs, I'm going to perform them, then he's publishing my novel, roughly in that order."

"I'll come to your opening. The publicity will be good for you."

"I'm calling to find out about the Chins."

"The Chins! Mel wants you to work with the Chins? Did they make you run up the stairs?"

"Yes."

He was laughing.

"They are crazy, you know?" Manuelo said.

"I think I got that."

"But they are genius."

"No. Say it ain't so, Manuelo."

"They will do good for you. Sometime we'll get together and run up the stairs."

"A great invitation."

"Good luck in your new career, amigo. Soon you'll be fixing faucets."

. . .

The following morning, regretfully, I entered the Chins' loft. They were waiting for me, with a rolling cart covered by a tablecloth. Mr. Chin snapped the tablecloth off the cart, revealing an array of food; everything I indicated I had eaten in one day—a toasted bagel with cream cheese, a corned beef sandwich with a side of potato salad, a blueberry muffin, a Planters Peanut Bar, half a barbecued chicken, cole slaw, diet cherry soda, a dish of chocolate chip ice cream, and four Pecan Sandies. I must admit, lined up on a tray like that at eight in the morning, it looked disgusting.

"I bet you like Twinkies, too," Mr. Chin said.

"I'm not a Twinkies man, but I do love an occasional Peanut Bar."

"You poison your body," Mrs. Chin said. "Assassin!"

"One day of your food, throw it on floor, you know what have? Garbage!"

Chin held his arm out rigidly. "Push down my arm. Use both arms if you need. Push down." This did not require a Herculean effort. I pushed down on the man's arm and prevailed. "Now eat your Peanut Bar."

"I go for these around four in the afternoon. I'm not a morning man."

"Eat!"

Slowly and with effort I ate the candy bar.

"Now, sit."

I sat on the floor for a few minutes.

"Candy in system now. Stand up. Push down my arm."

He held out his arm, I tried to push it down and I couldn't. I didn't know if he had tricked me, if he had some method of re- sisting, or if as he suggested it was the candy.

"Sugar steals strength. You want to live half-strength, eat sugar."

"Also make you depressed," Mrs. Chin volunteered. "Gives quick jolt, then lets you down fast. Are you ever depressed?"

"Yes, but they're sophisticated depressions, brought on by money, rent, career problems, the aging process—and then you've got cost-of-living-increases on the depression. I don't think we want to put all that on the occasional candy bar."

"Eat only this," she said, handing me a printed list, standard health food fare. "No more candy bars, no more cookies, no more ice cream."

"I'll give you the cookies and the ice cream. Let me keep the Peanut Bar."

"Mr. Steiner's orders. Is required," she insisted. "Now voice." She placed my shoulders against a wall. "Voice comes from dia- phragm, not throat. You squeak like Mickey Mouse."

"I should have his recognition."

"You have his voice," she said, apparently capable of trading remarks across cultures.

She ran me through a thirty-minute exercise for breath control and projection. Then I was to practice for a half-hour on my own while the Chins worked with electronics equipment that measured the volume of my voice. Next Mr. Chin brought a half-dozen orange traffic cones into the gym and placed them at intervals. I was supposed to run a pattern around the cones, while singing "God Bless America." This, too, was "required." Great patriotic moments in history: A man singing "God Bless America," spurred on by Oriental crazies and struggling to breathe. "You doing good," Mr. Chin offered. "Manuelo, he fainted." Smiling proudly they showed me they had oxygen equipment in a storage closet.

"Now stairs!"

"You throw that in? Every once in a while, *now stairs?*"

"Not every once in while. At definite times."

"You mean this insanity is on a schedule?"

"Carefully worked out. Now stairs!"

I ran down, I ran up. I got to the third floor running and walked the rest.

"Want more candy bars?" Mr. Chin shouted out derisively. He took me to a room off the gym, which contained a treadmill. "Now, walk."

"Practice breathing," Mrs. Chin instructed. "One hour."

"I can't think of anything more boring than to walk on a treadmill for an hour."

"We have TV," Mr. Chin said triumphantly.

He turned on a television set connected to a video recorder. I walked, watching a home video of Mrs. Chin demonstrating the voice projection and breathing techniques, followed by the main feature, a lecture by Mr. Chin on the evils of sugar.

. . .

I went through the madness every morning for three weeks. The Chins considered that I was making sufficient progress for them to add a specialty. After I had run the stairs and done the treadmill they brought out shoes with taps on them, which had been fitted for my feet.

"You tap dance?" Mrs. Chin asked.

"Only through free-lance life."

"We teach."

They brought out their own tap shoes and put them on. Mrs. Chin showed me some basic techniques. Then she played an audio cassette, an album of Fred Astaire vocals taken from sound tracks of his movies.

"Must sing, too," Mrs. Chin said. "You know words?"

"Some."

"You learn. Come on, Mr. Brock. *I'm puttin' on my top hat . . .*"

I tap danced with these two robed maniacs, who were singing and dancing along with me to the songs of Fred Astaire as they called out instructions for my dance and vocal techniques.

"Now can go," Mr. Chin said when the album was over. "Put on street shoes, run downstairs. Don't have to run up."

I ran down the stairs thinking I surely was going insane because

I felt Astaire had saved it for me. The madness of capping off these grueling physical exercises singing and tap dancing to Fred Astaire was so bizarre and, in a way, wonderful, that the physical training suddenly began to seem manageable.

· · ·

The regimen was unwavering. I ached, I took long, warm baths every night. I could have killed for a Peanut Bar. In time, the muscle soreness subsided and I was able to run up the goddamned stairs. I lost a total of ten pounds during the period. The love handles did not disappear altogether, but they did diminish. My sexual ardor increased and so did my narcissism. I looked at myself often in mirrors. I became a proselytizer for physical fitness, urging every-body in the family to ride bicycles through Central Park on weekend mornings. Sandy had been going to an exercise class twice a week for years—the years when I had been descending into the bloated, sugary state that so agitated the Chins. She was in excellent shape and seemed to enjoy the feeling of the entire family out on our bicycles, everyone eating ice cream after bicycling, but for Dad who dutifully ate from his own little bag of unsalted nuts and raisins.

The highlight of training with the Chins was, of course, the Fred Astaire segment. They stopped barking instructions and joined me each day for the last ten minutes of the album.

"Bet you do this with all your clients," I said as we were tapping away.

"No, you especially good," Mr. Chin said.

"Don't tell me white novelists have rhythm."

"You good for white novelist," he answered.

Mel arrived one morning during our last few minutes of Astaire. As we danced and sang, he applauded with approval.

"Inspirational," he said.

"You think this act has a future?"

"You look in good shape. The act may be too much of a novelty."

"Too bad we have to break it up when the training is over. Maybe Twyla Tharp could have used us."

· · ·

Ending each morning's workout with singing and tap dancing, I always left the Chins feeling exuberant. I was nearly skipping along the street after coming out of their building one day when I almost collided with Michael Jackson. He was strolling along with a small entourage surrounding him. I tap danced a few moves around him, spun around, kicked out to the left and the right, the toe of one foot to the side of the other foot and did a tap flourish at the end.

"Sorry. But it was irresistible—to see someone who moves like you. So long now," and I started to walk on.

"Say, wait a minute," Michael Jackson said to me. "You're good!"

"I am?"

"Who are you?"

"Paul Brock, a novelist. And I'm working on an act."

"Tap?"

"No, I've been studying tap to get in shape."

"You're really excellent."

"I've only been doing this a few weeks," I said modestly.

"A few weeks? Amazing," Michael Jackson said.

He turned to one of his people.

"Are you thinking what I'm thinking?"

The man nodded his head.

"Mr. Brock, I'm part of a benefit performance for United Way at Carnegie Hall tonight. I'll be doing a few numbers. It would be terrific if you'd come up on stage and join me on one of them."

"With Michael Jackson? In Carnegie Hall?"

"I'd introduce you as a person I met on the street, so joyful and talented I couldn't resist dancing with him," he said.

"I'm very honored."

And Michael Jackson was supposed to be so reclusive.

"Just wear regular clothes and tap shoes. I'll call you up from the audience. People will love it. See you backstage at seven tonight."

Sandy and the boys came with me to Carnegie Hall. The show was a parade of stars. Michael Jackson performed his numbers and was dazzling, of course. After his third number he spoke to the audience and told about our meeting and called me up out of my seat to join him for the song "Man in the Mirror." At several points in the song he turned, pointed to me and I did a tap solo. He joined me at the end, Michael Jackson and I tapping away together. The audience loved us.

At the conclusion of the show, Sandy, the boys, and I moved along the street with the people leaving Carnegie Hall. I was momentarily separated from them and found myself standing right next to Cher.

"Mr. Brock, you're a wonder. Such talent. And you've gotten so lean!"

"Guess you could say I got here with practice."

"I'm going to have to retract what I said about not ever considering sleeping with you."

"I didn't mention it before, but I'm in a relationship. Actually I'm married."

I walked away. Poor thing. I left Cher looking thin, gorgeous, and disappointed.

10.

THE CHINS PLACED ME on maintenance. I no longer went to their loft and was entrusted to keep my own regimen and not slide into sloth and gluttony. I bought a treadmill, which I put in the bedroom and worked out on each morning for an hour. I jogged a few miles a week. Tap dancing was optional, but dancing fool that I had become, I did it for fifteen minutes a day. The sloth and gluttony I planned to avoid, but I binged every few days on a Peanut Bar. One can only travel so far on New York's tension-producing byways with saltless nuts and raisins.

Henry called to tell me rehearsals with his musical arrangements were going to begin. He was planning on an ensemble the same size as the group he had first assembled for me.

They will hate me. They will dine out on this charade, this guy with no talent, a musical ignoramus. We're the performers, they will say, for having to keep straight faces while he attempts to sing. He has this song, "Chicken Lips," and when he's not looking we purse our lips. That's our symbol; how we greet each other when we arrive for rehearsals.

I sympathized with the position they would be taking. The musicians were professionals and drew *me* as an assignment. The first time I sang with Henry Ross and the orchestra was only for a song or two. This was for an entire act. I watched Itzhak Perlman on television playing with the New York Philharmonic and I came away with even more sympathy for what professional musicians would have to endure, playing for me.

. . .

While walking along Central Park West the next day I came upon the very Itzhak Perlman sitting on a bench reading a newspaper.

"Excuse me, but I just saw you last night on television. You were outstanding."

"Thank you. We had fun."

"Yes, there was a real zest to it. I'm in awe of people in the world of music."

"It takes years and commitment. But I'm sure whatever you do, *I* would have difficulty doing."

"I write."

"See? What kind of writing?"

"I finished a novel recently. I hesitate to tell you what I'm working on now. A musical act. Comic songs with an orchestra behind me. I'm terrified. The musicians are going to laugh me off the stage."

"Why would they? They were all newcomers sometime or other. Is this going to be like when Jack Benny and Danny Kaye appeared with orchestras?"

"If only it could be that good."

"I'd love to hear your songs. Would you give me a preview?"

"Do you mean it?"

"I have a car and driver over there. A concert promoter sent it for the day. We'll sit in the car and you'll give me a sampling."

"This won't qualify as music by your standards."

"I love all kinds of music. Come."

In the car I sang the first few songs for him.

"Very charming! But is that how you're going to perform? So solemn?"

"I'm very worried."

"But there's a comic sensibility to the material that's not re-flected in that anxious face. Making music is a joy. Show us the joy and the comic spirit of your songs. That should be your atti-tude."

Itzhak Perlman was directing me! I sang another song, taking his instructions, and he was pleased with the result.

"Much better. You know, I'd love to accompany you on a song. Let me get my violin."

He asked the driver to hand him his violin, he tuned it, and then we did "Cynthia Rosenbloom," me singing with Itzhak Perlman accompanying me.

"You'll do beautifully," he said. We shook hands and said goodbye, and as I left the car Itzhak Perlman was still playing the song on the violin for his own enjoyment.

. . .

I entered the sound studio and Henry was already rehearsing the orchestra. The sound was extraordinary. He had created an amalgam of musical styles, big-band music, such as the Artie Shaw Orchestra, combined with rock music such as the Band when the group played with a brass section.

"I don't have the material to stand up to it," I told him. "I can't stand up to it."

"You don't have rinky-tink arrangements. You have this full, rich sound. And that's part of the fun."

I looked at the musicians looking at me. I recognized a few of them from the first time I sang in the studio. Others I had not seen before, women and men in their thirties and forties and several men who must have been in their sixties.

"I've been worrying about this. When they see who they're playing for—"

"Paul, you've got studio musicians here who've been working steadily for years. But you've also got musicians who used to play in rock groups and got too old for the business, and some old-timers from the big bands who've been out of the business altogether."

"All pros and one amateur."

"You're giving them work. You're letting them get back into what they love. They're not the enemy, they're your band."

He took me by the arm and introduced me to the players, several of whose names I recognized from record albums. He positioned me in front of the orchestra, motioned to the engineers in the booth who were going to tape the rehearsals, and we began.

The first couple of hours were a mess. I came in at the wrong times, I was either ahead or behind the music. "You're doing fine," Henry repeatedly told me. We concentrated on the first few songs, and through sheer repetition and the excellence of the musicians I finally settled into some sort of consistent pacing. But this took hours. The Chins had earned their money. The old me would have been hoarse and drained. I would have liked to think the musicians respected me for that, if for nothing else. I was able to withstand rehearsing.

At about four in the afternoon, Mel walked into the studio and I was thrown back decades to the feeling I had in elementary school when the principal appeared in our classroom.

"I'm very pleased," Henry told him.

"I'd like to listen."

We went through a couple of songs; Mel took on his distant, serious face. I anticipated Mel saying, "We're going to keep the orchestra and do an album of instrumentals instead." When we were finished, he said, "Outstanding! Good work!" and left the studio, beaming. We worked another hour and then concluded the rehearsal. I was exhausted at the end, but it was a great day. I felt like a real musician.

. . .

"This is going to be the same as a bar mitzvah," Henry told me the next morning at the start of proceedings. "We're going to do everything over and over until we could wake you in the middle of the night and say, 'sing,' and you'd be able to do it."

"I made mistakes at my bar mitzvah."

"Everybody does, but nobody can tell. Same here. If you make mistakes, they'll be glossed over."

As the days went on Henry made adjustments, adding solos for the musicians, which were written down and became incorporated into the arrangements. After he was satisfied with the rendition it was frozen and we always did the song the same way, which gave security to the amateur.

One of the old-timers, Vinnie Palmeri, became a favorite of the younger musicians. He had played trumpet with big bands in the old days. In his late sixties, thin, stooped with a hawklike face, he had a constant stubbled beard and wore wide-lapel suits from the 1940s with handpainted ties.

"Jesus, we backed some palookas," he was saying when we were taking a lunch break one day. "I was with the Randy Treadwell Orchestra and there was this guy, Mack Dodd. He was Tarzan in one Tarzan movie. We're on the West Coast and Treadwell signs him to be a singer and the headlines on it was 'Tarzan Sings!' He sang like he came out of the jungle—a big, booming, lousy voice. They didn't know what songs to give him so they tried to find a nature theme. He did 'Indian Love Song' and like that."

I put my arms over my head in a hiding gesture.

"What is it?" Henry asked.

"I can see myself being added to musical history: *And then there was this novelist. He had this really elaborate orchestra behind him and he went out to sing songs about contemporary life. The thing is, he couldn't sing, but he couldn't write either—*"

"No, you're doing good," Vinnie said. "And without you, we don't have the gig."

"You're just saying that."

"I mean it. To be in a band when it gets put together is the best. And for what it's worth, singing-wise I got you over Tarzan."

. . .

Mel arrived at our apartment with his latest girlfriend—Sandy and I again asked to bestow him with social legitimacy. The woman was someone Sandy had met previously, Laura Waits, a former magazine art director who had opened an art gallery in SoHo. She was in her mid-thirties, tall with dark features and a striking angular face. During dinner the conversation was largely about the art world. At one point Mel said self-deprecatingly, "My taste in art runs along the lines of eight-by-ten glossies." I was beginning to wonder how he and Laura could get along on a regular basis, but there may have been a clue in Mel's appearance. He was not wearing a shirt open at the neck with the Liberace chain. He wore a conservative grey suit, white shirt, and quiet tie. He also was not attempting to dominate the conversation with show-business talk. A beeper he carried with him sounded and he went into the bedroom to make a phone call. The cultural gap between them was

obvious enough for Laura to explain to us why *she* was going out
with *him,* that beneath the high-level energy and the beeper and
the deals he was a good man.

"You don't have to tell us," I said. "We've known him forever."

"He says he's going to settle down, not travel so much. That
he has this important project in New York for an old friend of
his."

"I'm the project."

Mel returned to the room apologizing; something had to be
straightened out with a group on tour.

"You didn't say that Paul was the reason you're staying around
New York," Laura remarked.

"And you, honey. By the way, I meant to give you this when
we left, but since the subject's been raised—"

He reached into his pocket, removed an index card, and
handed it to me. A date was written on it, six weeks hence.

"Yes?" I said.

"That's it, pal. You open in Radio City Music Hall."

The talk shifted to the act, Mel describing it to Laura with
enthusiasm, the remainder of the evening having the contours of
a social engagement. I was talking, smiling, all the while waiting
for them to leave so I could get under the covers. Nothing that
had preceded this—meeting Henry the first day when they produced the musicians, the Chins, then rehearsing the songs—nothing
could have prepared me for that one announcement. It had no
relation to anything previously in my life. Yes, I had written those
lyrics, and Henry had modified the music, and I had been working
with the orchestra. But that announcement had nothing to do with
me; it belonged to someone else. Manuelo. Liza Minnelli. Me open
in Radio City Music Hall? I don't open in Radio City Music Hall,
I *go* to Radio City Music Hall.

We sat and talked. Mel said he was rediscovering the pleasure
of being in New York with a woman he liked. Pleasant talk. And
I was sitting there shouting internally, *I open in Radio City Music
Hall!* We gave them their coats, everyone kissed, all calm and lovely,
and suddenly I blurted out, "In six weeks!"

"We'll get you ready."

"What if nobody comes? That's wrong. What if people *do* come?" I said, dissembling.

"They'll come. It's going to be standing room only."

"Standing room only for me at Radio City Music Hall?"

"How can you know that?" Laura asked.

"That's my business," he said with total assurance.

. . .

Sandy and I made love that night after I suggested it would be a good idea to do so before I declined into a catatonic, terror-induced state. I couldn't fall asleep. A nice fantasy would have been welcome. Judy Garland to tell me not to worry, that I was born in a trunk. Or Jimmy Durante to say things would look better because I was starting each day with a song. I never got a good fantasy going. What I had were blinking lights spelling out the words "YOU OPEN IN RADIO CITY IN SIX WEEKS!" I saw it all. I walked out in my tweeds in that huge theater with the high tiers. Mel was wrong. He couldn't fill the place. Forty-six people were there. Henry motioned to the orchestra, they played, and I didn't bomb—I *died*. "Performer Dies in Radio City Music Hall. Medical Expert Cites Panic-Humiliation Syndrome."

I finally fell asleep at about 4 A.M. Bless Jimmy Durante. He showed up and said, "Don't worry, kid. When you're a performer you don't die from performing, you die from *not* performing. So you might bomb, but you won't die." Then he sang me a lullaby, "Ink-a-dink-a-doo . . ."

. . .

I asked Henry at the next rehearsal if he had worries about the concert date. He said, "This is going to be a well-oiled machine. We should be able to pick up an in-concert album right off the first performance." He was calm. Mel came by and listened to a few songs and he, too, was calm.

"It's going to be fabulous," Mel said. "A smash with audiences and the critics."

"This could be reviewed! Why didn't I think of that?"

"It better be. I pay my publicists a lot of money to get coverage."

"Twenty years from now the leads of the reviews, the sheer savagery of them, will be studied in journalism schools."

Mel dismissed this with a wave of his hand and talked directly to Henry.

"I'd like to borrow Paul tomorrow morning."

"We can start at one-thirty."

"Good. I have to work on his finesse."

"My finesse?"

"For all the TV interviews you're going to be doing."

. . .

Mel picked me up at the apartment in the morning in his Rolls. He started discussing other bookings—Boston, Philadelphia, Chicago, Denver, Houston, Los Angeles.

"What are you *saying?*"

"You weren't thinking this was a one-shot, just Radio City?"

Our destination was Blair and Rothman Enterprises on West 57th Street. Mel introduced me to Bobby Blair and Steve Rothman, both in their thirties, Blair five feet eight, blond, with a round face, and Rothman, six feet two, gangly, dark, and curly-haired.

"Here we are, Abbott and Costello," Blair said extending his hand.

"Frank Sinatra," I replied.

"I give that about a two," Rothman said.

"Right. But not bad for an ad lib," Blair commented. "Maybe a three."

"Bobby and Steve worked for Carson. They're brilliant at the talk show interview."

"We also do radio," Blair said. "That's thrown in as a bonus."

They were dressed for work in jeans, sweatshirts, sneakers, and I thought, *They're dressed the way I should be dressed. I'm dressed stuffy and these guys get to be me.*

"I like your clothes," I said forlornly.

"Energy level about a one there," Blair announced.

"Definitely needs work," his partner suggested.

"Here's the strategy," Mel explained to me. "Before you appear at Radio City you're going on TV to establish yourself. We want you to be so well known we could just call you 'Brock.' When you don't need your first name anymore you're at the pinnacle. Sinatra. Streisand."

"Mussolini," I suggested.

"That's a three," Blair said.

"I give it a zero," Rothman declared. "The man doesn't understand what he's being told."

"He understands," I said. "Brando. Lassie."

"Bobby and Steve are the ones to package you for TV. They're my aces."

"We've done people so big, we can't even tell you who they are," Blair declared.

"We've signed contracts not to tell, they were so big," Rothman added.

"The secret about talk shows, and this is information you don't get anywhere," Blair said, whispering in my ear. "The secret is— *to have a great six minutes.*"

We went into the next room, which was a simulated set for a television talk show, with a video camera facing the set.

"We're going to run a sample segment without any coaching to see how you check out," Rothman said.

"The world is divided between two kinds of people," Mel said to me. "The ones who watch the 'Tonight Show' and the ones who know what it takes to get on it."

"That's brilliant," Blair said. "Now that's a ten."

Rothman operated the video camera connected to a television monitor. Blair took a seat in the host's chair behind the desk. He looked into the camera and said, "Our next guest is a novelist and a musical performer. He's making his performing debut this week in Radio City Music Hall. Give a warm welcome to Paul Brock!" Rothman turned a dial on a machine and through a speaker came the sound of audience applause. As I approached the couch, I tripped on a wire; he turned a dial and produced laughter. I sat on the couch next to Blair.

"Why are you making this entry into performing?"

"An old friend, Mel Steiner, encouraged me and we've put together an act."

"But what qualifies you to have an act?"

"I've put in quite a few hours working with Henry Ross, a

very gifted composer and producer. And I was a performer in my college years, in the Catskills Mountains.''

"So your act is nostalgia?''

"No, it's contemporary. Comic songs about middle-class life today. All original material.''

"Is anybody still awake?'' Rothman called over from behind the camera. "I make it about a two.''

"You're being generous," Blair responded. "As Joan Rivers says, 'Can we talk?' Paul, you've got nothing.''

"I heard a two.''

"Nothing. Let's look at it, since we must.''

Rothman tinkered with his equipment and we watched Blair interviewing me on the monitor.

"Are you attending a funeral?'' Blair asked me.

"You're so stiff, you look like you're taking a chest X-ray,'' Rothman said.

"I was trying to concentrate on the questions,'' I offered.

"A flicker of life there when he says 'Catskills,' '' Blair commented. "But no, moving along quickly back into death.'' The tape ended. "Mel, we could cast this guy in a zombie movie.''

"*Zombies Speak at Midnight*,'' Rothman suggested.

"What the guys are saying," Mel interpreted, "is you have to get control of this medium. What did you think of the way you came off?''

"I wasn't ecstatic about seeing myself on camera. My voice isn't deep enough. I'm not tall enough. While you're at it, do you think you fellas could add a few inches to my height?''

"That's a six,'' Blair said.

"We might try to work that in," Rothman commented, "physical shortcoming jokes at his own expense.''

"They're going to guide you. Just the way Henry's been directing you with the music, they'll help you perfect the interview.''

"We have six weeks. We could lighten up Bill Bradley in six weeks," Blair said, pointing to himself with his fingers, giving himself an eight.

"This is what we're going to stress for promotion," Mel said opening his attaché case. "Your personal theme, Paul.''

"My personal theme? Is this something that plays wherever I go, like *Peter and the Wolf?*"

"Your copy theme. *I* give myself a ten."

He removed a printed poster from the attaché case and taped the poster to the wall. It was the size of the posters that are plastered to construction sites. I was shown wearing my tweeds, smiling. Superimposed was the skyline of Manhattan. The copy said: "Live at Radio City Music Hall, Paul Brock, America's Balladeer of the Middle Class," with the date and ticket prices.

"Fabulous, if I don't say so myself. Everybody's always ignoring the middle class, like you say in the songs. And now you're going to be their official spokesman. You're going to speak to them, for them. They won't be ignored anymore. They have you, America's Balladeer of the Middle Class."

"Brilliant," Blair said.

"Beyond brilliant," Rothman suggested. "Orgasmic."

I looked at myself taped to the wall. It was eerie seeing myself looming so large. I wondered how I could possibly live up to my own poster.

11.

WITH THEIR TOYS, the sound machine, the video camera, the playback mechanism, Blair and Rothman were like demonic little boys. I went to their office each day at lunchtime while Henry and the musicians took a break and I was trained in the talk show format. We watched videotapes of celebrities as they had been interviewed, my instructors pointing out differences in presentation, focus, publicity value. They interviewed me, taped the interviews, and then analyzed them. For their intensity you would have thought we were watching masterpieces of the cinema, these six-minute segments.

Now that we had the theme, we worked on a series of responses for me. Through these daily sessions, fielding the questions, viewing myself over and over, being prodded about technique, eventually I did develop a talk show interview. "There are so many commercials catering to yuppies and singles, did the middle class disappear from the culture? The lines are getting so divided, we're like separate nations with our own customs, language, food. Seared tuna with tiny little undercooked vegetables. That's yuppie food. Paying for children's orthodontia. A middle-class person's concept. Well, my concern is about *us*. This is like our own town meeting we're running . . ."

· · ·

On a weekend morning I went to buy a newspaper. I passed a construction site near our apartment house and plastered across the temporary boards was me, one block long, multiples of the poster, *Paul Brock . . . Paul Brock . . . Paul Brock . . . Radio City . . . Radio City . . . Radio City . . .* What if I caught a cold, the flu, what if I broke a leg, broke both legs? I knew the answer. Mel would set another date. I was booked.

• • •

As I walked along I saw Paul Simon leaning against a fence, strumming on a guitar.

"Say, isn't that you?" he asked, referring to the posters above his head.

"Who is to say *that* is me?" I responded philosophically. I figured someone who wrote "The Sounds of Silence" would have a philosophic bent. "Who is to say that who we are, as presented to the public, is really who we are?"

"Are you on drugs?"

"No, I'm having a reaction to seeing my first billboard. I saw it on a wall, but this one is on the street."

"Looks like a clever idea."

"Mel Steiner thought of it."

"You're with Mel Steiner? You have nothing to worry about. What kind of material do you do?"

"At its best it would be comments on the times. If you'd like to hear, I have a neat six-minute segment for talk shows that tells all about it, like catalog copy."

"I think I can figure it out from the poster. Songs about the middle class. I'm going to be there to see this. For a fellow artist."

"Are we fellow artists?"

"You've got a booking and a poster to prove it."

"You mean, I'm in that community of people like you and Bette Midler?"

"Why, here she comes now," he said.

Sure enough, Bette Midler sashayed down the street.

"Hi, guys. Don't I look simultaneously cute and tacky?"

"Bette, this is Paul Brock."

"A poster boy!"

"Paul was worrying about blanking out during his act."

"You've got to worry about the *audience* blanking out, sweetheart."

"Why don't you give us a sample of one of your songs?" Paul Simon asked.

I started to sing "Chicken Lips." Brilliantly, Paul Simon filled in on the guitar. Bette Midler removed a tambourine from her purse and we sat on the curb, me singing, the two of them playing. To be sitting under a poster of yourself singing your own song accompanied by Paul Simon and Bette Midler. That's a great New York moment. I don't guess it happens that often.

.   .   .

Both our parents came to the apartment to celebrate Sammy's eighth birthday. Mel's office had sent over a poster and Sandy taped it to the wall of the foyer. My father-in-law wanted to know if we had it printed ourselves. He thought it was like one of those imitation newspaper headlines you can get printed to order. I explained it was for the act that I had told them about. The four of them were speechless, looking at the poster, looking at me.

"Are you trying to tell which is real? We both are."

"My friend Myra, she saw this poster," my mother-in-law said. "She asked her son, Fred, who works in advertising. He said people have done that. People who want to get, say, signed to do a record, or sell a song, they make up a poster."

"That's one of the wild things about this," I said to Sandy. "Do you realize I'm already signed for records?"

"Daddy's going to be in Radio City Music Hall," Sammy told them. "And we're all going to get in free."

"Is this like when people rent Carnegie Hall to conduct an orchestra?" my father-in-law said, still trying to place it.

"No," Sandy said. "Paul's friend Mel Steiner is a powerful entrepreneur in show business and he thinks Paul has a great act, which Paul wrote himself, and there's an orchestra and arrangements and it's going to be fabulous."

"Mel is doing this?" my mother said.

"Mel made Manuelo a star. He's going to make Daddy a star," Joey explained.

"This is an important person. This is Mel Steiner," my mother said to my in-laws.

"He's very successful," my father added.

"Are you going to do your act from the Mountains?" my mother said, somewhat bewildered.

"With the help of a small battalion of people I will be out there performing a new act."

I broke into a tap dance, singing à la Astaire, "I go my way by myself . . ."

"This is your act?" my mother-in-law asked.

"I learned that for discipline."

"I'm sure Mel knows what he's doing," my mother said, closing ranks behind me, but it was apparent that this was straining even her loyalty.

"If Paul says he's going to do this, he's going to do this," my father added, trying to contribute by vouching for my word.

"And you're going to come," Sandy said.

"Yes, we'll order tickets," my father-in-law said grandly.

"We'll get them for you," I offered.

"I don't want charity," he answered, somehow challenged in his manhood. "We'll buy our own."

"Dad!" Sandy said.

"We'll buy!" he declared.

"I just moved a couple of tickets," I said to Sandy. "I'm hot."

. . .

My agent, Peter Raskin, called for a meeting with Mel to discuss the business implications of this new area of endeavor. Since Peter knew nothing about the variety performer's world, he did not presume to take a commission on any bookings. He pointed out, though, that in order to give me the best representation, he had co-agented the publishing side with Martha Sipes. And now he had lost, via the novel and stage, a successful scriptwriting client. They agreed that Mel would give Peter a percentage of his share of my performer's earnings in exchange for a percentage of Peter's share of my publishing earnings. I kept thinking, *Alleged* earnings, guys.

. . .

Helen Baskin was the person in Mel's public relations department assigned to oversee my publicity. She was a heavy-set brunette in her late fifties whose office was not adorned with photographs of celebrities. In my recent experience it was notable for this feature. She straightened a flap on my tweed jacket pocket.

"Mel says this is your look."

"He picked it out."

"I like it. I couldn't improve on it."

"Do you get into what people wear?"

"If need be. My claim to fame is, I'm the one who dressed Manuelo in white. I get offered jobs on that. *She dressed Manuelo in white.*" Helen chuckled at the notion.

She asked me questions for about a half-hour, straight auto-biographical material. I realized I was answering her questions with my television talk show approach, eyes fixed on her, good voice projection.

"It's like I'm on camera. Am I locked into this forever?"

"Print interviews aren't as stagy."

"Don't tell me I'm going to be trained now in print interviews."

"By me. Can't let you go out there saying anything that comes into your head. That's for your novels."

She explained the publicity procedures. One of her staff members would be arranging appearances for me on television talk shows, another person handled newspaper and magazine interviews, a publicity writer would prepare a press kit with a press release.

"I look at Mel sometimes," she said, "and I think, *Nobody can be that smart.* America's Balladeer of the Middle Class. I can't tell you how important a line like that is from a publicity standpoint."

"I hope we don't lose the fact that I'm a novelist. *He writes novels, too.*"

"We won't lose it. Isn't that the whole idea?"

She had a sample of my television interview on a videocassette sent over by Blair and Rothman, and we watched it and discussed how to tailor that material for print interviews.

A few days later I received a package by messenger with a note from Helen: "You may not know how fast this is. But Mel wants us to get on this. And when Mel wants . . ." A press kit was enclosed, which was a folder with a reproduction of the poster on the cover. Inside was an eight-by-ten glossy of me in the same pose as the poster. I was presented in a press release as speaking to and for my people. Several of the song titles were listed. Then I was quoted:

"The middle class has been sorely neglected. Home and hearth isn't 'hot' in our culture. Well, it's time we had the spotlight on us."

As I read it I thought, *When did I say that?* Then I remembered it had come out of a Blair-Rothman segment. At some point I could no longer tell where I ended and my press release began.

. . .

Mel invited us to dinner at his apartment, a dinner that Laura Waits had prepared.

"You follow a long line of Mel's women who could barely order a meal by phone," Sandy said to her.

"I'm settling in," and teasingly she pinched Mel on the cheek. "Look how nervous it makes him. He's squirming."

"I'm happy," he said, his voice a bit tense.

"It's an interesting environment here," Laura said. "The art looks like it was ordered by phone."

"I think it was," Mel quipped.

"I like those photos very much. Mel said they're your father's."

Years before, Mel had been kind enough to buy four of my father's landscapes, which were framed and hanging in the entrance area to the apartment.

"It's my father's pastime."

"With all of you being so close, you might think I'm saying this to get on your good side, and I am. But I also really like them."

"I have an order pad here," I said.

"Mostly I do prints in the gallery. But I'm doing a group photography show. I'd like to include your dad. Presuming he has other pictures on this level."

"That's very nice of you," Sandy said. "And I don't care if you're doing it to get on our good side."

"They're lovely pictures," Laura said.

"Marry this woman," I told Mel.

"Subtle," he answered.

• • •

I called my father the next day and told him about Laura's offer. He was very pleased and I introduced him to Laura at her gallery the next Saturday morning. He placed his portfolio on her table and she studied the pictures carefully.

"These are very good," she said. "Beautifully printed, too."

"Thank you," my father said.

"I'd be very happy to include you in the show."

I believed she was being honest with my father; his landscapes were lovely and always had been so, by my estimation.

"You really like them?" he said. I was on the verge of melting into tears. "How much is this going to cost me?" my father asked.

"It isn't going to cost you anything," Laura said, looking over at me in confusion.

"Once I saw an ad in a magazine, a gallery would show your pictures, but you had to pay five hundred dollars for the expenses."

"This is not a co-op gallery," Laura said. "We show the images, we do take a 30-percent commission on any photography that's sold. But you don't pay out of your own pocket."

"Oh, then this is really special," he said.

"What do you think of choosing six and making editions of twenty-five," Laura said. "And establishing a price of $250 per print?"

"Do you think you'll sell any?" he asked.

"I think so."

They selected six photographs, a geographic sampling: City Island, Central Park, the Hudson River, a woodland scene in the Catskills, a cityscape of a sunrise over the city, and the New Jersey shore.

• • •

The gallery was crowded for the opening. People had been invited from the gallery's mailing list and the five other photographers on exhibit had invited friends and family. My father was, by thirty years, the oldest of the photographers. We brought the children, Mel was there, and a few of my parents' cronies came. They stood around my parents in a group. Laura introduced my father to a trio of Japanese men in business suits. They praised his work and self-consciously he thanked them. A few minutes later Laura walked over to us and said:

"They bought a set of six for their office!"

"My first big sale!" he said, beaming.

By evening's end a set had been purchased by the New York Historical Society and a Manhattan real-estate firm, and there were several other prospects. When the crowd dispersed my father was still smiling, much as he had been from the beginning of the evening.

"A great night," I told him. "A great success."

"It could have come a little earlier, but it's very nice."

.   .   .

When I was about seven I sat in his darkroom as he developed some landscape pictures. He told me, "Whatever you do for others, there has to be something you own for yourself." "I own my marble collection," I responded, not quite getting it at the time.

My father had been recognized by people with artistic taste, and now had a passageway into his later years. Others would be looking for activities to do, but he had been given important approval for his work. I was proud of him for having always kept something of his own for himself, his art, through all those years. I hoped I had learned about integrity from my father. But I was also a child of my culture and I lacked the modesty of his ambitions, and his patience.

12.

THERE WERE TWO WEEKS to go before the concert. We were scurrying to get the children off to school when the phone rang.

"It's Liz Smith!" Sandy called out.

"Mr. Brock," Liz Smith said, "I'm planning to run something in my column and I wanted to talk to you directly. Would you object to single people coming to your concert?"

"Why would they? I don't go to their bars or eat their seared tuna."

"What would you say is a middle-class food?"

"Chicken you broil in your kitchen. Yuppies usually get it take-out."

"Interesting. That's word-for-word from your press kit. You have to say that Mel Steiner's acts are well coached. *Have* you been well coached, Mr. Brock?"

I almost responded, "I don't know what you mean," and probably should have. Instead I answered, "Yes, I have been."

"That's the best thing you've said."

The following day an item appeared in Liz Smith's syndicated column.

Let's hear it for the middle class! That's the intriguing premise for a concert by Paul Brock, billed as America's Balladeer of the Middle Class. This new comedy song performer debuts in two weeks at Radio City Music Hall. Pulling the strings is impresario Mel Steiner. Henry Ross did the musical arrangements. Paul Brock is a novelist you may never have heard of, but in Mel Steiner fashion, you will now. It sounds like fun and I'll be there. Brock seems to be an engaging type. When asked if he had been well coached for talking to interviewers he answered honestly, "Yes, I have been."

My first call after the column appeared was from Helen Baskin, the publicist, and it was not to compliment me.

"What was that about? You don't say you're well coached!"

"It just came out. I was trying to be honest."

"You follow the structure we set up. Liz liked the premise. But there are sharks out there who could eat you alive. Do not do that again!"

. . .

I had reached the point of rehearsing the act where it *was* like a bar mitzvah. I knew the material that well, and was as nervous as for my bar mitzvah. Mel was at the next rehearsal and when we took a break he whispered in my ear: "Bigger than Manuelo."

"You're crazy as a loon," I whispered back.

"You're going to be SRO."

"I happened to have called the box office. Tickets are available at every location. Does SRO have a new meaning?"

"You're doing the 'Today Show' tomorrow. Then on the following days, 'Good Morning America,' 'This Morning' on CBS, and Letterman."

"I am?"

"The ball game has begun."

. . .

At 7:15 the following morning I went downstairs where a limousine was waiting for me. Helen Baskin and Blair and Rothman were in the back seat, the team.

"We'll run through a few final pointers on the way over there," Blair told me.

"This is as final as you could get, unless you're planning to come out on the set and interview me yourselves."

"If only we could," Rothman said.

In the limousine was a television set connected to a VCR. They put on a tape of me being interviewed by Blair.

"See how he sits up?" Rothman said, referring to me.

"See how he keeps eye contact?" Blair offered. "This is a great six minutes. Pattern yourself after that man."

When the interview was over, they ran it again.

"How are you going to account for the lull between the time I get out of this car and go in front of the camera?"

"We'll have to take our chances," Blair said.

"We could have a portable unit for the Green Room," Rothman told his partner.

"We can try that next time."

"You mean this isn't state-of-the-art?" I protested.

Blair and Rothman looked at each other uneasily.

"I was teasing."

"You're doing too much talking, Paul," Helen said. "Focus on the interview."

We went up to the studio in the elevator and I felt uncomfortable about the way Helen had said, "Focus on the interview," in a flat, emotionless voice, a hypnotist's voice. Was there some weird hypnotism going on? Had I been programmed to perform in ways I didn't realize? The Manchurian Novelist.

When Helen did not repeat the phrase, I assumed I was having nothing more than the jitters. We sat in the Green Room and watched the show. Bryant Gumbel was in the process of interviewing a willowy blonde in her thirties, Veronica Lawson, who wore a jogging suit and sneakers. They were discussing her book, *Winning at Everything,* a title she managed to insert nearly every other sentence.

"As I explain in my book, *Winning at Everything,* 80 percent of success is in having a winning attitude, Bryant. I get up each day and say, *I'm going to win today. I'm going to win at this Thursday or Friday. I'm going to win at eating my breakfast, the best breakfast I can eat.*"

"And what would that be—not a jelly doughnut with chocolate milk?"

"It's right in my book, *Winning at Everything,* under 'Winning

Breakfasts.' Usually, I'm writing a book and I say, *I'm going to win at writing today*. The point is, Bryant, if you win, you can't lose, which is why I called the book *Winning at Everything*."

Blair and Rothman were taking notes, transfixed.

"Well, you win at slipping in the most mentions of your book in a single interview," Bryant Gumbel said.

Unfazed, she smiled broadly, a winning smile. After her segment, she came bounding into the room, taking a seat on a couch, followed by her publicist, also a blonde in her thirties, wearing a jogging suit. On their backs it said, "Winning at Everything."

A man in his forties wearing a blue suit and a bow tie came in and was introduced by his publicist as Dr. Philip Maxwell.

"What brings you to the show?" I asked.

"Depression," he replied, smiling.

I was sitting next to Veronica Lawson, who rummaged through a tote bag that said, "Winning at Everything."

"You did that very well," I told her. She was consulting her schedule for the day and she checked off the "Today Show."

"What?"

"Do you have many other interviews?" I asked.

She wrote a note to herself.

"What?"

"Just passing the time with another guest. Maybe trying to keep my mind off my nervousness."

She kept writing.

"Your first time on?" her publicist said to me, to deflect me from her client.

"My first."

"What do you do?"

"I'm a writer-performer."

During this exchange Veronica Lawson never looked up from her notes, oblivious to everyone in the room. She seemed to embody the worst clichés about young careerists.

"Let's get out of here," she said to the publicist and without acknowledging anyone else, Veronica Lawson rushed out, on her way to win.

. . .

The depression man was interviewed by Joe Garagiola. He was promoting an audiocassette, "Smile at Depression." You were supposed to play it for yourself whenever you felt depressed. We heard an excerpt, syrupy music and cheerful, inane messages. Maxwell smiled constantly as if he was appearing for a dental hygiene product. He said his cassette was selling fantastically well, which struck me as truly depressing.

I was taken to the set by a production person, fitted with a microphone, and introduced to Bryant Gumbel. Then we were quickly on the air. He asked about the origin of the act and I said, as rehearsed, that it was an extension of my previous writing and that I had no pretensions about being a great singer. He wanted me to talk about the act, and I did my home-and-hearth-isn't-hot routine, smiling, though not as broadly as Maxwell. To give Blair and Rothman their due, I had gone through this kind of interview so often that I was poised and focused. When I went back into the Green Room you would have thought I was Mario Andretti embraced by his pit crew.

"A ten!" Blair said. "A genuine ten!"

"You looked like you were back in our studio, you were so perfect," Rothman said.

"Outstanding," Helen contributed.

"You killed the other guests," Blair announced.

"Killed them," Rothman said. "Wiped them away."

I had thought the competition was within myself, to be able to do this and not self-destruct on camera—but apparently I was also supposed to kill the others.

. . .

The pattern continued over the next days; my people picked me up in the limousine, I watched myself on the VCR being interviewed, and then conducted the actual interviews. I was supposed to have "killed" the guests on the other shows, too.

A producer from "Late Night with David Letterman" called to say they had seen me on my interviews and were wondering if they could try for a variation. They wanted me to ask yuppies on the street what they thought about the premise behind my songs. I suggested we go to a singles bar and show me, a fish out of water, in that setting. The producer was intrigued with the idea, and Letterman concurred, but when we arrived at the studio Helen, Blair, and Rothman found out about it and they were furious.

"You can't break the format," Rothman said.

"We haven't rehearsed this," Blair complained.

"Paul, this is not advisable," Helen said.

This became my small attempt to retain ownership of myself. We left the studio, my staff trailing behind me in protest. The location shooting was at Ernie's, a Columbus Avenue restaurant with a popular singles bar. Outside the restaurant David Letterman asked me questions about my act for a few minutes, then the camera trailed me as I went inside.

"What do you think of middle-class males?" I asked a woman standing at the bar.

"Is this 'Candid Camera'?"

"David Letterman."

"You're kidding. Middle-class males? It's hard to tell," she said laughing. "You all look alike to me."

"What can I say to that, David? These people all look alike to me, too," I commented to the camera. I turned to a young man at the bar, a classic young stockbroker type. "How would you respond to a concert that advertised it was *for* the middle class?"

"I wouldn't go."

"Do you mind that I, a married, middle-class kind of guy, decided to come in here?"

"Not as long as you don't skim off the best-looking women."

"Do I have a chance?"

"Are they shooting this?"

I nodded, yes.

"No chance," and he laughed and moved along the bar.

"This is Paul Brock from a place where I don't belong. And if you wouldn't belong here, and for more on this subject, come hear my concert."

The segment ended with David Letterman saying goodbye to

me under a poster for the concert at a nearby construction site.

"We'll have to analyze this," Blair said, sulking on the side-walk.

"You broke every rule," Rothman said.

"It was good," Helen offered. "But dangerous."

. . .

My mother-in-law informed me that Phil of advertising saw me on Letterman and he was going to buy tickets. "It's only out of curiosity," she said.

"Curiosity is what this is about," I answered.

I called Mel's office and said to his secretary that I was going to stop by before my rehearsal to pick up a few posters; the boys wanted them for their rooms. When I arrived at the office, the receptionist said Mel asked for me to stop in and say hello. He was in a meeting attended by Blair, Rothman, Helen, and three young women who were introduced as publicity associates. Mel told me ticket sales were going well and he had made arrangements with WNEW, a station that played nonrock music, to air a rehearsal tape of me performing "Lost in the Middle" as part of a promotion that would offer free concert tickets to listeners.

As I waited for the elevator I found myself next to one of the publicity associates, a young woman in her twenties named Marcy, gushing with enthusiasm over finally meeting me. In the elevator she said:

"It's going to be a terrific debut. With a standing ovation at the end."

"You never know."

"Oh, it's for sure. Mr. Steiner said so in the meeting. He bought you a standing ovation."

"He *bought* me a standing ovation?"

I wondered where you bought one. Were there agencies? Did people have résumés? *I stood and cheered for Judy Garland. My other credits include Sting and Madonna.*

. . .

Having been on the network television morning shows, I was interviewed on several local shows. Meanwhile, the WNEW radio promotion was airing the song and mentioning the concert several times a day. Liz Smith ran a column item referring to the amount of publicity: "If Paul Brock gets through his interviews without suffering battle fatigue, it should be an entertaining concert." I didn't have to be concerned with that; the Chins' work was holding up so far.

I entered our apartment and found myself facing about fifty balloons with the letters SRO printed on them. They were from Mel, whose note read: "SRO, as promised. You'll be great, as promised." The children played with the balloons, which bobbed around the house advertising false gaiety to me. As Sandy and I were about to go to sleep I said, "Now I have to deliver. It would have been better with an empty theater."

"Then you would have been upset that it was empty."

"Do you think Mel bought up the tickets himself?"

"Honey, you *have* been on TV night and day."

"Will you answer a question honestly?"

"No."

"You know what I want to know."

"I can't give you an honest answer."

"You've heard me."

"I can't get past the fact that it's you. I love the writing because I love your writing. Beyond that, I don't know how well you're doing it."

"Are you scared?" She didn't answer, but I could see it in her face. "So we're both scared. You think the people are scared in my claque? You think they practice yelling bravo?"

"Mel wouldn't have to pay me to yell bravo. Bravo, honey."

. . .

We were scheduled to rehearse for the last time on the day before the concert, the rehearsal to take place in Radio City Music Hall. I walked on stage and looked out at the size of the place, deep, high with the sweeping rows of seats, and I went right back into my star dressing room and threw up.

I felt queasy all through the day of the concert. We asked the boys to wear jackets, shirts, and ties for the event, and this was helpful, having to fuss over them, which served as a distraction.

Just before we left the apartment they gave me greeting cards that they had made, "Good luck, Daddy" cards with stick figures. I put them inside my jacket pocket for good luck and we left for the concert in the chauffeured limousine that was sent for us.

. . .

At the Music Hall, I stood in the wings, not wanting to look out at the audience. If looking at empty seats made me ill, the idea that people were in them was certainly worse. Mel stepped out and introduced me: "Ladies and gentlemen, your spokesman and mine. Here he is. America's Balladeer of the Middle Class. With great pleasure—" and he turned and grinned at me like the kid I knew "—Paul Brock!"

The applause was respectful. I walked out, nodded in appreciation, Henry began the music, I looked at the audience—and I panicked. Nothing came out. Not a word. Maybe something you could call a gasp. I turned to Henry who was gesturing with his hands, I turned back to the audience and by now, the orchestra was so far ahead of me, it was hopeless. Henry stopped the musicians. A few titters and some coughing could be heard from the audience.

"Paul! What's going on?" Henry said.

"I panicked."

"I see that. Start again."

Mel was calling from behind the curtain and I went over to him.

"I forgot the words!"

"Okay, listen to me. Take the music with you." He gestured for one of the backstage assistants to give me copies of the material. "Go back, tell the audience you're sorry. That you're a little nervous."

I did this. I walked back, faced the audience, and said, "I'm sorry. I'm nervous. This wasn't in the act."

We began again. After the first few words, I remembered the songs. The nervousness did not disappear. Several times my voice quivered from the tension, but we kept going. The reception of the audience was warm throughout. After I sang the last of the songs, in waves, starting out front and spilling back to the rear was my paid-for standing ovation.

"You did it!" Mel said, embracing me.

As planned, I performed "Yuppies Don't Know Chinese Food" for an encore and when it was over, ending the concert, people all through the theater were standing and applauding; people on all sides, some applauding with their hands over their heads so I could see them. A few were making V-for-victory signs. A sea of people applauding me.

I don't know what they'd think of this over at the Writers Guild or at the Authors Guild, but I have to admit it felt wonderful.

13.

MEL RENTED AN English valet, Mr. Pembroke, to be in my service in the dressing room. I wondered if that was his real name or whether it was generic packaging. A shiningly bald, portly fellow in his sixties, he informed me that he had dressed the late Laurence Olivier when "Sir Larry" had been in New York. I was to call him "Pembroke." I told him he could call me "Sir Paulie," if it made him more comfortable. Pembroke was grievously disappointed to realize his gentleman for the evening arrived in the same clothing he was performing in and was planning on going home in the same outfit. "No dressing robe, sir?" he said. And I don't think Pembroke thought much of my gift to the orchestra and technical crew, which he helped me distribute when the curtain came down. "T-shirts, sir?" in a voice that could have chilled the champagne Mel provided. On the front of the T-shirts it said: "I Was with Paul Brock in Concert and Survived." I suppose I was being optimistic when I ordered them.

Caterers arrived backstage with carts of food and drink for everyone connected with the concert. Sandy, ebullient, said I would have had a standing ovation even if Mel hadn't bought one, and Laura agreed. I confronted Mel on that point and asked what the going rates were for standing ovations. He said it cost $950 and the women were right, he could have saved the money. The children were lovely, both saying how much they liked the concert and then they clung to me, as if to retain ownership of their daddy during the excitement.

"I knew you'd do it," my mother said. "Even when he was in the Mountains, he had a talent. He just never concentrated on it."

"I'm so proud," my father said. "To see you get up in front of all those people—"

"And live through it. Thank you, Dad."

"Amazing," my father-in-law announced. "Simply amazing."

"It's like a dream," my mother-in-law told us. "Paul on stage. I said to Milt, I couldn't believe it. You expect it's going to be terrible and you're so relieved when it's not."

"I'm very happy for you," I said.

"How much do you figure to make for a concert like this?" Milt asked me.

"I don't know. I still owe for the clothes."

. . .

What is it like to see your very father performing on stage at Radio City? I figured sitting quietly for that gets you an ice cream sundae. On the way home we stopped at an espresso–ice cream parlor. I became aware of a couple in their fifties at a nearby table staring at us. They were whispering, both looking over. The man came toward me.

"You're Paul Brock."

"Yes."

"We were just at your concert! I said to my wife, *There he is, a regular person, eating*. Could you autograph my program?"

"Of course."

I signed my name on the concert program.

"Tell him he was better than Wayne Newton," his wife called over.

"We were in Las Vegas last month. We saw Wayne Newton. You were better."

"Daddy, that must happen a lot," Joey said after the man returned to his table. "People know you from your writing and ask you for your autograph."

Sandy and I looked at each other. That had never happened to me as a writer.

. . .

The reviews turned out to be good. Most critics accepted that the material was more important than my ability to present it. In the *New York Times* the reviewer wrote:

>The middle class has been set to music. Articulating the anxieties of people "lost in the middle," that's the title of one of the songs, is Paul Brock. He is a 47-year-old Emmy award–winning television writer and soon-to-be novelist.
>
>Brock has written comic songs for himself whose music parodies Piaf and Aznavour with a nod in the direction of Allan Sherman of "Sarah Jockman" fame. The lyrics cover a range of preoccupations of the middle class: bills, parenthood, and the slighting of the middle class in the culture. As a lyricist Brock writes felicitously. Among the titles are "Children's Shoes Blues," "Me and My Car," and "Taxes" about the economics of life in the middle. "Chicken Lips" is about a father working hard to make his children laugh. "Sports Heroes," a comment on those mind-boggling salaries. And "Yuppies Don't Know Chinese Food" on the discomfort of seeing young singles coming into their own when they have demonstrated such poor taste in their choice of Chinese restaurants.
>
>The music is serviceable and has been cleverly arranged by Henry Ross. Paul Brock would be unlikely to put anybody out of business in competing for an audience as a conventional singer. He does sing well enough to tell the stories of his own songs.
>
>In Paul Brock, billed wryly as America's Balladeer of the Middle Class, we have met an appealing, new performer whose songs have substance and wit.

"Incredible!" I yelled.

"Honey, it's so fantastic," Sandy shouted.

I didn't know if that was the kind of reaction to a favorable review you would get from Tony and Mrs. Tony Bennett, but we were jumping up and down, arms around each other like ballplayers who had just won the pennant.

. . .

"We're on our way!" Mel called to say. "You're going to do two more concerts at Radio City."

"I am?"

"We'll fill the place on the reviews alone. Then you're going on tour."

"I *am?*" I said, my voice rising in desperation.

"You don't quit when you're ahead; you move ahead when you're ahead. You'll do the tour, maybe I'll throw something else in, we'll time the book for the right moment, and there you are."

"When you say *tour*—"

"I mean, America. America needs you."

. . .

"Such a review," my mother said after seeing the *New York Times*. "I'm having the Xeroxes made right now. I thought I'd slip them under a few doors." My parents lived in Co-op City in the northern section of the Bronx, where there were fifteen thousand high-rise apartments.

I could count on my mother-in-law to give equal time to the negative side.

"What can you do?" she called to say.

"About what?"

"A mixed review in the *Times*. They can't all be good."

"You call that a mixed review?"

"Phil said it to his mother. Wait, I wrote down what he said."

"Yes, I wouldn't want to miss anything here."

"Mixed, but a selling review."

"That was not mixed. And if that's the use of language our Phil the advertising man has, he should be in another field."

"It said the music was serviceable."

"I'll live with that."

"So what happens now?"

"Trepidation, anxiety. Because I'm doing two more concerts and going on tour. I have to hang up now, Belle. I have to read my mixed review again."

. . .

The two additional Radio City concerts were set for Friday and
Saturday nights, three weeks hence. A rehearsal schedule was established to keep me on top of the material. I was going to sing
with the orchestra for two hours each day and increase the rehearsal
time as we got closer to the concert. When rehearsals resumed, in
a gesture of camaraderie, everyone was wearing the T-shirt I had
given them.

. . .

I left the studio after the first rehearsal, and standing outside the
building was Bruce Springsteen. He was wearing jeans, a bandana,
and an "I Was with Paul Brock in Concert and Survived" T-shirt.

"I heard from one of the technicians that you were rehearsing
today. I'm Bruce Springsteen."

"Yes, I know who you are."

"I was at your concert. I stood and applauded."

"How much did Mel Steiner pay you?"

"Is he still doing that? It was a terrific show."

"I can't believe you're wearing that T-shirt."

"I saw Pembroke. He worked a couple of press parties my
record company threw. He had an armful of the shirts and I asked
him for one."

"I have one of *your* T-shirts. I wear it to go jogging."

"Aren't I the enemy?"

"*You're* a performer. How do you do it? And when you tour,
how do you keep up the energy, city after city?"

"To tell you the truth, I was coached by the Chins," he said.

"You were?"

"I know you're into your own material, but maybe someday
you might like to write a song for me."

"Golly."

"I don't think you want to use a word like 'golly' if you're
writing for me."

"Of course. Fuckin' A."

"And I'm not Eddie Murphy."

"Sorry. Sure. I'd be honored."

"What's next for you?" Bruce Springsteen asked me.

"A tour, but I have doubts about doing it."

"You shouldn't. While I was watching you it occurred to me, you've got the knack. Some artists can only play small rooms, but to be an arena performer is something not a lot of people can be."

"I've only played one concert."

"You've got it. I can tell. And I'd like to ask you to join our club. It's called the Arena Performer Club."

"You want me to be in your club?"

"It's only for people who can perform in an arena and really move a crowd. We get together, watch videos, talk about technique. All on the highest level. So far it's me, Madonna, Neil Diamond, Mick Jagger, Michael Jackson, the boys from U-2, and you."

"Golly. I mean, wow!"

"Good luck on your tour. Meantime, I'd be interested if you've got any extra T-shirts."

. . .

I worked on the new novel in whatever free time I had and I answered the mail I received after the concert. I had received dozens of letters from people who must have taken my name and address from the telephone book. The letters kept arriving. Most were variations of the theme: "We finally have somebody to speak for us."

One letter was from the person who, in fact, inspired the song "Cynthia Rosenbloom," about the girls of our youth. It was sent to me by someone I had dated in the Bronx, Ellen Moskowitz. I had poured so much Chinese food and pizza money into that girl, my total assets, and she never did more than neck, spurning me for Marty Shuman, who said he was going to be a doctor. (See also "The Undoctor of Love.") And here was Ellen Moskowitz writing to tell me she had gone to my concert and had greatly enjoyed it. She was going to be in New York that week; could we meet for a drink? I couldn't resist the temptation to find out what had become of her and, I suppose, to say to someone who had rejected me, *This is who you turned down.* I called and we arranged to meet at the Algonquin for a drink. She was seated when I arrived, a heavy-set, middle-aged woman in a print dress, her brunette hair in a permanent. What had been a cute, insolently sexy face was now a round saucer, as if another image had been printed over the original. I knew someone would have the same reaction suddenly seeing me after twenty-five years.

"Paul, I'd know you anywhere. But then I just saw you on stage."

"It was nice of you to go."

"Well, after all, my old lover."

"Not exactly lover. We never got past necking, Ellen."

"It's an expression, to say 'lover.' "

We talked for a while, filling each other in. She had a sixteen-year-old boy and fourteen-year-old girl and was married to Bob Kaplow of Interiors by Kaplow, Rockville Center. She "helped out in the store with sales." She didn't know I had become a writer and had never seen my name until the promotion for the concert.

"I couldn't believe it was you up there."

"Neither could I. Whatever happened to the guy you were going out with, Marty Shuman?"

"Oh, him. He became a salesman. He sells to drugstores."

"Wait a minute! He was supposed to be a doctor! You turned me down for him because of that!"

"I did always like you."

"Ellen, I must have taken you out on twenty dates. I saw you longer than some people stay married, and you never let me get to first base."

"I couldn't. When I was going out with you, I was sleeping with Marty."

"Sleeping with? *Actual?*"

"To tell you the truth, after I met Marty I still went out with you because my parents didn't want me to go steady. And I couldn't do anything with you if I was sleeping with Marty. I was no *whooa*."

"The guy claimed he was going to be a doctor. He got credit for that! And he slept with you! How many times do you think you did it during the time you were going out with me?"

"Twenty-two."

"You have the number in your head?"

"I'm sure of it. But, Paul, if you want, I mean, I'm no virgin. We could make it now upstairs in the hotel. For old times' sake."

"I think old times' sake only works if we did it before!"

We talked a while longer but I simply couldn't concentrate and eventually I called for the check.

"Do you have to go so soon? Well, if you don't want to make it with me, can I have your autograph?"

Sometimes these things just don't work out the way you had in mind. I get to meet the Cynthia Rosenbloom of my youth and I learn I had lost out to a make-believe doctor! Twenty-two times! While I was paying for her meals!

. . .

I had completed an interview for *Parade* magazine and was leaving the Steiner office when Mel's secretary intercepted me, saying that Mel wanted to see me.

He was at his desk, a dark, brooding expression on his face. In the room with him were Blair, Rothman, and Helen Baskin and they, too, looked grim.

"We've had a little bad luck, buddy."

He handed me a copy of *Variety* and pointed to a story. A woman named Priscilla Blake was debuting a new act at the Ballroom, "Confessions of a Yuppie." The songs included "What Do Yuppies Eat and Think?" "Yuppies Get a Bad Press," and "When a Yuppie Goes with an Older Man."

"Basically, the act is a complete rip-off of yours," Mel said. "She's managed by a guy named Art Bergman, a wily sonofabitch. He's looking to get her a free ride off of you."

"Is she good?" I asked.

"The question is—is she getting exposure?" Mel said.

"She was on with Regis and Kathie Lee," Helen said.

"If she catches on, doing the yuppie angle on what you're doing about the middle class, it's going to take away from you," Mel told me. "You'll get total overload on this kind of act."

"So if she's good, it's not good. And is she's not good, it's not good," I said.

"You got it," Mel replied. "It's not good."

. . .

We went to see her perform that night, Mel, Laura, Sandy and I, Helen, Blair, and Rothman, seated at tables in the rear. Priscilla Blake was about thirty, a pretty redhead with long hair and a clear, professionally trained voice. She was accompanied by a pianist. Mel said she had come out of musical theater and it was apparent. She was playing a part. She performed in a tailored suit wearing Reeboks, carrying a briefcase. The songs were the reverse spin on my songs and were all about single people's interests. The melodies even sounded so much like mine that the entire act was virtually a parody of mine. She was fairly well received in the nightclub by an audience predominantly of people her age.

"I give them a ten for chutzpah," Blair said after the show.

"Tonight she's doing Letterman," Helen said. "She's such a natural for Letterman, she could be a regular."

"The only plus I can see so far is that Art hasn't booked her into Radio City. Yet," Mel said.

Nobody in our group knew what to do. Largely, we were in shock. In a sense, my act had been stolen. Mel and Laura came back to our apartment and we watched Priscilla Blake on Letterman. After preliminaries about her background and information about where she was appearing, Letterman said:

"There's someone named Paul Brock, who does songs about the middle class—"

"I don't know about middle-class people," she said. "They don't come into the bars where I hang out with my friends, and I don't go into the orthodontists' offices where they hang out with their kids."

"Have you seen his act?" Letterman asked her.

"All middle-class guys look alike to me," she said, the audience laughing. "Remember that Nichols and May routine where she talks about dating Albert Schweitzer. Well, I believe I did date him, this Paul Brock. Bourgeois. Pudgy. Kind of bitter."

She then sang "Yuppies Get a Bad Press," and looked to be a big hit with the audience.

"*I believe I did date him!* What is that about? How can she say such a thing?" I shouted.

"Why *would* she claim she dated him?" Laura asked Mel. "I don't understand."

"It's insidious," Mel answered. "If Paul is taking a stand on home and hearth, what does it say about him if he actually went out with one of these yuppies he sings about?"

"Who'd believe such a thing?" Sandy said.

"It doesn't matter. It's about publicity," Mel said.

They left soon after, Mel looking miserable.

"I didn't think she was very good," Sandy offered. "Her voice was good, but the songs weren't. But I guess that's not the point."

"Remember the battle of the baritones? The battle of the big bands? Maybe I should take her on, *mano a mano*." Thinking I had the answer I immediately called Mel on his private line, and on his way home, he picked up from his car.

"What if I have a shootout with her, like in Radio City?"

"You don't want to give her any extra attention. You don't want to be associated with her in any way. It detracts from you. This whole goddamn thing detracts from you," he said, his voice tired and trailing off.

. . .

Priscilla Blake appeared on the morning network programs, the local morning shows. She usually managed to weave into the interview the insinuation that I had dated her. A yuppie interviewer on a cable entertainment show, playing right into her strategy, said, "It doesn't speak too well of this man if he's doing songs disparaging your age group while he's going out with people in it."

She answered, "I really don't understand their rituals."

Newsday ran a story on Priscilla Blake and again she took a run at me. "Bourgeois. Pudgy. A little bitter." Bitter? Yes, I was getting very bitter. And I was not pudgy!

Helen tried to counter with publicity for me, and I went on a few radio shows. She couldn't get me back on television, however, or in the newspapers. What Mel had feared was happening: my act was, in effect, being jammed in the media by Priscilla Blake.

An ad appeared in the *New York Times* announcing a concert by Priscilla Blake in Town Hall, devilishly scheduled the week before my additional concerts at Radio City were to take place. Mel ran ads to announce the two new concert dates for me. But ticket sales for my concerts were sluggish. I was rehearsing with the orchestra; Mel came by to watch one day, observed the proceedings with a brooding expression, and left without talking to anyone.

"Is there any truth to the rumor the concerts may be canceled?" one of the musicians asked me.

"I don't know. I only work here," I said.

. . .

"Think I could get a song out of this?" I said to Sandy that night. " 'When a Yuppie Steals Your Act, Jams Your Publicity, Cancels Your Concerts, Wrecks the Publishing of Your Novel, Drives You Back into Television.' It doesn't scan too well."

"Not all of those things are true. She hasn't put you out of business."

"Not yet. What we're looking at is: My tour doesn't happen. The book is published modestly, but not terrifically. And I go back to writing scripts."

"Maybe this is providential. Maybe it's gotten out of hand, all this merchandising of you that Mel cooked up. Why don't we just take the gains and call it a day?"

"What gains?"

"More people know your name now than before. That could help the book."

"Not enough, honey. Basically, I'm right back where I was. Plus I put all that time and work into the act and I never got to play it out."

"You've got a novel done. You're a novelist now. We'll move out of New York. We'll live on less. You'll write what you want to write."

"How much less do you think we can live on? And if someone isn't making a living as a novelist, he still has to do something for a living. And what about you? You'd have to give up being near your contacts. We're stuck, honey."

· · ·

"Here he is, Mr. Q-u-a-l-i-t-y!" With an emcee singing to the Miss America melody, I made my triumphant return to the Polo Lounge. Behind him was a backup group of singers, six suntanned men in sports shirts, white jeans, Gucci loafers, with gold chains around their necks. In counterpoint with him, they were singing:

> Brock is back, it's a reason for jollity.
> Brock is back, he's our Mr. Quality.

I walked around the room, shaking hands with people who were eating salads.

"He's our quality guy, whose first drafts alone would rank him in the Polo Lounge Hall of Fame. But his fast, effective re-writes are surely the stuff of legends. He had a little sabbatical to get his novel out of his system and to try to move it along. But once a television writer, always a television writer. So let's give a big Polo Lounge welcome to your writer for hire and mine, Paul Brock!"

Like a trader on the floor of Wall Street, I circulated through the Polo Lounge, taking orders. Producers and television executives were seated at the tables and they started shouting story ideas at me. The Secret Loves of Lyndon Johnson. The Secret Loves of Dwight D. Eisenhower. Competing with the ideas for political figures, others were shouting diseases: Sickle cell, Tay-Sachs, Lyme disease. "Hasn't that been done by now?" I said. "It's been waiting for you," Tod Martin called out. "A football player on scholarship wrecks his knee," Ronnie Hill yelled over the crowd. "Does he stay in school, or return to the farm?" "You did that already." "For a *basketball* player. This is football," she said. "The Secret Loves of Charles de Gaulle," a producer yelled, "for European television." "The common cold!" someone else called out. I moved through the room, signing on for projects. I had enough work for years, for the rest of my life.

· · ·

"Paul, we've lost our momentum here," Mel said to me in his office. He showed me Priscilla Blake's press clippings, which now included a wire-service story and a feature in *USA Today*. "Our ticket sales are all right. We'll have acceptable houses in New York, but to try touring with you—it could be disastrous. So let's put the tour on the back burner for a while. And I'll try to think of something."

I looked through the news articles. There were plans of touring *her*. We had been out-hyped.

14.

Dear Mr. Brock:

I was in the audience for your Radio City concert. I, too, am lost in the middle. Everything you touched on struck a chord in me. Recently, my niece came to New York and we went to see Priscilla Blake at the Ballroom. I found her to be uninteresting and an imitation of you. I don't write fan letters but I had to say that you really speak for us.

I had received about seventy letters since the concert. The idea that I spoke for "us" was a recurring theme in the fan mail. Sandy commented that the mail was almost political, and I passed this observation on to Mel when we next spoke.

"How many letters came in?" he asked.

"About seventy."

"Seventy? Could you bring them here? Right away?"

Mel's cabinet was in session when I arrived; Helen, Blair, and Rothman were seated in his office. On Mel's desk was another pile of letters. This was the mail that had been sent to me in care of Radio City Music Hall or Steiner Varieties.

"We've got about a hundred letters here. Plus your seventy. This is a very heavy amount of fan mail," Mel said. "Let's see that footage again."

Blair and Rothman screened a videotape that we watched on

Mel's television monitor, showing reaction shots of the audience at the concert, which included several couples flashing the V-for-victory signs. Mel said they were not people he had hired.

"Something's there," Mel said. "What?"

They reran the footage, Mel freezing the frame on a man making the V sign. Mel kept studying it.

"If I didn't tell you what this was, where would you say it was shot?"

"A political rally," I said.

"Exactly."

Mel studied the freeze-frame image, squinting. We sat in silence for a while. Then Mel said, "Okay! Here's what we do. We promote this like a political campaign. The campaign is the middle class against everybody else. We use sound trucks, literature we give out on the streets. We give it the look and feel of an election. And how do middle-class people get to be heard, how do they vote? They come to Paul's concerts! And what happens at the concerts? They applaud, they wave pennants, just like at political rallies. We can even get them to sing along like at old-fashioned hootenannies!"

"Helen hasn't even been able to get me on the air."

"Helen has something new to work with. We launch the campaign with a big kickoff event. We pull a Richard Nixon."

"Come again?"

"We do a Checkers speech. We get you on 'Entertainment Tonight.' You sit there with your wife and sons and your dog. You deny you ever met this Priscilla Blake. And you say the fact that she would falsely suggest such a thing is exactly the kind of yuppie values you oppose. You tell about how you speak for the middle class in your songs. And how they get to vote for their concerns by going to your concerts. Then we'll roll out the campaign. This is great! Better than what we had. Boys, you'll work with him on the presentation. Paul, think of this as an extension of your act. And we're in business all over again!"

"Hold on here. Richard Nixon? You *do* mean this as satiric."

"Of course. We'll even put an American flag behind you. But you have to deny the affair; that engages the battle. Then you do a basic sell."

"I am very proud to be working with you, Mel," Blair said with deep emotion.

"I know. I'm great. So let's do it, folks. Paul, we're going to win, after all. You'll be the ultimate cross-over artist. You'll cut across ethnic lines to all people in the middle class. You are America!"

.   .   .

I worked with Mel, Blair, and Rothman. At one point in my television presentation I was to say: "I notice that Priscilla Blake never actually claims we had an affair. She says, cleverly, 'I *believe* I did date him.' Well, I *know* she didn't. And that kind of playing fast and loose with language and the truth is what we've seen too much of from younger people in our society. I thought that went out with the greed and excesses of the eighties."

I went on to state that the middle class struggling with bills and family life resented the materialism and the self-involvement of people from the Me Generation. For a long time we had been feeling left out, the "forgotten middle." I came along with my songs about middle-class life and people like me finally had someone to express their point of view. Their support for me was almost political.

"Profound," Blair said. "I got to give him a ten in the profoundness area."

.   .   .

On my way home I was buoyant, knowing that we were going to outflank those poachers. I explained the strategy to Sandy at home and then delivered my "Entertainment Tonight" presentation.

"This is absurd," Sandy said in response to it.

"What do you mean?"

"What do *you* mean? I'm not going on television with you and the boys and the dog. You're not using your children, your family in that manner."

"It's satire. Richard Nixon."

"It's Mel's manipulations."

"What am I supposed to do, allow these people to do me in?"

"If that's what results from all this, then that's what you get."

"Absolutely not. Priscilla Blake is a liar and a thief. That kind of behavior went out with the greed and excesses of the eighties."

"You just said that."

"And I'm going to say it on television with you or without you."

"Without me. Without the boys. Without the dog."

"You don't speak for Skippy."

"Paul, you don't get to deliver your wife and children to do this."

"Then I'll take my trusted dog and do it without you."

"Talk to him about it."

. . .

Sandy missed the point and the Nixon satire entirely. Fortunately many of the television critics did not. Marvin Kitman in his syndicated column called it "tongue-in-cheek Nixon" and named it the "Skippy Speech." (Ultimately, I was able to deliver my own dog.) I rebutted Priscilla Blake's insinuations. I made my statement about articulating the concerns of the "forgotten middle." I did it with Skippy at my feet and the American flag in the background and upheld my virtue and appealed to my constituency. Throughout this enlightened land, television critics had fun writing about my Nixonian turn.

The "campaign" was under way. Large trucks rolled through business districts of Manhattan, billboards on each side of the trucks showing me, larger than life. From loudspeakers on the trucks, intercut with my singing of "Lost in the Middle," in the cadence of a political announcement, a man's voice intoned: "If you're middle class and you've had enough of being ignored, Paul Brock speaks for you. See Paul Brock in concert!" Trailing behind the trucks were "campaign workers" distributing handbills advertising the concert to people on the street. The workers were women in red, white, and blue aprons, wearing straw hats with "Paul Brock Speaks for You" across the hatbands.

The visual aspects of the new promotion, the trucks and "campaign workers," made it a natural for television news coverage. Items about the promotion effort appeared on all the local news television programs, which in turn generated coverage in the newspapers. A story about the promotion appeared in the metropolitan section of the *New York Times* with a picture of one of the trucks in midtown Manhattan. There were stories in the tabloids, as well. As the comic spokesman for the "forgotten middle" with my trucks and campaign workers in the background, I was perfect upbeat material to close out the network nightly news. Both CBS and NBC concluded programs with items about me. A piece appeared in the Sunday Arts and Leisure section of the *New York Times,* an interview and discussion of my songs. And then MacNeil/Lehrer did a feature on me.

In the wake of this new media blitz Priscilla Blake with her yuppie act was simply overshadowed. Quickly she had gone from being an obstacle to me to someone who illustrated the basic contention that yuppies get too much attention and the middle class had heard enough about them. What about us?

. . .

I had been given a schedule indicating where the trucks would be appearing next and I brought Sandy and the children to watch. Sandy had been reacting to the "campaign" in a subdued manner. The children were very excited. We stood on 57th Street and Fifth Avenue as one of my trucks approached, the image of me towering over the real me.

"Daddy, here you are!" Sammy shouted.

"It's a parade," Joey said, seeing the workers filing along the street.

"You've gotten very big," Sandy commented drolly.

"You were wrong about the 'Skippy Speech.' I was right to do it."

"It obviously worked out for you."

"And for Skippy. I bet he could get a book out of it," I joked.

. . .

New posters for America's Balladeer of the Middle Class appeared around the city promoting the upcoming concerts. The posters carried a new line: "It's the Forgotten Middle against the World and Paul Brock Speaks for You!" Newspaper advertising began appearing, which reproduced the poster and featured quotes from reviews of my first concert. As a result of the "campaign" both Radio City concerts sold out. And the tour was on again.

"Mel has just come up with a last little wrinkle for publicity," Helen Baskin called to say. "From now on we refer to the 'Paul Brock Phenomenon.'"

"Isn't that a bit of an exaggeration?" I asked.

"That response is exactly why I'm calling," she said. "We're going to be referring to the Paul Brock Phenomenon with the media, and we don't want Paul Brock himself engaging in philosophic discussions about whether this is, or is not, a phenomenon."

"I can't refer to myself that way."

"A few weeks ago nobody ever heard of you. Suddenly, you're selling out concerts, fan mail is pouring in, you're going on tour. Paul, that *is* a phenomenon."

. . .

Mel came to the final rehearsals before the Radio City concerts to implement the sing-along idea. He was going to print lyrics in the program for the audience to follow. Along with my feelings of panic, which would naturally arise from being on stage again—forgetting my lines, fainting—I was now frightened about Mel tampering with the material. I, who would never have thought of doing an act, was now worried about the sanctity of it.

"I don't want you turning this into a circus," I said.

"What I'm looking for is like when Springsteen performs and the audience is so at one with him, they sing the songs along with him."

I had to separate my fantasies from reality and restrain myself from saying, "Oh, sure, Bruce. We're club members together."

We ran through several numbers with me singing first, then everyone in the studio—the musicians, the technicians—singing the songs with me the second time around.

"Beautiful," Mel said. "Keep rehearsing it that way. Think of Springsteen. Think of an old-fashioned hootenanny. It won't get out of hand. Trust me."

. . .

Pembroke's services were engaged for the second concert, and something must have been going on in terms of my popularity because Pembroke asked me for an autograph. He still was not happy that I showed up in my street clothes-performing outfit. "Perhaps I could lend you a dressing gown, sir."

"This is it, Pembroke. The real new me."

Mel came into the room to report that he had been circulating through the auditorium and people were getting settled, busy going over the song lyrics.

"Paul, I want you to know I reread the novel the other day. To stay focused on the goal line. We're doing right, pal. It's a terrific book."

"Thanks, Mel. But maybe tonight I should just do a reading from it. What is it going to sound like if you have a sing-along and no one sings along?"

"They will."

"Did you pay people to sing?" He didn't answer. "You *bought* a sing-along?"

"I scattered a few people here and there, just to get the thing going."

. . .

Having done one concert before didn't mean I would be relaxed for this one. I put the lyrics on index cards so I wouldn't be thrown by the new element of the audience participation. Mel introduced me to the audience by saying, "Welcome to the Paul Brock Phenomenon! Here he is, America's Balladeer of the Middle Class! The Spokesman for the Forgotten Middle! Brock!"

I received a standing ovation *to begin*. Mel must have bought it. I think I performed at about the same level as the earlier concert. The spot that concerned me was when the audience would begin to sing. This was to take place on the third song. After I sang it through once I was to call out, hootenanny-style, "Everybody sing!" Even with paid-for singers within the audience I could feel an awkwardness about singing out. As we went along the sound was building, though. By the time I reached the concluding "Yuppies Don't Know Chinese Food," people were very much in the spirit of the lyrics and the event, and it seemed like the entire audience was singing along. I was given another standing ovation, applauded the audience in return, and walked off stage.

"It worked!" Mel said.

"It was really nice, wasn't it? All those people singing."

"Yes, it was really nice," he mimicked, impatient with my naiveté. "You're a star."

. . .

A party was held afterward at the Pierre Hotel and Sandy and I were applauded when we entered the room.

"I feel like we're Fred and Ginger," Sandy said.

"I thought the first concert was great, but the sing-along!" Laura said. "It was like a happening."

"So is this," I said, regarding the room, which was filled with celebrities. Samantha Reilly rushed up to kiss me as photographers took our picture. Her book had been published to favorable reviews and she told me her next project was a magazine about life in Manhattan. Financed by her new boyfriend from Houston, the magazine would be patterned after the book and would be called *Samantha*.

A commotion was taking place in the room, and out of it Manuelo materialized. The photographers who had been working the party gravitated around him and then the two of us together as he embraced me.

"You were great, amigo." He whispered so no one could hear him speaking in English. "The singing—that's our Mel, no?"

"Yes."

"Mel, I want that, too. Song sheets, English and Spanish."

Helen Baskin pushed through the crowd.

"Paul, I have a writer from *People* magazine. He wants to talk to you about what's going on with you and your audiences. This is important!"

Helen and I separated from the crowd and she led me to a corner of the room, where I was introduced to a man in his thirties carrying a tape recorder.

"Mr. Brock, another sold-out concert. Tremendous crowd re-action. How do you account for it?"

"Well—" I looked over at Helen for a beat, then I proceeded. "What we have here is—a phenomenon . . . "

. . .

I was featured on the cover of *People* magazine. There I was, peering out from supermarket racks and newsstands. The story began with a double-spread photograph of me standing on the stage of Radio City Music Hall at the conclusion of the second concert, the people in the audience standing, applauding. The photo was captioned "The Paul Brock Phenomenon Hits New York. Other Cities to Follow."

"In just a few weeks, through his humorous songs, Brock has become a comic flag-bearer for the middle class." I was quoted on my basic interview, that the middle class had been lacking a forum for the concerns that I was expressing. Next came a statement from a Manhattan psychologist, Dr. Ernest Tolentine, who said, "The Phenomenon has strong and valid psychological roots. Brock addresses the sense of neglect experienced by many people today. When he performs, they see themselves in him. The sing-along concept we noticed in the second of his concerts is a chance for these people to hearken back to the freer times of their own youth, when they felt special, and to sing out and behave like young people themselves."

Mel was then quoted, listing every city on the tour, saying, "Not since Manuelo have we seen anything like this. We'll be sold out all across the country."

Helen called to congratulate me for the article—which is strange when you think about it. I wasn't being congratulated for anything real that I'd accomplished, but only for being publicized.

. . .

I bought the morning newspapers and was crossing the street on my way back to the apartment. A chauffeured Bentley was waiting for a red light. A window lowered and I heard a woman's voice call out to me in a British accent.

"Aren't you Paul Brock?"

It was Princess Di!

"Yes, I'm Paul Brock."

"I thought it was you. Would you mind chatting with me?" She opened the car door and I entered and sat next to her. "Imagine my good luck. I just read about you in *People*."

"Oh, do you read *People?*"

"I have a subscription. I like to keep up with what they're saying about me."

"How are things going?" Not too brilliant a remark, but what do you say to a person like that?

"Smashingly," she answered.

You've got to love the British. We couldn't get away with a word like "smashingly."

"I love the way you're dressed," she said. "So relaxed and American. British men can get a little too Turnbull & Asser."

"This is my image."

"Very pleasant. You're obviously a man in control of yourself. You handled the *People* interview extremely well."

She was holding the magazine open to my story and had written little remarks in the margins—"Excellent," "Good turn of phrase."

"It's so easy to be made the fool," she said. "You handled it perfectly."

"I appreciate hearing that from you."

"You must come over to us in London. We should set up a command performance."

"It's been a pleasure. I'm a great admirer of your publicity coverage."

"You're much better looking in person," she said. "Lovely to meet you." Princess Di kissed me on the cheek, then blushed and said, "Please don't make too much of that. I'm a little too tall for you."

· · ·

At dinner with Mel and Laura, they announced to us that they were getting married. We were thrilled for them. He asked me to be his best man and over the next few days we had several conversations concerning a bachelor event. I would have had a dinner for him, taken him out for the evening, whatever he wished. He said what he wanted more than anything was for him and me to go to the Lum Fong Chinese Restaurant on Fordham Road in the Bronx, where we used to take girls after movie dates. We went by Rolls—probably a first for the Lum Fong—and it was like stepping into a time machine. The restaurant was still there, the same dark, narrow place we remembered, the food exactly as it had been. We ordered the chicken chow mein of our youth, and it seemed to have been sitting in the kitchen from back then.

We tried to remember every girl we had ever dated when we were growing up.

"The women I went out with over the years—" Mel said. "Crazies, near-hookers. I hold the record for going out with the most women comfortable wearing false eyelashes." He was thoughtful for a beat, then his eyes began to water. "Maybe this is why I wanted to come here. How many restaurants can I sit in and cry?" I reached out and squeezed his hand. "I never thought I'd end up with anybody nice," he said.

"She's lovely."

"She is. After all these years, *I'm* marrying a nice girl, too."

. . .

The wedding was small, held at the home of Laura's parents in New Rochelle. After the ceremony I introduced Sandy to Mel's parents, who came from Florida where they now lived. They were tan, healthy-looking, a prosperous, elderly couple, a long way from the Benny the Great I remembered.

"Congratulations to all of us," I said. "Mel finally got married."

"Congratulations to you," his mother said. "You're a big star."

"Thanks to your son."

"He's very proud of you. We are too. We always keep up with the things you write."

"We knew him when he wasn't so big," Benny said to Sandy.

"I know," she answered. "So did I."

I offered a toast to Mel and Laura and as part of it, I sang a song to them, "I've Never Been in Love Before," from *Guys and Dolls*. I felt as if I were floating as I sang it, that it existed in a sphere outside show business and the activity of the past months. It was like the point at a wedding when the uncle who thinks he can sing and has had too much to drink gets up to do a number with the band.

. . .

The *Wall Street Journal* ran an article about the Paul Brock Phenomenon that included a breakdown of which current stars appealed to which segments of the population. According to their chart, I shared an audience with Barbra Streisand and Frank Sinatra. *I'll buy that,* I said to myself. *Time* magazine had a piece, heavily researched, with childhood photographs supplied by my mother. "Even when he sang in the Mountains with his friend Mel, we knew he would be a star," she said. Sandy was referred to as my "illustrator-wife" with the hyphenation often favored by the media. My "illustrator-wife" was besieged with inquiries from potential accounts and people she had done business with in the past who hadn't used her services lately. "We just happened to see you in *Time* magazine."

Joe Bosso, the booking agent, came out of retirement to make a statement about the Journeymen. "They had a great little act, those two boys. I encouraged them to stay with it, but they had other plans." *U.S. News* and *Newsweek* also ran pieces referring to the Paul Brock Phenomenon, and somewhere amid all this I felt the real phenomenon was that they were all calling it a Phenomenon.

. . .

The Paul Brock Phenomenon was also the subject of a Ted Koppel "Nightline" program. Jeff Greenfield opened the show with a report that included footage of my concerts. In his remarks he said:

> Paul Brock is not a hayseed who wandered into town spilling lyrics from a song bag. He has been a working writer, and this enterprise has been masterminded by entertainment impresario Mel Steiner. Whether Paul Brock is, as advertised, a phenomenon, or a well-designed product, in the end it probably doesn't matter to his public. His fans like his man-

ner and, more important, his substance. His comedy songs seem to connect to the middle class—and *that,* people are telling us, is a welcome addition to the world of show biz.

A professor from Columbia University whose specialty was popular culture said, "We're starved for community in our culture, and a Paul Brock concert is a temporary but clearly defined community." A free-lance music critic who wrote for *Rolling Stone* said, "Not since the Archies," which was a musical group created for an animated version of the comic book characters, "has there been such a contrivance on the musical scene." I was in the studio and asked to answer that, and replied that "even if my act has been produced, so to speak, that doesn't mean my lyrics were written for me. I write my own material and that has to give me credibility." Koppel then asked me for my bona fides as a writer, and I mentioned having won the Emmys and the fact that the novel was going to be published. Mel was interviewed from Los Angeles. At one point he raised himself up slightly in his chair, and I knew that somewhere along the line Mel had had himself coached for television. He talked about how my appearances resembled political rallies more than they did conventional concerts. Koppel then challenged me to characterize my performing ability. "I'm not great, but I'm good enough. The main thing is the material, which speaks to people in the Forgotten Middle." The program ended with that remark. What Mel and his staff had accomplished was that I could talk to the media and handle the situation. The big guns—I, Alan Dershowitz, Henry Kissinger—we could all go on "Nightline" and nail the interview.

15.

"WE'RE IN GREAT SHAPE," Mel said to me. "We do the movie and then the tour, we release the movie, then publish the book, and you're home free."

"Could you back up a little?" I said. We were sitting in his office, eating sandwiches for lunch, casually, and just as casually he said all that. "What movie?"

"The movie with you as the star, coming soon to a theater near you. The cross-country tour, of course, to give America a piece of the Phenomenon. The book, I think you know."

He reached into his drawer and handed me a script.

"I've got the financing. Took me one phone call. We do it fast. A few weeks, in, out, done."

"Like those old Republic Pictures westerns? I have to warn you before you get in any deeper. I'm not Hopalong Cassidy. And I don't ride."

The title of the script was *Harold against the Yuppies*. It was written by a writer whose name I knew, Barry Redden, who had written a couple of recent movie comedies.

"I've got Jim Hedges to direct. He just did a Steve Martin. It's a perfect vehicle for you. We shoot it now. While we're in post-production, you're on tour. We release it when you come off tour. Then we'll bring out the novel. We'll get out a concert album from the act. We'll sell the album in bookstores. We'll sell the book in record stores. When the video of the movie comes out, we'll time that for the paperback. We'll sell the paperback in video stores, the video in bookstores."

"Slow down. A movie! I can't act."

He put his hands on his hips, the way you would express consternation with a small child.

"That's not an issue. Haven't you learned *anything?*"

. . .

Harold against the Yuppies was about a burned-out television producer, estranged from his wife, who dashes out of his office on a Friday, impulsively announces he is going on vacation, quickly books a package with a travel agent and discovers he has landed in a singles resort where everyone is considerably younger than he is. Several of the songs from my act with me singing them were to be inserted in the action. According to Mel, the main casting was to draw on the cast from "Saturday Night Live."

In the story, feeling alienated from the younger people—and they don't have much affection for him—Harold is playing out the string on his week at the resort, waiting for the plane home. A blizzard hits the northeast, no flights can get out of New York to bring them back, and everyone is stranded at the resort. Several of the young people are worried about losing their jobs. Harold overhears their concerns and offers strategies for dealing with their situations. Over the next couple of days Harold becomes a kind of ombudsman for them. On their last night on the island, everyone puts on a talent show. Harold is so impressed with the abilities and enthusiasm of the people in their talent show that back in New York he produces a TV special with them. In the process of dealing with the young people, Harold is drawn out of himself and reconciles with his wife as the story ends.

The screenplay certainly didn't seem right to me. I gave it to Sandy to read; she felt as I did, that the story was working too hard and didn't mesh.

We spent an evening with Mel and Laura at our apartment. Laura was of the opinion that doing the movie could be fun. The idea was to shoot in Florida. We would all go down there for a couple of weeks; the children had a springtime school break coming up. It would be like a big family vacation, except that I would be acting in a movie.

"We have twenty million dollars for production and distribution," Mel said. "All our friend here has to do is agree."

"Isn't this amazing?" Sandy said. "To sit around and talk about whether or not Paul is going to be in a movie."

"Oh, go on, Paul. Be a movie star," Mel teased.

"Mel, the screenplay needs work—and the star is shaky," I said.

"Fix the screenplay. And don't worry about the star."

"I'll go this far. I'll think about doing it, but the script has to be right."

"He already sounds like an actor," Mel teased.

The main problem with the script was overplotting. Basically, it most resembled the old-fashioned Hollywood studio musicals, where various stars did a star turn, like *The Big Broadcast of 1936*. But if you were going to do that kind of movie, then I felt you should do it. So I made cuts in the script, and rewrote the protagonist's scenes so it had more of a feeling of someone not taking anything too seriously. And I wrote in asides to the camera like in the old Hope-Crosby road movies. If the movie didn't take itself too seriously and the character didn't either, then maybe it could work and I had a chance of walking through the action. To make it a purer version of what it was, I changed the character to really be me, in the style of people playing "themselves" in those old movies, and retitled it *Paul Brock against the Yuppies*. When I gave it to Mel, he started using words like "brilliant" and "inspired."

"Mel, it's just a little movie. An old-fashioned studio musical. That's what it aspires to be and that's all it is."

"*That's* what's brilliant!" he said.

. . .

I found myself back in the Russian Tea Room where I thought I would never be again, this time not as the Writer but as the Star. Mel and I met with Jim Hedges, the director, a lithe, tall, redheaded man in his thirties, with a freckled, affable face, who wore an L.A. Dodgers hat in the restaurant.

"Are you orthodox Jewish?" I asked him.

"Box office quality here, Mel."

"Please. I just want to be able to walk through this thing."

"And you set up the script that way. A great idea," Hedges said.

"He could keep doing movies like this," Mel said. "On and on."

"Like Bulldog Drummond," I suggested. "This is a one-time-only deal, fellas. My goal is to escape with my life."

. . .

My musical numbers were shot in a studio in New York and, Republic Pictures–style, took two days. I am sure the MGM extravaganzas spent more time than that on one musical number. But it was fine with me. We went down to a hotel in Key West where the location shooting was to take place. Sandy and the kids were there, we swam and played ball when I was not required to be on the set. It really was a kind of vacation.

I had very little to do with the other cast members, who all knew one another from New York. The real-life me was as estranged from the younger cast members as was the character in the movie. As for my acting, basically I wandered through with my hands in my pockets. I expressed my concern to Hedges, and he said, "That's exactly the effect we want, exactly what you wrote. You're Jimmy Stewart here." Hedges and Mel reviewed the film that had been shot each day and I asked if I should be sitting in on those sessions. Hedges said, "Don't trouble yourself with that. Jimmy Stewart never did." So Jimmy Stewart spent his evenings with his family and with Laura, Mel sometimes joining us.

The distance between me and the younger performers began to decrease as the script called for more interaction among us. I played volleyball with them after work, the staff nurse taping my ankles so the valuable property would not sprain an ankle. When the scenes were shot for the show that the young people perform, I was on the set laughing along. A wrap party was held on the last night of shooting and I was very much part of the group.

. . .

After the party, a bit keyed-up from the idea that I had actually been in a movie, I took a walk down to the water's edge and saw Steven Spielberg leaning against a tree.

"I didn't know you were here," I said.

"I'm a friend of Jim Hedges. I just dropped by to say hello. He showed me some of the footage. You know, you've got a great, casual style. The hands in the pockets. The asides. Very natural."

"I don't look like I'm walking through, dazed?"

"There's a real easygoing quality to you. Where it doesn't look like acting."

"That's because it isn't."

"I'd say the singing helped. You did those concerts. It's given you the confidence to take this on."

"I've just been trying to do my best, not faint, and keep an image in my mind of Jimmy Stewart."

"Well, you've got a screen personality you can bank on for a long time to come."

"Do you think so? Mel Steiner said we could go on and on with these movies."

"I'd love at least one of those movies to be mine. Let's talk about it when you're back in New York. We can meet for lunch sometime. You know, you *are* very Jimmy Stewart."

"Well, gee whiz."

"Cary Grant comes to mind, too."

"I admired him very much. I guess it comes through."

"Listen, I have my friends for the most part. But based on what I've seen of you on the screen, I'd really like to get to know you personally. Well, here's my helicopter. I'd certainly be thrilled to direct you in a film. Very soon, I hope."

"Thank you, Mr. Spielberg."

"Steve."

. . .

The movie went into postproduction and Mel worked on details for the tour. For my part in rewriting the movie and acting in it, really no more than a few weeks' work, I received a check for

$250,000. When it arrived Sandy and I looked at it, overwhelmed. We didn't even cash it for a few days.

"Maybe we should just frame it," I said. "Leave it on the wall like the first money received in a luncheonette."

"Maybe we should buy a luncheonette," Sandy quipped. "Security for the future if the bubble bursts."

. . .

Mel put us in touch with his business manager, Sonya Hall, a slim redhead in her forties with an office on Madison Avenue. She sat in a room with nothing on the walls—no art, no bookshelves, no nonsense. She stared at us with piercing eyes.

"We need to create a solid financial plan," she said. "You have to be careful. A playwright I know made a fortune, invested badly, fell so far behind, the IRS attached penalties that meant if he had a hit every single year he still couldn't get even. He did what any sensible person would do under the circumstances. He died."

"That is a very inspiring story," I said.

"Then there was a ball-player, I don't want to mention his name, put his money into sporting goods stores. They fleeced him for everything. Man was devastated. Nearly died."

"Do you have any of the good stories?" I asked. "The kind you read about in paperbacks, parlaying ten dollars into ten million?"

"Don't be deceived. Wait, I have another one. An actor. His business manager put him into dairy farms. Went sour. Lost it all with the drop in the price of milk."

"I think you've sufficiently sold us on the fragility of new income, Ms. Hall," Sandy told her.

"Stay involved," she said to Sandy. "Wife of a textile manufacturer, he died of a heart attack. She went to get the money. It was gone. To his bimbo."

"Then the wife died," I said.

"She did. How do you know?"

"Free-lancing," I said. "You get to be an expert on worst-case scenarios."

She said we should start looking at luxury co-ops to take

advantage of the soft real-estate market, but we were operating on the bubble-burst theory. If we made any untoward moves that resembled hubris—and moving up to a fancy co-op would be one of them—the gods, who audited materialistic free-lancers, would descend on us and the bubble would burst. We decided we were going to stay where we were and keep the money in the bank; protection if the co-op plan in our house came through. Nothing profligate. That should have kept the gods out of our building.

. . .

"You did such a good job in the movie," Mel said to me, "I'm thinking of starring you in the next one."

"Next one?"

"The movie of *Upward Mobility*. I might produce it myself. Nah, it'd be better to get a real actor."

"Fine. I am not insulted."

"Want to write it?"

"I'm kind of booked, if you haven't noticed. There's a novel I'm writing and I seemed to be scheduled for a nationwide tour."

"We can put the script on the back burner for a little while. But think about sqeezing it in."

"I just want to get through this tour."

"And you will. America awaits you, buddy."

. . .

The tour cities were Boston, Philadelphia, Washington, Detroit, St. Louis, Chicago, New Orleans, Houston, Dallas, Denver, Minneapolis, Seattle, San Francisco, San Diego, and Los Angeles. The tour was being promoted as the Paul Brock Phenomenon. Mel reported that on the basis of the publicity to date, the tour was 90 percent booked. The remainder of the tickets, he predicted, would be sold with some preconcert publicity in each city. I had a meeting with Tom Riggs and Barbara Moss and they reported a complete turnaround in orders for the novel. They were going ahead with the five hundred thousand first printing. Because it was somewhat incalcuable that all this was actually happening, I ran a few bubble-bursts through my mind and tried them out on Sandy.

"The book will bomb, the reviews will be nasty, there'll be a vicious backlash against me and my publicity, and *Upward Mobility* will have the largest number of returns in the history of the publishing industry."

"That's pretty complete. But for someone who's seen Sonya Hall and her tales from the crypt, you've left out death."

"Yes, death. I will die from a display of my very own books falling on me in a bookstore. Remaindered books."

. . .

Either Helen Baskin or one of her assistants would be with me to oversee interviews during the tour. Mel asked me to wear a beeper in case anything broke for publicity purposes along the way. At an appropriate time in the interviews I was supposed to say, "I'd also like to mention that my newest novel, *Upward Mobility*, will be published shortly."

Booths were to be set up in the lobbies at the concerts for the sale of Paul Brock Phenomenon souvenirs: programs, buttons, pennants, and T-shirts with my picture on the front and the tour dates listed on the back.

We set out for Boston. Mel was to follow, and on my plane was Helen, two assistants from Mel's office, Pembroke, Henry Ross, who was signed on to conduct during the tour, the musicians with their instruments, my entire entourage. I had become the Soviet Army Chorus and Band.

. . .

We did a final run-through at the theater on the day before the concert in Boston. Mel stopped by, stayed a while, and pronounced us ready. At the hotel, Pembroke stood over me, having taken his disapproval of my clothing on the road.

"To have been on tour with Sir Larry in the provinces, helping him with his attire," he said, rearranging my underwear in a drawer. Some people regretted never having seen Olivier on stage. This man regretted not having helped him unpack.

"Would you like anything, sir? Mints?"

"Pembroke, this is an idea whose time has not yet come. I can take care of my own underwear and get my own mints."

"The stars, sir, they don't unpack their underwear, they don't get their own mints."

"It doesn't go with me. It doesn't even go with my act. I can't have a personal valet."

"I would be happy to return to New York. I would have had a lovely engagement at the Metropolitan Opera House, but for this tour of yours. And frankly, sir, your attire is really not to my taste."

"Great. Go home, we'll work out the money. The way they used to pay farmers not to plant potatoes, we'll pay you not to fold my underwear."

I felt liberated as soon as he left. I didn't need to spend the next six weeks of my life with the disapproval of Eric Blore.

•   •   •

Mel came in to see me backstage at the theater before the concert.

"I'm here to tell you to enjoy it. I don't have to wish you luck. I've already removed this from luck."

"Did you buy a standing ovation, paid-for singers?"

"Nothing."

"I'm out there with no net?"

"You'll be fine. All I want to say—and this is the pep talk—is that you're in great shape, physically, musically. What you have to do is keep it fresh emotionally, which isn't so easy city after city. Just remember, for the people who are out there each night, this is their first time. Nobody gets anywhere cheating on an audience. And it's your obligation to give them their money's worth."

"Mel, that's very sweet. That was a real speech."

"I'm very proud of you for what you've accomplished. Of course, I'm also very proud of me for what I've accomplished."

•   •   •

The concert went "smashingly." People waved pennants; the sing-along portion was spirited. The next day I had a few hours to myself before the second of the two Boston concerts and was strolling along the street when I was beeped on the beeper. I called in to an answering service and was told to contact Helen at the hotel. She wanted me to be back there within the hour for a special press conference. A public room was set up for the media, several re-

porters were present, along with television cameramen and photographers. Helen introduced me to four middle-aged ladies
wearing Paul Brock straw hats. They were friends who lived in
Brookline and had been to the concert the previous night with their
husbands. The leader of the group explained that when they spoke
that morning the women decided they would start a Paul Brock
fan club. They called the theater and were directed to Helen, who
told them they would be the first fan club. I said that I was flattered
and managed to mention that I hoped they would also be fans of
my novel. The ladies kissed me for the cameras and as I was leaving,
the fan club president said to me, "This has been so much fun. We
haven't done anything like this for years. We used to be for Perry
Como."

. . .

I played sold-out concerts in the East and the Midwest. I kept Mel's
advice in mind and tried to give people what they came for, and I
don't know if I got better as the tour progressed; the main thing
was that I didn't get worse.

I returned to New York a couple of times for a day or two to
see Sandy and the children. The bad stretch for me was the western
portion, when I was going to be away from home for three weeks.
I took along a laptop computer and in my spare time I worked on
the new novel to the extent that I could. My working title was *The
Schoolyard*. I thought I was on the right track with the main character, who was based on someone like me. The black ball-player
he befriends was a composite of the ball-players I had met when
I was researching the television script. I really admired the gracefulness, the athleticism of those schoolyard ball-players. I wanted
to convey in this novel that for most of them—good ball-players
but none of them future NBA stars—their gracefulness would have
no arena in society beyond the basketball court.

. . .

In San Francisco I did some sightseeing wearing sunglasses and a
Stetson as a disguise. A tourist on the cable car in his own Stetson
said, "Where're ya from, pardner?" and I said, "The Bronx."

One of my interviews in San Francisco was with a reporter

for a newspaper feature service and, as was sometimes the case, it would be conducted in my hotel room. This was a Thursday afternoon before the Friday-night concert. The reporter arrived, Debby Chandler, a stunning woman about thirty, five feet six with light-brown hair, pale blue eyes, a porcelainlike smooth face, beautiful enough to have been a model. She was wearing a blazer, skirt, and blouse, the jacket open revealing a bosomy figure and slender waist. She was the most attractive woman I had met on the tour.

She conducted the interview with a technique I had noticed only among some of the older reporters. When I answered a question, she smiled as though that was exactly the right answer, and this had the effect of putting me at ease.

"You've been on the road so long, are you getting tired of performing?"

"Not at all. Each concert is a new audience. People are there for the first time and you have to remember that." (From the trunk of standard replies.)

"Are you getting tired of being interviewed?" (Not a standard question.)

"That depends on the interview."

"Is it lonely on the road?"

"I have my audiences to compensate."

"Well, I'm not in the demographic group of your fans, so in preparation for this I went to the Seattle concert. I enjoyed it. The audience certainly liked the singing."

"Did you sing?"

"I hummed."

The interview continued along factual lines; she needed to know the cities I had visited, my future plans, and I mentioned the novel.

"What will you be doing the rest of the time in San Francisco?" she asked.

"Doing some writing, if I can."

"And eating alone?"

"Probably."

"Interviews are curious little relationships, aren't they?" she said. "You have a half-hour or so of near-intimacy with someone, then you never see that person again."

"That's show business, I'm told."

We shook hands, she looked at me for what was an uncomfortably long time, and she left. A few minutes later the phone rang and she was on the line.

"I was thinking. The idea that you would be by yourself, possibly ordering room service, eating alone, doesn't seem right. Would you like company for dinner?"

She said "for dinner," but unquestionably that was not all that was on the table here.

"I'm not sure."

"Suppose I call you back in an hour. Maybe you'll be sure then."

I had never slept with anyone other than my wife since we were married, and that was the truth of it. I was on my own in San Francisco, I had spoken to Sandy and the children earlier. Who would know if I went to bed with this beautiful woman? Maybe this kind of thing went with the territory, with stardom. Maybe I wasn't living to the fullest experience of life. Perplexed, sexually agitated, I decided to go for a stroll through the hotel lobby.

. . .

Sitting on a couch in the lobby was Dr. Ruth. I could go right to the expert on this. I'd ask Dr. Ruth.

"Excuse me, I'm Paul Brock—"

"Yes. I was at your concert in Chicago. Very good."

"People must do this to you all the time," I said, "but I need your advice. I'm married. I love my wife. I'm out here on the road, lonely. And a beautiful young woman has just asked to come to my hotel room tonight."

"Hmm. A classic dilemma."

"Some of the thoughts I'm having against it are, *What if someone finds out? What if this woman writes about it? What if I get a sexually transmitted disease?*"

"My, you're morbid. Is your novel so morbid?"

"What would you advise me to do?"

"Have your own TV show. You could sing a few songs, talk to the audience."

"Do you think that having sex with this woman is part of living a full, rich life, experiencing all the world has to offer?"

"Go for syndication, cable. You don't have the same limitations as with the networks. I'm in touch with good people who could produce this for you."

"Dr. Ruth, you're evading the issue. Do I sleep with her or not?"

"How would I know?"

"This is your specialty."

"I'm not a rabbi. Technique, I can talk to you about. Basically, my main contention is—you should try new positions."

"I never slept with her. They're *all* new positions!"

"My advice is, you should think of syndication."

. . .

I returned to the room; Debby called a while later and I thanked her and said I had a headache. I just couldn't do it. Maybe if Dr. Ruth had said it was all right—

. . .

Mel was planning an end-of-tour party in Los Angeles and Sandy came out to join me, the boys remaining in New York with my parents. We were staying at the Beverly Wilshire and as we entered the lobby I saw Joe Staples, the scriptwriter from New York, probably in California to look for work. It was likely that he had been sitting in the lobby to check on people's comings and goings.

"Hello, Joe, how are you? My wife, Sandy."

"Nice to meet you. So, Paul, whatdaya got?"

"I'm not out here looking for anything."

"Don't kid a kidder."

"Joe, I'm not."

"Please—"

"Haven't you heard of the Paul Brock Phenomenon?"

"What's that, your own production company? You producing now?"

"Where have you been the last couple of months?"

"In New York, working on a script. I just came up for air."

"And you've been totally immersed in it, right? No other life."

"But I fell behind on work. So I came out here."

"Joe, I wrote a novel and I couldn't get it promoted, so I wrote an act, singing songs about middle-class life and I made a movie to help the novel along, and tomorrow night I'm doing a big concert."

"Beautiful. A lot of good elements there. Who you selling it to?"

"That's not a story idea!"

"Come on, who you looking to sell it to?"

"Nobody. Really."

"He's a cutie pie, your husband."

. . .

I was booked to appear on the "Tonight Show." Blair and Rothman came to Los Angeles specifically to guide me through it. They ran tapes for me in the hotel room of previous episodes of the "Tonight Show," they took turns playing the host and asking me questions, they went over the rules: don't depart from the basic interview, sit straight, stay focused, keep your eye contact.

"You guys are so keyed-up, it's like I'm going to do Lear."

"Norman Lear?" Rothman said, suddenly confused.

"King Lear. I've done interviews. I won't mess up."

Jay Leno was the host. The guests were Burt Reynolds, Charro, and me. My interview was like batting practice. I did the seared tuna, the paying for children's orthodontia, I talked about the movie and the novel.

"You've been playing to sell-out crowds all over the country," Jay Leno said.

"It's sort of a natural phenomenon, Jay . . . "

Everything went as planned. When I came off the set, Blair and Rothman were so moved by the perfection of the segment they practically had tears in their eyes.

The last concert of the tour was a great, cheerful event, the audience singing along boisterously, the musicians breaking their own procedures and singing, too. In a Mel Steiner gala, I was joined for my last few numbers by Hot Cats *and* Manuelo. I called people out and we all held hands on stage, Sandy, Mel, Laura, Helen, Blair, and Rothman.

We were taken by the obligatory limousines to the postconcert party at a factory building that had been converted to a huge deco restaurant. Mel had flown in the Chins and they raced up and cheerfully punched me in the stomach. Then we did a little Fred Astaire tapping together. A society orchestra played and Sandy and I danced among such intimates as Kevin Costner and Julia Roberts—and we were dancing to the songs *I* wrote.

"If it all ended right here it would be a thrill beyond my imagining," I said to Sandy.

"The amazing thing is, it isn't ending."

. . .

Paul Brock against the Yuppies opened five weeks later in 750 movie theaters. The old Republic Pictures people would have marveled at the speed with which this movie was released. We attended a premiere with klieg lights, paparazzi, onlookers behind velvet ropes, then a party at the Four Seasons.

"So what did you think of the movie?" I whispered to Sandy when we were in a corner alone.

"It was good enough," she said and I knew exactly what she meant. I hadn't disgraced myself. By having a casual attitude on screen I couldn't have been accused of taking the enterprise, or myself, too seriously. It was a musical revue—no more, no less. The "Saturday Night Live" people got to do their routines, and I performed my best songs. I'd like to think my rewrite saved the script.

It opened on a Friday when several other movies were released and it received, appropriately, the third or fourth review in the newspapers, in order of priority. Critics, for the most part, accepted the movie within its limited aspirations, as a musical revue, and the reviews were generally favorable. Siskel and Ebert, accurately by my standards, said it invoked memories of the old-fashioned musicals, mentioning *The Big Broadcast of 1936* and *Winter Carnival.* I was this year's Sonya Henie. Which was great. Nobody said I was this year's dog.

The movie, as they write in the trade papers, "did business." People who were now in my audience—my fans as well as the middle-class curious—came to see it, while younger devotees of

"Saturday Night Live" wanted to see their favorites. Mel, not about to lose the thread, included a prominent line in all movie advertising, "Look for the new novel by Paul Brock, *Upward Mobility,* coming soon to a bookstore near you."

An album was released, *The Paul Brock Phenomenon: Live in Concert.* In record stores, merchandising displays for the album included an announcement about the novel, which was to be sold in both bookstores and record stores, while the album was to be sold in both record stores and bookstores.

The novel was shipped to stores when the movie went to another tier of distribution and was being screened in fifteen hundred theaters across the country. Sandy and I took the children with us on a Saturday for a celebration—the Children's Zoo, lunch at Tavern on the Green, and then a tour of midtown bookstores to see "Daddy's book with Mommy's artwork." The displays of the book in the stores were immense. The book was prominently placed in store windows, and a large poster had been made from the cover, which the stores were using. Along the top of the poster were the words "The Paul Brock Phenomenon Brings You a Wonderful New Novel."

"Unbelievable," Sandy said as we stood looking at a huge display of books in a store.

With appropriate irony I said, "Easy as pie."

16.

THE NUMBER ONE bestseller. Within days of publication, *Upward Mobility* was number one on all the fiction bestseller lists. It hadn't even been reviewed yet in many of the major book columns. In terms of sales Mel had published the book so that it was essentially review-proof. I could have settled into the position of novelists whose books are blasted by critics but sell anyway. "My intention is to communicate not with reviewers but with my readers." "I never read reviews." "I'm laughing all the way to the bank."

I was prepared to draw on that particular tradition, but the reviews were excellent. A couple of critics treated it patronizingly as another celebrity book, as if Billy Joel had written a novel. By and large, though, it was regarded as a respectable book, well written, and about something, and it had always been my hope that it would be seen that way. The *Time* magazine review said:

> The Paul Brock Phenomenon has arrived in print. *Upward Mobility* by Paul Brock, if not, well, phenomenal, is surprisingly a first novel of considerable literary merit. Before he recently became "America's Balladeer of the Middle Class," Brock published three short stories in *Esquire* and won four Emmys as a scriptwriter. There is a real writer's hand at work here. *Upward Mobility* is a well-observed narrative of middle-class people who resemble many of us.

The review went on in positive terms to describe the struggles of my leading characters to recapture the passion and idealism of their lives and their marriage. The reviewer then wrote:

Paul Brock is enjoying big-time success as a 1990s Allan Sherman—and why deny him his banners waving? However, variety performers come and go. And where is Allan Sherman today? The arrival on the scene of an interesting novelist, not by way of academia but out of the maelstrom of middle-class urban life, is more of a phenomenon. We are tempted to say, "Sing out, Paul, if you must." We prefer the quieter Brock, the one who writes quality fiction.

My in-laws finally gave in to the national trends. They came to dinner and, in a victory long in coming, did not say one negative word about me, or about the publication of the book. They even asked if I would autograph some copies for their friends. As for my mother, in what had to be the apotheosis of her maternal pride, she went beyond photocopies of reviews and had a printer run off a four-page flyer on newsprint, "The Paul Brock News," containing my reviews and copies of news stories, which she distributed in the lobbies and handed out to people at Co-op City.

"Mother, are you sure that's dignified?"

"Do you know how many mothers here would want to have something like this to work with?"

. . .

At Mel's invitation Sandy and I went with him and Laura to dinner at the Rainbow Room to celebrate the book's reaching number one. Mel raised a glass and toasted me, "To an acceptable singer of song and not a bad novelist."

"To Mel, a pretty good promoter."

"I've never known anybody like him," Laura said of Mel. "He says he's going to do something and he does it."

"We never had any doubts," Sandy said, facetiously.

"From now on," Mel said, "the sky's the limit."

"Mel, since we are already sitting in the sky, practically, and you have fulfilled every possible dream I could have had about my book and becoming a novelist, what are you saying?"

"The European tour. They'll love you there."

"I'm not doing any European tour!"

"You have to."

"Send Manuelo."

"He's been. You'll do it for European book sales."

"No!"

"Could I interest you in Japan?"

"Only if we bring back the Journeymen and you tour with me."

He did a long, comic take as if he were considering it.

"Who are the Journeymen?" Laura said.

"You keep secrets from your own wife?" I said.

To the chagrin of the maître d', Mel and I launched into the stirring strains of "The Undoctor of Love," our Rainbow Room debut.

.   .   .

I met with Barbara Moss and Tom Riggs and talked in general terms about the novel in progress. They were diplomatically enthusiastic, not as yet having read any pages; I didn't think it was ready to show. Tom Riggs confirmed that the paperback for *Upward Mobility* would be timed to the videocassette of *Paul Brock against the Yuppies,* and the paperback would be sold in video stores and bookstores, while the videocassette of the movie would be sold in bookstores and video stores. We talked about some of the additional promotional activity for *Upward Mobility*. At Barbara's and Tom's request, I had been doing more author interviews and a few book signings at bookstores. At the signings people actually stood on line in advance of my arrivals. I thought that happened only for books by Pavarotti or Sophia Loren.

.   .   .

In the Bronx a few blocks east of the Grand Concourse was the Fordham branch of the public library. When I was growing up I used to go there on Saturday mornings. A librarian would light candles to set the mood for story hour and we would sit on the floor and listen to her tales. When I was old enough to read books myself, I would carry them home, armloads of books. I called and asked if they had *Upward Mobility* and the librarian said they did and would hold a copy for me. I took a taxi uptown to the library and asked for the book. The librarian said, "Here you are. Our last copy. It's your lucky day."

"It is that."

I took the book and placed it in the section for "new arrivals" and just looked at it there. Nothing I had ever done as a writer made me prouder than seeing my novel on a shelf in my childhood library.

. . .

Mel was pressing me about his proposed European tour. He said that he needed to start booking halls. I turned him down once and for all to work on the new novel. And for the next three months I concentrated on *The Schoolyard*.

"When will the new book be done, Daddy?" Sammy asked me at breakfast. I was going over some sales figures on *Upward Mobility* and happened to be preoccupied when I answered him.

"We're working on it. We hope it will have the same accuracy of observation as *Upward Mobility*," which happened to be a line I used in interviews.

"Huh?" he said.

"Who's *we*?" Joey asked. "I thought you wrote your novels by yourself."

"That's the first-person pretentious," Sandy commented.

I had done so many interviews that it had become difficult to get out of the mode.

. . .

I was still doing publicity because it was, after all, in the service of selling the book. Sandy saw it otherwise, and we had a running argument about how much time I was giving over to promotion.

"I think you just adore doing these interviews," she said to me one morning. I was preparing for a visit of a reporter who worked for a Brazilian magazine.

"I don't. I have to do them. This is my moment. It sells books."

"This is your moment to write. Money coming in, no worries, no scripts to do."

"It's maintenance, like with the Chins. You have to maintain the thing."

The interview was conducted in our living room. I had met the reporter before at a foreign media press conference organized for me, and she was stunning, but the overriding fact was that the circulation of her magazine was substantial. Dolores Vida was in her early thirties with a sensual face and an astonishing figure. Sandy had told me she was not planning to be home when the reporter was there, but it looked like Sandy might have been spying on me because she came back into the apartment from her studio while the interview was still going on. I introduced them and Sandy was abrupt and walked back out.

"Interesting-looking maintenance," she said to me that evening.

"It was just an interview."

"You didn't know she looked like that?"

"We met a few weeks ago and she asked if we could talk. Her magazine has a two million circulation in Brazil, so I said yes. It's business."

"Your business, Paul, is writing, not spending time with Brazilian bombshells, Mister Phenomenon."

"Are you jealous?"

"Well, I know I don't look like Miss Brazil. And I know I'm not so enthralled with every wonderful word you say that I write it all down."

"Then you're jealous of my success."

"Wrong. I happen to be proud of it. You wrote a cute act and a lovely book, but I'm getting tired of the act. It doesn't end. It's in my home. And you should get on with your writing."

"Maybe we should get you an album or something. You don't have a bad voice yourself," I said, trying to lighten the atmosphere.

"That's a talk show response. I didn't marry a talk show guest."

. . .

Mel was becoming restless and called at least once a week to check on the progress of the new book.

"Who gets this kind of recognition? Let's move it out," he said.

"I'm working on it."

"Well, don't be a dilettante. You want to get the next one out while you're still hot."

Considering the momentum I had going for me, too much rewriting did seem to me a dilettante's indulgence. I managed to increase my pace and was writing faster on this book than I usually did. The slow, deliberate way in which I wrote my first novel didn't feel right for this material. I was writing about loose, free-wheeling, inner-city characters. My first, freest expressions seemed the best in the long run.

. . .

Mel asked me to come to his office for a meeting and when I arrived two people I had not met before were in the room with him. One was a fashionably dressed slim brunette in her thirties, and sitting next to her was a man in his forties, handsome with perfectly greying hair, dressed in an impeccable grey pinstriped suit.

"Paul, this is Sherry Stone and Bob Reynolds."

We shook hands all around.

"May I?" Sherry Stone said and she came over to me—and *smelled* me. She ran her nose along my neck and face. "Old Spice," she announced definitively.

"That's so wonderfully mass-market," Reynolds said.

"What is this?" I said.

"Show him," Mel said to Reynolds.

From a leather attaché case Reynolds produced four atomizers and placed them on Mel's desk. Stone took my hand, turned it over, and sprayed a substance on the heel of my hand.

"Do you like it?" she asked.

"I don't know."

"If you had to choose, do you like this better?"

She sprayed my other hand with a substance.

"You brought me in here for market research?"

"Put your ol' shnozzola to work," Mel said. "Which cologne smells best to you?"

She sprayed the back of one hand with the third cologne, the other with the fourth.

"The first is cheeky, the second an assertive little devil. Come on, Mel, what do I know about this?"

"You know what you like."

"The second. It's not as pungent as the others."

"Are you sure?" Reynolds said.

I sniffed my hands.

"As sure as I want to be."

"Splendid. Number two it is," he said, and looked over at his associate, both of them seemingly pleased.

"He selected it himself," Mel said.

"I'm getting a very uncomfortable feeling here."

"Paul, there's something a writer wouldn't want to accept. You can't go on forever. Even a major player like you've become— it has to end. I'm giving you something that can go on into your old age, and, you should pardon me, after you're gone. And this is it."

He held my hand up.

"Your own fragrance."

"My what?"

"We'll call it 'Brock.' A man's cologne for thinking men. 'Brock.' It's a good brand name."

"I don't want a cologne named after me!"

"We're breaking ground," Mel said. "You don't get too many licensing shots like this."

"And what are you going to have, commercials with middle-class guys?"

"Yes, we would have advertising that showed average-type people using the product," Stone responded.

"I draw the line here. This is totally exploitive."

"Of course it is," Mel said casually.

"You've chosen a very nice, mass-marketable fragrance, Mr. Brock," Reynolds said. "Not unlike Old Spice. Mel is right. Your cologne could very well be in existence long after you're gone."

"If I could point this out—I'd really like my legacy to be what I wrote, not what you said I smelled like."

"Use it in the mornings. Live with it a little," Mel said, handing me a bottle. "It's nothing to look down your nose at, as it were. The first novelist with his own fragrance!"

I brought the bottle home and told Sandy about this meeting, thinking she would find it amusing.

"Are you going to say yes to it?"

"No! Do you think I would?"

"It's certainly possible with you."

And she turned and walked away.

. . .

I completed a first draft of the new novel and although there had been a frost between us of late, I still asked Sandy to read it. She had always been my first reader. I went off with the children for the day on a Saturday. When I came back to the apartment she did not greet me with celebration.

"Maybe your editor will have some thoughts. It just doesn't make it for me."

"What doesn't?"

"A lot of it, I'm sorry to say. You keep sidestepping scenes, emotions, like you're hurrying to get to the end."

"It *is* a first draft—"

"It's rushed, Paul."

"You're saying that because you know I wanted to finish it. Maybe you have too much information about that."

"I'm saying that because it's the way it reads. I'm sorry. The relationship between the guy and the ghetto kid, the central relationship in the book, doesn't ring true. And I don't think you get into ghetto life enough to capture the kid's life-style. It's not your direct experience, so you have to spend more time on those sections, really work on them. Right now it's hurried, glib. But don't put this on me. Show it to other people."

. . .

I gave it to the agent, Martha Sipes, and to the editor, Barbara Moss. They were more conciliatory, pointing out the strengths of what I had accomplished, certain scenes, certain exchanges within scenes that worked for them. But overall, they agreed with Sandy. I was given pages of notes from both of them, which amounted to the same comments Sandy made in a few words. It felt rushed. It lacked authenticity.

. . .

We went out to Fire Island for the weekend. The weather turned cold and grey. I was walking along the bay when I saw Sandy alone on the dock looking out toward the mainland. I went over to her.

"What are you doing out here?" I asked.

She did not respond.

"What's going on?"

"I'm waiting for the 'Daddy Boat.' "

"What are you talking about? I'm here."

"Who are *you?*"

It was like she never had seen me before.

"Sandy!"

She kept staring at the mainland.

"I'm waiting for the man I fell in love with."

"This is spooky. Stop it."

"He was going to write wonderful things."

"Enough!"

"His father always kept his integrity." Then she laughed rue-fully. "Think my husband's over there looking for his?"

"It's cold out here. Let's go."

I went to grab her arm and she pulled away.

"What do you want from me?" she said sharply.

"Some time," I found myself saying.

"Time? I can't give you time. I don't even know you."

She moved several steps away from me.

"Are you coming?"

She did not respond. I walked back and she stayed out on the dock, looking for me.

. . .

Upward Mobility continued to be number one. *USA Today* ran a cover story: "The Paul Brock Phenomenon Has Legs." I picked up a copy when I was in the supermarket for a few items that we needed in the house. It was close to ten at night. I was walking back to the apartment and I noticed a van cruising along, moving at my pace. A man with sunglasses was watching me through the window. I quickened my pace and so did the van. I started to run. The man leaped out of the van and yelled for me to stop. He was holding a gun. I froze. He rushed up and held the gun to my head.

"Speak and I blow brains out," he said.

A second man rushed up, also holding a gun. They forced me into the back of the van. Then they put a blindfold around my eyes and tied my hands behind my back.

"One word, you dead, Brock."

They knew me by name. I had been followed, seized. I was terrified. I sat on the floor of the van, feeling ill. My captors began speaking Arabic, arguing with each other. After what seemed like an hour of driving around, the two arguing, it was evident that I had been kidnapped by terrorists. And they had gotten lost.

I prayed this was a fantasy gone awry. But it was real. We came to a stop, they took me out of the van, the blindfold still covering my eyes, and I was pushed along outside and then up a few steps. We seemed to have entered a building. A door was opened and the blindfold was removed. My captors were both slightly built men wearing leather jackets, sports shirts, and slacks. We were in a small apartment, a metal cot with a mattress and no linens was to the side, a worn sofa faced a table that held a television set. One man pointed the gun at me while the other secured a clamp to my ankles with a chain that was locked to the metal frame of the cot.

"You political prisoner," the man with the sunglasses said. "I am Abdullah. This is Omar."

"What do you want of me?"

"We are Palestine Freedom Front."

"What do *I* have to do with Palestinian freedom?"

"Our demands—immediate give up of lands to Palestinians."

"Now!" Omar added.

"Immediate give up of lands? What do you want, my house on Fire Island?"

"From Israel! Give up of lands from Israel!"

"Now!" Omar contributed.

"You kidnapped me to get land from Israel?"

"You famous American person. You in *USA Today*," Abdullah explained.

"Look, this is a terrible mistake. I don't have any power over Israeli policy. I have no power over American policy. I'm just another citizen."

"You famous. Be big media of our demands. If no good answer, we kill you."

"How can I make you understand? I am meaningless in what you want."

"We are smart. We get famous American person. America, world opinion push Israel. We get lands. You go free." He smiled, pleased with his scenario.

"It won't work. What lands? The West Bank? Gaza?"

"All Israel."

"All? You think Israel is going to give up its *entire* territory because you kidnapped one American citizen?"

I had been abducted by the Two Stooges of Terrorism.

"We call police now. Tell them we have you. Let everyone wait, worry. Tomorrow we make demands."

Abdullah left the apartment, which did not have a phone, locking the door from the outside. Omar guarded me with his gun.

"I have money. If you let me go, I will make you a rich man for the rest of your life."

"Want land!" he answered, turning away from me.

Abdullah returned in a while, said he had notified the police and we would wait until morning. Chained to the cot I lay down and spent the night thinking how terrible it would be for Sandy and the children to hear about this. I summoned up every wrong thing I had ever done to them, every burst of egotism, temper, impatience. Did they know how much I loved them?

At some point in the night I must have fallen asleep out of exhaustion. Abdullah went out early in the morning, returning soon after with a toothbrush and toothpaste for me, orange juice, bread and cheese—a civilized gesture, but more importantly, it told me we were near population. He turned on the television set. My kidnapping was reported on the news. Paul Brock of Phenomenon fame had been abducted by members of the Palestine Freedom Front. A State Department spokesperson said they had no knowledge of such an organization, which was likely one of the many splinter groups operating outside the control of the main organizations. Completing the report was the information that my book was a bestseller and my movie was in general release across the country. That was when it occurred to me that the kidnapping was a hoax masterminded by Mel for publicity purposes.

Taking comfort from it I spent the morning with my alleged captors, watching game shows. At noon a news report showed Mel on camera outside his apartment. He said how upset he was and that he wanted the kidnappers to know he would meet demands for money if only they would release me unharmed. In the corner of the screen I could see Laura standing behind Mel. She was crying. My stomach collapsed. Laura would never have been an accomplice to anything like this. It was no hoax. And the goal of my kidnappers, that Israel relinquish *all* its territory on demand, placed them to the left of just about every Arab political faction.

"What you want is unreasonable," I said to them. "Nobody responsible on the Arab side is asking Israel to totally disband. And if the Arabs had only honored the 1947 partition and respected Israel's right to exist all along, we wouldn't be having the problems we have today," I pointed out to an unreceptive audience.

"All land," Omar said.

"Do you accept Resolution 242 as a basis for negotiations? That, as you recall, calls for a gradual Israeli withdrawal from Arab territory in exchange for permanent peace," I said informatively.

"All land!" Omar growled.

So much for my attempt at raising the intellectual level of the abduction. Abdullah showed me the note he had been writing containing the demands. He was going to call the police and tell them where to find it. In pathetic, scrawly letters he had written: "Palisdin Fredun Frund Keel Brock Unlais Isrel Geev Arab Awl Lan Beelon Arab. Meenin Evreedin."

"What does this say? Nobody will be able to figure this out!"

Abdullah left to post the note and Omar fell asleep in front of the television set. I managed to crawl to a window, dragging the cot with me. The window opened on a courtyard.

. . .

Looking out a window of a nearby building was John le Carré.

"Psst. Over here!" I called out, trying not to wake Omar.

"Hello, there."

"I know who you are. You can help me. I'm being held captive by Arab terrorists."

"Oh, people say those kinds of things to me all the time. When you write my kind of novels—"

"No, this is the truth! Call the police, please!"

"I'm afraid I can't do that, my good man. I was in the States for a while not getting a book done that I'd been working on. And I said to an American friend, *Lock me in. Take me somewhere with provisions and no phone and lock me in until I finish*."

"They've threatened to kill me."

"Who?"

"Two Arab terrorists. They're from some fringe terrorist group. I'm a well-known writer here, Paul Brock. They grabbed me off the street and they're holding me captive unless Israel gives up all its territory. The spelling and handwriting of their note was terrible. And if the demands aren't met, they said they'd kill me."

"That's the plot of this? It's very banal."

"I grant that you're a master. But I don't need an editorial critique. I need help!"

"I'm just not in a position to help. Tell me, though—if the spelling and the handwriting of their note is so terrible, how will anybody know their demands?"

"Exactly!"

"My advice is—rewrite their note," John le Carré said.

"That's all you can offer?"

"It's good advice. I'll be out in a week. If you're still there, I'll tell the authorities first thing."

"Please! And listen, this is mine. I don't want to see you using it in one of your books."

"You needn't fear. If *that's* your plot, you can have it."

. . .

On the evening news it was reported that the only lead in my case so far was a note from the terrorists that was "unintelligible." I offered to help Abdullah with his English and his spelling so the demands would at least be understood. I wrote out for him, "We are the Palestine Freedom Front. We hold Paul Brock hostage and will kill him unless Israel relinquishes all territory that is now the state of Israel and returns it to Arab rule." Interesting demands. I was a dead man.

On a morning television news report the next day a State Department spokesperson said a note had been received from the terrorists and the requirements were impossible for the United States or Israel to fulfill.

.   .   .

Abdullah and Omar argued furiously, then Abdullah turned to me.

"Omar thinks it better to kill you right now. Might be better for deal."

"What deal?"

"My cousin, he owns restaurant in Hollywood. He knows many people from movies. He says if we don't get demands, we still have good story to sell to movies."

"What! You're in this for the movie rights?"

"For land. But also for movie rights. Omar thinks better story if you dead."

"Omar doesn't know shit about story! It's better if I live!"

They had another argument, a script conference where they decided whether or not to literally kill off a character. Abdullah seemed to prevail for the moment and he rushed out of the apartment with the latest note, which I helped him write, accepting Golan, the West Bank, and *half* of Israel. If I lived long enough they were going to have me writing a note to get them an agent.

Preoccupied with his argument, Abdullah neglected to lock the door on leaving. He must have gotten lost again. Hours passed. Omar fell asleep on the sofa, the gun tucked in his waist. He was snoring, the television set was on. I turned the cot on its side, sliding the mattress off and slowly made my way to the door, carrying the cot to which I was chained. I opened the door, carried the cot into the hallway of the building and then outside to the street. It looked like I was somewhere in Queens. Three-story buildings lined both sides of the street. I screamed for help, for the police, and faces began appearing in apartment windows. Someone, evidently looking to pick up a $25 hotline reward, called a local television station before the police and a film crew arrived to film a man chained to a cot in the middle of a city street. That image was widely circulated the next day with stories of "The Phenomenal Escape," as it was called in the tabloids. By the time the police stormed the apartment where I had been held, Omar was gone. Abdullah may still be lost.

• • •

I hugged Sandy and the boys a long time when we were reunited. In my first statements to the press I had kind words for my captors, whom I said treated me well. After all, I didn't want them coming after me for a second draft.

"It's gone too far," I said to Sandy as we sat together in our living room. "The celebrity-ness. Who I'm becoming. I have to get out of this."

"Fine with me."

"I hope I can. The way Mel put all this together I'm an entire industry."

"I wouldn't worry about Mel. He'll have somebody else to take your place in no time."

"Still, he did all this work. I don't know how I can possibly tell him."

"Once, a lifetime ago, Mel and I were together—"

"Yes?" I said apprehensively.

"It wasn't for long. It was all very whirlwind. But he asked me to marry him."

"*Marry* you?"

"It had nothing to do with my feelings about him."

"I never knew it was so serious! I thought you went together a little while."

"It was just a little while."

"My best friend and my wife!"

"Paul, you're losing the chronology. This was before I met you. I went with people before we met and so did you. The famous Roland Greenblatt, dentist, was a closer call."

"I'm in a French movie!"

"Please. Why I'm telling you this now, what's important for you to know about this is: *You can say no to Mel.*"

. . .

Looking at it objectively, their relationship wasn't exactly a current episode. I figured it happened between them roughly sixteen years, four months, and two weeks previously. In light of recent events, I really had more immediate concerns, such as what was to become of the rest of my life. So I tried to hear what Sandy was telling me; that I could say no to Mel.

Barreling along, he had instructed Helen Baskin to organize a press conference the following morning for me to answer questions about my abduction, and get the maximum promotional mileage out of it. A display of copies of the novel and the album occupied the area behind the lectern in a conference room at the Hilton Hotel. A couple of hundred members of the print and broadcast media were in attendance.

"It was unfortunate that it happened," Mel said to me before I went before the microphones. He was holding newspapers with stories recounting my escape. "But we couldn't buy this kind of attention," he said. "The foreign press, too. It will help the European tour. You have to do it now."

"I'm not doing any European tour."

"Suppose we do a movie of this experience, starring you."

"You'll be competing with the kidnappers for the rights," I said. "And then I guess you'd want to do a tie-in book in hardcover for the movie and in paperback for the video."

"You're learning."

"I think I'll pass on it, Mel."

"Then start thinking about an American tour for the new book. You know how they say, *Everybody's going to be famous for fifteen minutes.* Well, I'm trying to buy you another half-hour."

. . .

At the press conference I talked about the kidnapping and my escape and answered questions from the floor. Then I announced that I had a statement to make:

"Paul Brock, the celebrity, stands before you as someone who has been totally packaged. Professionals propped me up, coached me, taught me how to sit, stand, do interviews. It was like I was dubbed. I did write my own lyrics; I'll take credit for that. And I did my own singing, to the extent that it was singing. I'm grateful to the people who became my fans. But I'm not a performer. That was a creation. So I can't keep faith with myself and go on with this any longer. I'm a made-up act. I'm really a writer and that's all I want to be from now on. I'm announcing my retirement from show business, effective this minute. I'm pulling the plug. The Phenomenon is over."

I walked away from the lectern as people were shouting questions, cameras were clicking.

"What did you *do?!*" Mel said. "Now is when you capitalize. How much time do you think anybody gets in the spotlight?"

"Mel, I'm getting lost in this."

"We're talking income here for your *children's* children."

"They can get their own act. The word is—no. It's over."

. . .

I declined all interviews over the next few weeks. Clusters of media people waited near the entrance of our apartment house, but when I persisted in not making any further statements their ranks dwindled and eventually they left. Mel surprised me by respecting my decision. I stayed to myself and started working on a rewrite of the novel.

In June the children finished their school year and we went to Greece. Sandy knew an art director who spent his summers in Lindos on the island of Rhodes. The art director and his wife, who was a teacher, had three children aged seven, twelve, and fourteen. We rented a house there, the children played together, Sandy painted, I worked on the novel. Occasionally, an American tourist looked at me oddly. *Don't I know you from somewhere?* But the

Phenomenon had never reached Greece and among the local citizenry I was able to pass, blissfully, unrecognized.

. . .

I was on the beach with the boys making a sand castle one day and Joey asked me: "Daddy, are you famous?"

"I was for a minute."

"Mommy says you're not going to sing anymore," Sammy said.

"Only to you guys." I burst into a few lines from "Sing a Song" and threw in a great funny face at the end.

"Daddy, you're getting funnier," Joey declared solemnly.

"How do you like that? Just when I got out of the business."

. . .

I gave the rewritten novel to Sandy and sent copies to Martha Sipes and Barbara Moss.

"It's much improved," Sandy said. "You really feel for the guy and the kid now."

"Is it better than *Upward Mobility?*"

"That's not a fair question. It's different. *Upward Mobility* was more personal. This is more outside your experience, more of an invention, but good."

"Not as good, is what you're saying."

"Not everything can be at the same level."

"It's not supposed to be. One's work is supposed to get better."

"The *next* book will be better."

"Will it?"

. . .

The agent and editor agreed with Sandy that the rewrite was an improvement over my earlier draft. When I pressed them, they said it was publishable, if not quite at the level of my first novel. I knew I hadn't worked as deliberately as on the first book. Parts of it still seemed rushed. But I couldn't see how spending any more time was going to produce anything better than what I had. It was a decent book, not as good as my first. I always had the option of abandoning it. Barbara Moss insisted that I owed it to myself and my readers to see it in print. Sandy, true blue again in her loyalty, said it definitely should be published and I decided to go with the book as written. I had started out on this novel confidently thinking I didn't have to compare myself with Updike, but I was falling short of matching up to myself.

· · ·

I had spoken to Mel in August. He and Laura were back in New York, having gone to Japan for a month on a Manuelo tour. I told him I had been working on the new book. He said *Upward Mobility* was still on the bestseller list. It was a pleasant conversation. He was not judgmental about my decision to walk away from performing; nor did he even bring it up. The summer was such a complete entity unto itself, so removed from the events of the previous months, that the entire experience of being a performer began to feel distant to me.

· · ·

On our return we passed through customs at Kennedy airport and were about to enter the public area of the terminal when we stopped, stunned by the scene in front of us. People were holding Paul Brock banners. Photographers, reporters, TV crews with cameras and lights were pressing against the gate to get at me. Mel pushed past the guards and came rushing up to us.

"Welcome home," he said.

"What the hell is going on here?"

"I didn't want to tell you. You were working on your book and I didn't want to distract you. Your retirement speech—we took it and put it together with some clips of you performing. And we put it out as a video. It's a smash hit. The number one video. A hit single, too. Kids love it. It's considered a terrific example of integrity in the culture, that you could walk away like that. A marvelous antiestablishment statement."

"Oh, my God."

"And we've also lined up a TV special, 'The Big Hype.' The inside story of a phenomenon. All about how the act was manufactured, the publicity, Blair and Rothman, the Chins, footage of you performing, scenes from the movie, your retirement speech. Honest television. Television that informs."

He took me by the arm to nudge me toward the crowd. I didn't move.

"You're not hearing what he said," Sandy told him. "Paul doesn't want to be in show business anymore."

"He's not. Did I say tour? Perform? He doesn't have to do anything but write his books. And make the occasional author appearance. Maybe a nice press conference-by-satellite type of thing. Did you finish the new book?"

"I'm holding it."

"Hold it tight. It's going to be huge. Bigger even than your first one."

"Mel, the consensus is—it's not as good."

"What does that have to do with it? You're bigger than when you left."

"Daddy, didn't you say you're not going to sing anymore?" Joey asked, looking at the surging crowd.

"I did. But it looks like even my retirement has been packaged."

"Just say hello to everybody and go home, Paul. We'll take care of the rest. We're going to get the TV special on for the week we publish the new book, and we'll go with the paperback of the first book with the showing of your movie on TV, and I'm working on the movie of the first book, and we'll pop the TV special into syndication and time that out with the paperback of the second book."

"Mel!"

"What can I tell you? You're hot."

"You did this!"

"It's what I do."

"I am not performing ever again!"

"Absolutely. It's on the video. The integrity of that—" he said turning to Sandy. "It's why they love him."

The crowd was straining for me to come their way.

"Once you sign on, there's no getting out, is there?" I said to Sandy.

"All those people have been waiting for you," Mel told me. "So just go over and wave hello. From now on, you call the shots. Whatever the Grand Old Man of Integrity wants to do."

As I looked at the crowd some of the fans began to wave their Paul Brock banners.

"Come on. You're going to have another huge book," Mel said. "Smile; you're a culture hero."

Sandy shrugged her shoulders, resigned to the situation, placed her forehead against mine and said, "Chicken lips." We managed to smile and I went to greet the crowd and the media for Phenomenon Two, the Sequel.